No Game No Life 6

THE GAMER COUPLE WHO CHALLENGED THE WORLD!

YUU KAMIYA

—The One True God lies sprawled on the ground.

"Hey! Hey, you.
Didja kick the bucket, please?"

"...Let me stay, by your side—
forever and ever and ever..."

"Will you ignore all logic...and walk the same path as me? As my wife."

...Schwi, overwhelmed by feelings she still didn't know how to properly express, sank to her knees and with a damp voice squeezed out:

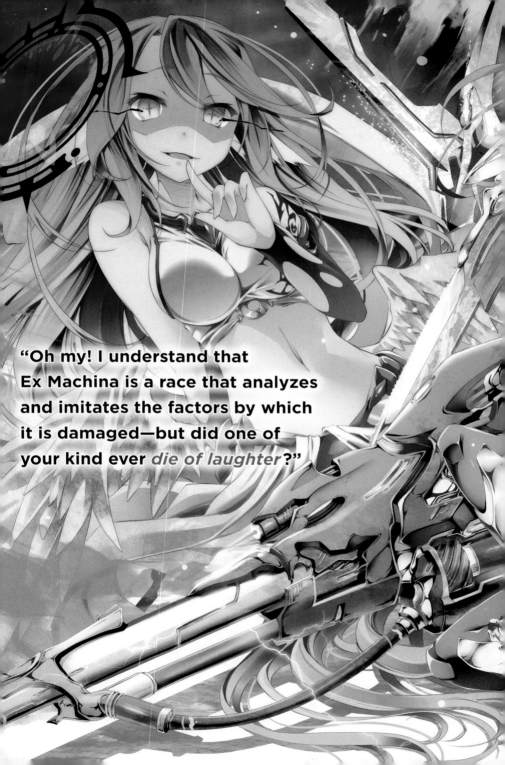

"Oh my! I understand that
Ex Machina is a race that analyzes
and imitates the factors by which
it is damaged—but did one of
your kind ever *die of laughter*?"

Enemy: *Flügel Jibril*.
Probability of success: nonexistent.
But...there's no such thing as zero
when it comes to probability.

"Lösen— All armaments...
Initiating supplication for
life with maximum output."

THE TEN COVENANTS

The absolute law of this world, created by the god Tet upon winning the throne of the One True God. Covenants that have forbidden all war among the intelligent Ixseeds—namely.

1. In this world, all bodily injury, war, and plunder is forbidden.
2. All conflicts shall be settled by victory and defeat in games.
3. Games shall be played for wagers that each agrees are of equal value.
4. Insofar as it does not conflict with "3," any game or wager is permitted.
5. The party challenged shall have the right to determine the game.
6. Wagers sworn by the Covenants are absolutely binding.
7. For conflicts between groups, an agent plenipotentiary shall be established.
8. If cheating is discovered in a game, it shall be counted as a loss.
9. The above shall be absolute and immutable rules, in the name of the God.
10. Let's all have fun together.

CONTENTS
06

No Game No Life

YUU KAMIYA

6

YEN
ON

NEW YORK

NO GAME NO LIFE, Volume 6
YUU KAMIYA

Translation by Daniel Komen
Cover art by Yuu Kamiya

NO GAME NO LIFE
©YUU KAMIYA 2014
First published in 2014 by KADOKAWA CORPORATION, Tokyo.
English translation rights reserved by Yen Press, LLC under the license from KADOKAWA CORPORATION, Tokyo, through Tuttle-Mori Agency, Inc., Tokyo.

English translation © 2017 by Yen Press, LLC

Yen On
1290 Avenue of the Americas
New York, NY 10104

Visit us at yenpress.com
facebook.com/yenpress
twitter.com/yenpress
yenpress.tumblr.com
instagram.com/yenpress

First Yen On Edition: July 2017

Yen On is an imprint of Yen Press, LLC. The Yen On name and logo are trademarks of Yen Press, LLC.

Library of Congress Cataloging-in-Publication Data

Names: Kamiya, Yu, 1984– author, illustrator. | Komen, Daniel, translator.
Title: No game no life / Yuu Kamiya, translation by Daniel Komen.
Other titles: No gemu no raifu. English
Description: First Yen On edition. | New York, NY : Yen ON, 2015–
Identifiers: LCCN 2015041321 | ISBN 9780316383110 (v. 1 : pbk.) | ISBN 9780316385176 (v. 2 : pbk.) | ISBN 9780316385190 (v. 3 : pbk.) | ISBN 9780316385213 (v. 4 : pbk.) | ISBN 9780316385237 (v. 5 : pbk.) | ISBN 9780316385268 (v. 6 : pbk.)
Subjects: | BISAC: FICTION / Fantasy / General. | GSAFD: Fantasy fiction.
Classification: LCC PL832.A58645 N6 2015 | DDC 895.63/6—dc23
LC record available at http://lccn.loc.gov/2015041321

ISBNs: 978-0-316-38526-8 (paperback)
          978-0-316-38527-5 (ebook)

10 9 8 7 6 5 4 3 2 1

LSC-C

Printed in the United States of America

⏻ OPENING TALK

When he was a child, he thought the world was simpler. That there was no contest you couldn't win. That hard work would be rewarded. That anything was possible. What he believed as a child, still foolish and ignorant—looking at the world with cloudless eyes—was it wrong?
......Was it really wrong...?
......──

In the cramped room, lit only by a faint lamp, the boy picked up a piece. He was the only figure there. But the boy looked intently at someone he knew he saw, deep in the darkness, and ruminated.

A game, after all, was only child's play. Alone in the room, the boy imagined an opponent of perfect strength, and carefully, he placed his piece on the board, just as he had done as far back as he could remember. Outside the room, terror and uncertainty—the despair of those who couldn't foresee even the day that would follow—froze the darkness of night. But inside the room, it was like another world. The faint light reflected with a burgeoning heat. Piece in hand, the boy ruminated once more.

* * *

Once they grew up, everyone naturally drifted away from games. Why? Because they didn't have time? Because the world wasn't as simple as games? Whatever the reason, when people grew up, games were inevitably discarded as childish things... But the boy—had never given this any thought. He simply considered his next move and then once more placed his piece on the board.

A child who went on and on playing games alone. He'd grown up the subject of strange looks from everyone around him, yet the boy kept playing. After all, he didn't understand the reason for those peculiar stares. Because if he squinted carefully into the darkness—"he" was there. Seemingly about the same age as the boy, "he" grinned boldly.

The boy thought "he" was strong. "He" was always far ahead of the boy, and the boy would always—lose. As if it was only natural. As if there was no chance he could win in the first place. And feeling this...*unbearably entertaining*, the boy challenged "him" again. As far as others were concerned, the boy was alone, but to the boy, they were two. That was all. In the darkness, "he" never spoke. But "he" greedily sought out the moves that surpassed the boy's—the more perfect play.

A more correct move. A more excellent tactic! A more advanced strategy!! "He" merrily gloated from the darkness, and the boy answered back with a bold grin of his own.

...As far as others could see, the boy was alone—but he didn't care. The world was simple and clean. Win, lose, or draw—that was all there was. And no matter the outcome—though in the end he always lost—he'd ponder how to win next time. That—was the boy's world.

But the outside world trampled his personal world mercilessly.

—No warning. The dim room lit up dazzlingly, and the boy turned to the window. The night sky, which was supposed to have been shrouded in red—had gone white. As his parents burst into the room, screaming and grabbing his hand, the boy, terribly slowly, looked at it. Connecting heaven and earth—a column of light. As his parents held him, shrieking something, their faces pale, the boy quickly reached out.

—The game wasn't over.

Abruptly, he pulled the chessboard on which he'd been playing "him" close, and then... When next he lifted his eyes, a light that seemed to sear his retinas—

——......

They were right: The world wasn't as simple as games. Awoken by the terrible smell, the boy came to this realization. Extricating himself from the charred arms of his mother, draped limply over him, the boy looked around. The scene left in the wake of the light that had violated his world, unreasonable and absurd, occupied his senses. The taste of blood in his mouth. The scent of scorched flesh in his nose. His ears rang with an abyss of silence. His skin baked with a burning heat. And his vision...swam with a world utterly changed. Not a vestige of life remained. Rubble, clouds of dust, and exposed earth stretching as far as the eye could see. The boy turned his eyes to the sky. Amid a scarlet canopy that looked poised to fall at any moment—destruction rampaged. Gods battled over petty squabbles, without so much as a glance at humanity below. Just one stray blast. A whole world of people—to say nothing of the boy's own private world—obliterated in its wake.

They were right: The world wasn't as simple as games. *Because the world had no rules.* No rules. No one to call foul. No, even from the start— Suddenly, as the boy stood, visible through the smoke and dust, a shadow lit upon the rubble. Wholly oblivious to the child, this silhouette casually—almost as an afterthought—noted the gaze directed its way.

The boy gaped at the one who had taken everything from him— the destroyer—and thought: *Yes, to them, human beings aren't even players.* It had swept away his—their—world without a care, as if it had been so much dust. This force of annihilation. Through the flames and sand, he could just make out a shape like a person, but—

".........."

Recognizing that his gaze had been met, the boy turned and staggered off, dragging his feet behind him. Shaking off the glare he felt at his back, he walked far—someplace far away. To survive. Clutching the chessboard hard enough to break it, that day the boy became a man.

This world is chaos. Devoid of fate. Filled only with random happenstance. Unreasonable, absurd, and meaningless. Amid all that, where could one find...time to play games...

■■■

It had already been six thousand–odd years since the endless Great War had torn heaven and earth asunder and murdered the planet. Since the conflict for the throne of the One True God for absolute sovereignty over the world. A world in which the God who had claimed the throne by default—Tet—had set forth the Ten Covenants. A world on a board where force of arms was forbidden and all quarrels had to be settled by games—Disboard. In this world, on the continent of Lucia in the west, there was a city.

The "Provisional Commonwealth" of Elkia—the capital, Elkia. A city which, until just a few months earlier, had been driven to the brink of doom, submerged in despair. The last city of Ixseed Rank Bottom, Immanity. But now things had changed. Three countries—

- The Eastern Union—the nation of the Werebeasts, comprised of countless islands
- Oceand—the nation in which the Sirens and Dhampirs lived symbiotically under the sea
- Avant Heim—the nation where the angelic Flügel graced the heavens

—populated by four races had been brought into the fold in a twinkling by the new king and queen just after their coronation. This city now found itself the capital of a sprawling commonwealth. The city's Main Street bristled with activity. Merchants and farmers who had just gained—or lost—vast resources. Craftspeople who purchased their goods. Each and every one of them traveling to and fro on foot or on horseback, haggling in voices overlapping without pause.

A world where all quarrels and conflicts were settled by games. Indeed, that must sound quite simple. But the reforms were all too rapid. Immanity was swallowing up other races and multiple countries in games and forcing them into their fold. No matter how you might dress it up, all it represented was a policy of aggression. Spouting off about how it was a commonwealth, united in cooperation—was entirely too kind. Under such circumstances, the administration should have been in chaos, a quagmire of political wrangling among realms and races. Under such circumstances, that was what one could rightly expect.

—That is, if it hadn't been the handiwork of the king and queen... the siblings named Sora and Shiro. Winning games with other nations—plays for dominion—swallowing them up whole and then—*achieving bloodless coups without anyone losing out.*

On the bustling street, here and there, one might find a few Werebeasts. The preposterous concept of building a multiracial commonwealth to transcend the barriers between the "sixteen seeds," the Ixseeds, little by little, subtle as it might be, was somehow showing progress.

The world was changing. With this place, Elkia, at its center. There must have been some for whom this unshakable premonition felt uncomfortable. But at the same time, people's hearts throbbed and their eyes glinted. For they were the witnesses—to the revolution of the world.

............So, back to the main topic. As described earlier, the Ten

Covenants set forth by the One True God caused everything to be decided by games. As for that One True God, Tet: Don't you wonder...how he passes the days? How a more or less omniscient and omnipotent One True God lives? Today, I'm going to do you a special favor and tell you about it. For now, in an alley of Elkia, being poked with a stick by a small Werebeast girl—

"Hey! Hey, you. Didja kick the bucket, please?"

—the One True God lies sprawled on the ground.

"...N-now that I think about it...Immanities...die if they don't eat, don't they...?"

"So do I, please. Are you a dumbass, please?"

At this insult delivered with wide, innocent eyes, Tet pressed his face more firmly to the ground. The Werebeast girl, with black hair and ears like those of a fennec fox—Izuna Hatsuse. Formerly the ambassador of the Eastern Union in Elkia, now the playmate of its king and queen—pardon, their adviser. While this Izuna prodded him, Tet considered: Though this might have been his first attempt at existing as an Immanity—he really shouldn't have.

—So, just what was the One True God doing in a place like this? He was just...killing time. Because being the One True God was deathly boring. You can say "I am the One True God" all you want, but looking out over the world gets old. On top of that, when you consider that Tet used to be the God of Play, it was no wonder that he craved a game once in a while. Disguised as a member of the race he'd be infiltrating, he'd limit his power. Wander the world, compete, and go home—that was what Tet, the One True God, did to fill eternity. Today, on a whim, he'd planned to pay a visit to Sora and Shiro—

Dropped by after all. Hee-hee! ♪

—but it seemed that before he'd have a chance to drop by, he'd be *dropping dead*. He'd turned himself into an Immanity, walking a few days without eating for the hell of it, and now look at him.

Tet could only be impressed at the imagination-defying frailty of this race, but fundamentally...the One True God was terribly angry—that is to say, hungry—

"...............Here. Eat this shit, please."

With these words, Izuna sloppily extended one of the fish she'd bought. The One True God—eyes glazed as if finding himself in the presence of a goddess—stared back at Izuna, asking:

"...R-really?"

"...Take the damn thing, please. Before I change my mind, please."

Izuna's tone was strained as, drooling, she deliberately averted her gaze from the fish.

"...They told me we'll be taking kind of a long trip, so I should go buy some shit to eat, please."

While Izuna muttered, Tet eyed the giant leather sack hefted on her back.

"Uh, so they asked you to get food for everyone?"

"...? For myself, please. Everyone went to buy their own shit, please."

That was Werebeast for you. It seemed they needed that many calories to sustain those physical abilities of theirs.

"I'm just giving you a little, please. They only gave me *three hundred en of snack money*, so I couldn't get that much, please."

—Tet understood that to mean *three hundred gold pieces*, but he didn't point it out. He gratefully accepted the goddess's charity, but—

"But I don't have anything to give you in exchange... Oh, I know—you wanna play a game?"

In response to Tet's proposal as he sank his teeth into the raw fish, Izuna's ears perked. *Wanna play a game?* Tet's expression when making this suggestion had triggered her Werebeast sense.

"...You must be good, huh, please?"

"Eh-heh-heh! I don't mean to brag, but I've never lost in my life—with one exception!"

"Bring it! Bring it, please!"

....

"Why—why can't I beat you, pleaaase?!"

—One hour. They'd played cards until Izuna had racked up nine losses and no wins.

"Ah-ha-haaa! If you can't beat those two, there's no way you're gonna beat me!"

"—Those two? You know Sora and Shiro, please?"

...*Nice call*, Tet laughed to himself—and then looking at this "young philosopher," he suggested:

"...All right, let's do this. I'll tell you a story while we play."

"You're just trying to distract me, please. Just like that bastard, Sora, please."

"Ah-ha-ha, don't worry. That's not an issue—I'm gonna win either way, you know!"

"...I'll kick your little bitch ass, please."

Izuna glared hard as if in so doing she might see through his cards to discern his hand.

"If you wanna talk, talk, please. I'm gonna win, damn it, please!"

To this, he responded with distant eyes and a smile.

"But this story, you know, it's not one you hear every day... I'm telling you, I'm pretty sure you haven't heard this one?"

"......I can't hear you, please."

She could totally hear him— Tet chuckled, dialing down his grin a bit.

"If you can't, then, sure, whatever. After all—this is a *myth that's never told*."

—And chasing after memories inspired by the figure of the Werebeast sitting across from him, the One True God began his tale—*Once upon a time...*

"There was a stupid, stupid...big old war, they say—"

⏻ CHAPTER 1
3 – 1 = HOPELESS

—It was said that, once, there was something called the "sun."

A white flame sparkled, and the sky spread clear and blue—that was the legend. They say it was the Great War of the gods and their creations that scorched the earth and closed off the heavens with ash. The ash collided with the power of the planet that flowed through the heavens—with "spirit corridors"—to give off the light that stained the sky red. That red blanketed all the land as the killing continued. Or perhaps it was just the wailing and blood of the planet itself… Either way, the only thing that fell from the sky was… that iridescent blue ash.

....

Ivan furrowed his brow and looked up to the murky red horizon. The "black ash" still glowed blue as it piled up like snow on the wasteland. Ivan vaguely called up all the knowledge a *human* could feasibly summon. They said that the blue light was the sparkling of spirits, otherwise invisible to humans—that the sky appeared red because of the polarization of light or something, and that the real color of spirits was translucent... As for why this glimmer should be visible to humans, who lacked spirit corridor junction nerves... Apparently, it was the last flash of spirits—broken colliding with the ash—as they died.

—Dead spirits: a lethal poison to almost all living things, including humans. If they got on your skin, you would be burned. If they got in your eyes, you would go blind. If they got in your mouth, your guts would melt. It was called "black ash" despite its azure sheen because what it meant was death. *Or maybe just for mercy's sake...* His face was covered by a particle mask. His body was protected from the waves of violent cold by pelt armor. If he threw all this off and lay down there, the earth and wind of death would lead him into repose.

He wanted to rest. He'd been working nonstop since morning. The feeling in his extremities had long since been lost. He wanted to sip some warm soup, wash off the ash, and doze off on the breast of his wife—but if he couldn't do that, then instead... At this *seduction*, Ivan trembled and cut off his thoughts. Having been born into this world, with no reason to either live or to die—

"—Ivan. Is the black ash getting to your head?"

Roused by the low voice of his comrade, Ivan blinked a few times and looked to his side—at his two allies.

"...I just had to rest for a moment, Alei. I'm getting old, you know."

"If you're getting old, wouldn't that mean we're in trouble soon, too?" Alei chuckled, and Ivan responded ironically to the lad a generation younger than himself.

"Get ready. One day, you'll find all of a sudden that you can't do the daft things you used to— Riku, that goes for you, too."

With this, Ivan faced Riku—their leader, whose name meant "Land"—standing at their point. The youngest among them—just a boy—his expression hidden by his mask and goggles, betraying nothing. All that pierced the goggles were those dark eyes...as black and unreflective as night.

"Thank you for the warning. So—if you're done with your 'rest'...
let's go."

Weaving through the cover of rocks, they'd crawled on their
hands and knees, the raw pelts of beasts covering them. No feeling
in their limbs, no food in their bellies—all so as to avoid detection
by the enemy. To survive. And—to make it here. Ivan nodded and
peered down at the base of the hill silently. What lay there was a
giant crater...with a mountain of steel imbedded in its center.

■■■

It was the corpse of an airship—a steel ship constructed by the
Dwarves to travel the sky. A remnant of the earthshaking "skir-
mishes" of recent weeks. Riku's party had come to dig through the
wreckage for resources. Slipping under the cover of a rent in the
hull's armor that looked as though it might give them access, Ivan
asked Riku:

"...Spirit compass?"

"It's no use. Too much black ash. It just spins meaninglessly at all
the corpses."

Ivan clucked to himself. So much for that lifeline. The spirit
compass—it combined pyroxene, which reacted to large spirit
responses, with mere obsidian. It was a tool made by Riku and
his older sister to detect the masses of spirits harbored in the bodies of the gods and their relations (those monsters) and show their
direction—but it was useless now. Which meant they were left with
only their own senses for their search. Against monsters with super-
natural abilities that left humans in the dust... It wasn't even funny.
And no one was laughing. Without so much as a smile, Riku gave
the order.

"...Stay sharp. We're going in."

Riku and Ivan's other companion, Alei, nodded wordlessly and
sank into the wreckage. Brushing off the accumulated ash, sitting
for a moment and savoring his good fortune at having made it this
far alive—

...Concentrate!

Ivan quickly reprimanded himself. Staying calm, suppressing his breath, even his heartbeat—becoming a speck of dust unworthy of notice, yet sharpening his senses so as not to miss a single speck himself—he began investigating the ship.

The danger was relatively modest. The front had already moved far away, leaving this place a discarded heap of rubbish. But it was far from safe. There could be monsters that had strayed from the front. Or creatures from other races wandering independently of the war. Or again, if, by some chance, one of the Dwarves stationed aboard this airship had survived— *Even if he's on his last breath, we'll more or less be done for.*

—That was reality. The unreasonable reality, at which one could only throw up one's hands. If a Dwarf held a catalyst and spoke a single word, it would be enough to turn hundreds of humans to dust. That was what they were facing. What they were hiding from to survive. And so—

"—Ivan, look! We hit it big!!"

At the loud cheer behind him, Ivan lifted his head and turned. A short distance away, Alei waved his right hand enthusiastically, his eyes sparkling with excitement.

"Get over here. This is amazing!"

Ivan stared coolly at Alei for a while, then shifted his attention to Riku standing beside him.

"......"

Riku said nothing, just slowly raised a hand—and motioned as if slitting his throat. That was enough to make the effusive Alei gasp and shake.

"S...sorry. B-but, anyway, come look at this."

What Alei had found, at first glance, looked like a small box. A puzzle made of several blocks intricately intermeshed. But when Alei held it and squeezed, twisting, it emitted a prismatic glow—

"This—"

At the large diagram projected in midair, even Ivan gasped, unable to conceal his surprise.

"Could it be—a world map?!"

"Yeah, and it's the latest version!"

—A world map. So far they had done what they could to make maps using the materials they had collected and measurements they could make, but the light before them demarcated the land and sea of the world in painstaking detail. In this world whose geography changed moment by moment due to the war, this indeed was—

"...That's not all," Riku muttered softly.

"It shows their strategy and current positions—some of it seems to be in code, but I can read Dwarven. It's not an issue."

"—Ha, ha-ha!"

It was no wonder Alei was excited. Ivan let out a smile. With this data, it was likely they could deduce the current state of the war. If they could guess where the next areas of conflict would arise, they might even be able to forecast a *relatively safe* place to live! With this monumental discovery, Riku's voice relaxed.

"Ivan, Alei—match the left and right sides up with our existing map. I'll copy the strategy and positions."

""*Achéte!*""

At his command, Ivan and Alei, still unable to hide their excitement, answered in unison with a vow to those who had passed before them, those who had willed them their resolve in death—*achéte* (I accept). Retrieving paper, ink, and measurement equipment from their backpacks, they set to work. Hurriedly, yet with precision, they measured the map and copied it over. But then a thought occurred to Alei, and he spoke.

"Hey, Riku, can't we just take the gadget that projects the map itself?"

As Riku slowly raised his head, Alei continued.

"Doesn't that make more sense? It's not like it's too big to carry. Aren't we just wasting paper and—"

"No. We can't take anything with us that uses spirits. Copy the damn thing."

"Sure, but, I mean..."

"*Alei.*"

With a voice as sharp as a knife, Riku stopped him short.

"*...If you want to die, just tell me*—I'll fulfill your wish."

Expression lost, eyes reflecting no light but filled with black slaughter, Riku growled.

"We don't need a monster detecting a spirit response and making a crater of our village."

"—A-all right—all right, I was out of line..." Shrinking from Riku's assertiveness, Alei shook his head. "B-but do you have to get so angry...?"

"Alei, what Riku said—it's our policy. Remember?"

Ivan interjected chidingly, his expression stern. Alei swallowed and recited:

"—'We do not exist. We must not exist, and thus, we are not perceived'..."

"You do remember, don't you? It may take some work to copy a map—but it's not worth dying over, is it?"

"...Sorry."

Alei apologized softly. Just then, ever so subtly, a dull tremor rocked the ground.

"—!"

In an instant, as if by agreement, they lowered their postures and leaped behind cover.

■ ■ ■

—Struggling to stifle his pounding heart. Suppressing his breath, shrinking his body, Ivan turned to Riku, who was likewise hiding. Riku removed a glove, produced a blade, and without a moment's hesitation made a small incision on the tip of his index finger.

...That's Riku for you...

Riku pressed his exposed nerves to the floor. Using the finger to feel out information from beneath them, he cocked his other hand to his ear. Watching was out of the question. Showing one's face would be suicidal. But putting an ear to the ground was also out of the question. They were needed for sounds above floor level. So Riku combined these *too* rational methods to analyze the data spilled by the enemy. Vibration and sound alone were sufficient to make quite detailed assumptions based on their intensity and rhythm. Licking his lips inside the particle mask, Ivan focused on Riku's hand signals.

—*...Distance about thirty bays, bipedal, one, heavy, slow*— Oh, *you've gotta be kidding.*

The height of the enemy, as estimated by Riku from its gait, was twenty feet. A behemoth over three times the height of a human, moving slowly—so was it searching for something...? A cold sweat stuck to Ivan's back. Then, an earsplitting bellow rocked their surroundings.

—*Son of a bitch! A Demonia!!*

He knew without waiting for Riku's hand signals. One of those fiends created by that mutation of the Phantasma—the "Devil" or whatever it was. These fiends had little in the way of brains. You could say they were beasts granted half a wit. They possessed fearsome strength combined with an awareness of what it meant to be prey—a half-assed intelligence, in exchange for silent predatory instinct. And this Demonia, wandering about a place like this, must have been one of the lowest among them. Perhaps an ogre or a troll... Then, was it within human ability to fight it?

—*No. Obviously not.*

Indeed, it wasn't feasible. No matter how low a Demonia it might be—it would reduce a human to a lump of meat in a flick. The fiends didn't employ bestial instincts such as caution or ambush because *they didn't need to.* They recognized, with their childish intellect, that they were strong and could solve every problem with brute strength. With the weapons the party had on hand...no, no matter how well they might have prepared, it was impossible for a human to kill *any* Demonia.

And it would be meaningless.

Even if they did manage to slay a single Demonia—what would that mean? What if a high Demonia, with significant intelligence, took note and came to regard humans as a threat?

—Humanity would be helplessly exterminated. Therefore, there was only one thing they could do now. Run. No alternative was even worth considering.

…"We do not exist. We must not exist, and thus, we are not perceived"… Humans couldn't resist. They had to play the role of the hunted. And so… Ivan saw it coming—Riku's next words as he turned slowly toward him:

"Ivan, this is an order," Riku commanded. "—Die here."

"*Achéte*, leave it to me."

Chuckling, Ivan assented without hesitation. He pressed the luggage from his back to Alei and casually strode forward.

"H-hey…"

Ivan smiled reassuringly at Alei, who'd taken the pack with quavering hands.

"You know how it is, Alei. Now, one of us has to die."

Yes—one would act as decoy while the other two ran. That was their only choice. Thirty bays—a distance a human could sprint in eight seconds. Having encountered a Demonia at such a *critical range*—they'd had no options from the start. Were all three to flee together, in the *best case* they'd be caught and annihilated. In the worst case, they'd be tracked back to the village… The enemy was at least that intelligent.

Riku must have considered *who should be sacrificed and where*… and that alone.

"We can't lose Riku, and, Alei, you're still young. It's a simple matter who should be weeded."

"But—that doesn't…!"

Ivan smiled gently. Then he loosened the band under his chin and slowly removed his particle mask.

"Ivan…?!"

The cold air brushing his skin strangely eased his tension. The wind felt good as it blew off his suffocating sweat and the smell of beast hide.

"Don't sweat it. Protecting friends and family—now that's something worth dying for, ain't it?"

With that, Ivan proffered his mask to Alei, whose shoulders shook.

"…Damn it. Shit—*shit!*"

Slapping the shoulder of his longtime friend and ally, Ivan turned. Gazing through the goggles into the black eyes of Riku, who considered him silently, he spoke:

"So long, Riku. Take care of my family—my kid."

Riku didn't flinch. Without averting his gaze, he faced Ivan squarely, answering with a nod.

"Yeah, I will."

……

"Sorry."

At this word inexplicably dropped, Riku asked dubiously, "…Why should you apologize?"

"Sorry."

Ivan just—repeated it.

"You know, Ivan. You…" Alei shakily addressed his comrade's back, but Ivan turned away with a wave over his shoulder as if too embarrassed to look.

"Alei, you take care of Riku for me… All right, I'll be passing ahead."

■■■

Ivan and the other two simultaneously—but in opposite directions—erupted from cover. In contrast to the low, controlled trots of Riku and Alei, Ivan sprinted madly and noisily. As the beast roared, Ivan glanced back while maintaining his speed. He saw the enemy, having noticed him, kicking away some steel remains and coming for him.

—The creature was large. As Riku had figured, a behemoth over three times the size of a human. Muscles swelled beneath its black fur. Turbid teeth protruded from a mouth that split its head in half. As this nightmare lit after him without a side glance, Ivan sneered.

Behind the beast, in the other direction, Riku and Alei could be seen scampering madly away. The monster had been too distracted by Ivan's flailing to notice at all—

"—Ha-haaa!"

Finding it suddenly amusing, Ivan let out a whoop. Focusing his attention ahead of him, he increased his speed. The decoy operation had been successful. Now he just needed to draw this monster as far as he could. Might as well aim for the best possible result, right? After all…it would be his last mission of his life.

—Yes, his role ended here. Just run like hell for as long as he could—a simple chore.

"I'm sorry, Riku—leaving you all the heavy lifting."

That Riku, like a little brother to him, would see missions that were more painful, more exacting, more difficult, by heaps. Unlike himself, who in a few minutes—possibly seconds—would be at peace—

"Yeah, it's a crying shame… But still, I'm counting on you— goddamn it."

Riku's black eyes, like darkness, crossed his mind. Even when he'd returned Ivan's gaze, they reflected…nothing. No fear, no doubt, no distress. No sadness or pain resided in them. And that was why Ivan trusted him. He'd lay down his life on orders from a boy who was his junior. Because he trusted that the person with those black eyes would discard his own life like trash if necessary—trusted he'd *expend that life better* than anyone else. But…

"I know what I'm putting ya through—but Riku, there's no one I can think of counting on but you."

That's why he'd spontaneously apologized. For letting Riku give him a reason to die… It wasn't like he wanted to die. Back in the village, his beautiful wife and wonderful daughter awaited his return. He wanted to escape somehow to experience a humble happiness with his family.

—But then…how different would that really be from being buried in the blue ash and drifting away into death?

"Aah, aaaah…!!"

Pathetic, Ivan thought. He could not have been more pathetic, surrendering the choice of such happiness at this hour. He didn't want it. This ending was the last thing he wanted. Anything but to die for no reason like that, with no meaning.

"I'm sorry, I'm sorry! But please, forgive me—"

—To live in such a broken, mad, hideous world. To be born without meaning, to live shivering, finding some shred of happiness, only to have it ripped away. To be slaughtered. What meaning could there be living in a world where this cycle repeated endlessly?

—The answer to that question had been given to him by that boy, Riku. Living to protect one's friends, one's family, and—*for the sake of one who would see the end of the War*—dying. It was magnificent. It was perfect. There could hardly be a better justification for one's existence. Was it not a sublime death? Of course it was—say it out loud and see.

"—I! Die to protect my friends and familyyyyyyy!!"

You see—? To whom, for what, whereupon must one bow one's head—?! A putrid stench. He realized that a death beyond human ability to avert was upon him.

"Ha—haaa! Say, Riku! This age someday will end, won't it—?"

No answer. But it wasn't as if he was asking for one.

—To begin with, "someday" was a concept foreign to Ivan. This world was too cruel to pin hopes to. This world was too harsh for the luxury of despair. The past and the future were out of reach and wholly irrelevant to the people living in the here and now. All one could do, all that was afforded, was to write the present, spin the tale of this moment, with whatever life remained. Even if it could be swept away in an instant like rubbish on the whim of someone, somewhere.

"Aahh…"

All that could be done was to keep running, maniacally, like this.

"Ah—ah-aaaaahhh-aaaaah!"

Maniacally forward. Screaming that you were here. If you fell along the way, you just had to pass the burden to someone else.

"Aaaaaaaaaaaahhhhh-ahhhh-aaaaaaaaa*ahhh*-aaah!!"
That was all humans could—
"Aa*ah*———ah—"
And another scream disappeared.

■■■

...It was such an age, the Great War. Humans were frail and power-less. They had to survive as a race, not individuals. No one could afford individual emotion. One was for all. Everyone had to work for the collective. In service of this, they were constantly forced to choose options that were perhaps not the best, but most expe-dient. Using all their cunning and reason, humans survived—no, *kept running.* Caked in mud and ash, trampling every small joy, leaving corpses behind—until someday there would be a full stop. With this strategy, they sacrificed one to save two, cut off the few for the many. Even if it meant leaving someone behind, they would prioritize saving everyone left in the village. They lacked the luxury of choice. The one who had insisted on these rules...had been Riku himself. It was too late for guilt or regret. But—without looking back or slowing down, when he'd reached the relative safety of the woods, suddenly—

"......!"

Riku was assailed by the sensation that his stomach was drop-ping out. The face of the man in his memory grew unidentifiable. An unbearable sense of loss and a violent disgust at something swelled within him simultaneously. Ivan—a generation older than himself—had been a brave, considerate, helpful man. Among those Riku's age, there was not one who wasn't indebted to the man. He'd been positively smitten with his wife and quite shy until they married...

And already, Riku was recalling him *in the past tense.*

"Riku... Hey, Riku!"

Alei, tears still staining the corners of his eyes, grabbed Riku's shoulder and shook it violently.

"You can't keep trying to take everything on yourself—you'll implode!"

But Riku maintained his dim—unlit—*ghostlike gaze*—

"When that happens, someone will take over for me."

At these words, delivered matter-of-factly, Alei fell silent. Judging that there was no one chasing them, the two began walking. Their feet were heavy as they headed for the village...and not just because of the heaps of ash. It was what they'd left behind. What they were left with. What they'd have to endure from here on——

"...Hey, Riku. This age... Someday...someday it will end, won't it...?"

They didn't know. It was the same question Ivan had screamed at the end. Riku didn't say anything, instead looking up at the red sky where the blue ash danced. Then something crossed his mind, words someone had said: "Every night gives way to light." Watching the bits of detritus drift through the air with their soft blue glow, quietly piling up...

"Yeah. It'll end."

If he didn't believe that, if he didn't hold that faith, right now...

...the weight would bring him to his knees.

■■■

The expedition had lasted four days, all told. Their return destination, the village, lay beyond the wasteland where the blue ash fell, deeper into the backcountry than even the snow-laden woods. At the base of a razor-steep crag, a cave was hidden. From the outside, it looked just like any old beast den. But when one went inside, decaying pillars loomed, and musty lanterns hung here and there. Riku took one and lit it with the tinderbox he produced from his breast pocket. Its dim orange light guided them into the cave, through the tunnel dug at its end. Proceeding farther, mindful of the traps set to ward off beasts, they saw a wall constructed of several sturdy logs. It was the gate, installed to stop the odd wolf or bear that wandered past the traps. Of course, if the intruder was of another race, such a bafflement was of utterly no comfort, but still— Riku approached the gate and knocked, forcefully and in a predetermined rhythm, and waited. Shortly, the gate creaked slowly inward, and a boy in a pelt coat peeked out.

"Welcome back. Thank you for your hard work."

Riku and Alei just nodded as they passed.

"...Mr. Ivan?"

Riku silently shook his head. The guard inhaled, and as if to hold something back, he repeated to Riku:

"Thank you for your hard...work."

......

Beyond the gate, the cave spread wide. Presently, it served as the hideout for almost two thousand people. They had sourced drinking water from a spring deep in the cavern, and they even raised livestock in an open-air enclave. The enclave had two entrances, the other connected to an inlet from the sea from which they could harvest salt and fish. For humans, who would be done for if they ran into anything outside, this was considered a relatively secure habitat. Its thick, stone walls could withstand at least the odd stray shot from the feuds of other races.

—That may have been an innocently optimistic assessment of the village, but Riku climbed the jointed wooden steps and strode inside. The residents working in the square noticed him and tossed their gazes his way—and from among them, a girl dashed up to him. She was small and thin, but her bright hair and blue eyes blazed with the light of life even in the cave. Approaching him, she hollered:

"You're soooooo late! Just how much do you want to make me worry, *little brother!*"

"Believe it or not, we did hurry."

Riku answered brusquely and dropped the load from his back onto the ground.

"Couron, has anything changed while we've been gone?"

"Call me 'big sister'! How many times do I have to tell you, you little—" Pouting and lecturing, the girl called Couron nodded fiercely. "Don't worry, though. At the very least, there hasn't been anything bad enough to report—now will you take off that *nasty* cloak and pelt? I'll drop them in the wash for you!"

Dusting off Riku's head unreservedly, Couron insisted, "You, too, Alei. Thanks for all you've done!"

Couron took Riku's cloak and other gear and addressed Alei, who stood behind him. Then she noticed that someone else who should be there wasn't— Before she could ask, Alei answered.

"...Ivan's dead."

Couron wrenched her face just as a voice rose from the corner of the square.

"Daddy!"

Riku turned to see a little girl running toward him, tripping over herself. Alei, seeing her, took in a short breath. The girl who'd exhausted herself on her approach, seeing Riku, beamed and shouted:

"Where's Daddy?!"

"..."

Riku didn't answer. Ivan's daughter—her sparkling blue eyes much like her father's.

"...Nonna."

"Riku, Riku. Where's Daddy?"

Nonna asked again, tugging at Riku's clothes. Her sunny face nevertheless seemed somehow clouded.

"You see, Nonna..."

Alei opened his leaden mouth to explain, but Riku motioned to stop him. Likewise, Couron was attempting to get between her little brother and Nonna, but Riku pierced her with his eyes. He touched his chest to check.

——It was all right. *It was locked.* In the same matter-of-fact tone as always, Riku delivered the news.

"Ivan—Daddy's not coming back."

——.

The girl opened her eyes wide as if she didn't understand, but when Riku went no further, she wobbled back. Large tears could be seen welling in the corners of her eyes, and her little lips trembled.

"—Why—?"

"……"

"Daddy promised he'd come back! He said, 'Be a good girl and wait for me'! I've been a good girl—I kept my promise! So why—? Why isn't Daddy coming back?!"

"…Because he's dead."

"You're a liar!!"

Nonna's shriek echoed through the cave.

"Daddy…promised me he'd come back!"

How long had it been? Riku vaguely wondered.

How long since a voice so tragic failed to move his heart in the slightest?

"Ivan tried to keep his promise. But we ran into a Demonia, and he drew it off and got left behind."

"I don't care about all that! Why won't Daddy come back?!"

—Nonna was right, Riku thought. Why and for whom her father had died were of no concern to her. Her beloved father wasn't coming back. No amount of explanation could ever change that fact.

"Daddy said humans would win!"

"We will. That's what Ivan fought for, with everything he had. He fought to protect us—so we all might win."

How long had it been? Riku vaguely wondered.

How long had he been able to lie so blithely? Nonna wrinkled up her little face.

"That's not winning! If you call that winning—"

"—Nonna!"

A sharp voice and a hand extending from behind the girl cut short what would have followed—

—Namely—*I wish it was you who'd died.*

The gaunt young woman, Nonna's mother, once Ivan's wife, appeared out of nowhere. Sympathetically, she clamped a hand over her daughter's mouth and looked into Riku's face. Seeing that her eyes held neither a grudge nor hatred, Riku swiftly *touched his chest again.*

—*It's all right.* It's fine.

"Riku…"

Marta, Nonna's mother, pronounced his name in a scratchy voice. *I'm sorry*—Riku felt an urge to say it aloud but swallowed the words.

"…Ivan acted as a decoy to allow us to escape. If he hadn't, we would all have died, and he had faith that if we managed to bring home what we found, it would protect you and Nonna."

"…Thank you, Riku."

Marta mumbled tearfully. She nodded a slight bow, then fled into the village, her fatherless daughter in her arms. Once she was out of sight, Couron muttered as if in prayer:

"…Ivan. He was a fine man."

Yes, he had been a good man. And the wife he'd chosen was a good woman. She uttered no curses or grievances, neither did she harbor them. She just believed him. Their daughter, meanwhile, was a smart girl who could see the truth. She stared right at Riku and let him know what he was—

—a liar.

"Riku!"

Suddenly, with a violence that caught him off balance, Couron embraced him.

"—Welcome back. I'm so glad you're safe…"

"……Yeah…here I am."

With that, Couron opened her mouth exaggeratedly in a deliberate attempt to change the subject.

"Riiight, right, right! It's time for you to take a bath. I'll get it ready!!"

"A bath!"

Alei cheered, but Riku frowned and grumbled.

"We can just wipe ourselves down. There's no need to waste fuel."

"Your *big sister*! Is telling you. 'Take a bath!' Frankly, you stink!" Couron complained, sniffing her own clothes as if worried it was coming off on her. Riku sighed but trudged off obediently. When they'd crossed the square and entered the terminus of the corridor, an older man spotted him and called out.

"Hey, Riku! It finally started working for us, that heap of junk!"

"Oh, come on, Simon!! Why'd you have to tell him?! I was hoping to surprise him!"

"Working…you mean that telescope?"

Riku gaped, at which Couron held her head high.

"Hm-hmm. What do you expect from me?"

"Well, you did explain the principle, Couron…but I still have no idea how you could put it together."

Led by Simon, Riku climbed the stairs to the workshop built in a widened horizontal hollow of the cave. In its center, he saw a cylinder installed. About a year ago, they'd salvaged it from the wreckage of a Dwarven tank—an ultra-long-distance telescope. When they'd picked it up, it had been snapped down the middle, hardly more than rubbish… Riku asked:

"Are you sure it doesn't use spirits?"

"Yeah, relax. It's like an ultra-enhanced version of the telescope you were making. Basically, it uses a bunch of glass disks all stacked together in a complicated way. Let me tell you, I had to work to get the lens ratios right!"

"—I see. Two people died for this. We'd better make the most of it."

Couron had been there when they'd picked it up. It had been Couron who'd identified it as an ultra-long-distance telescope and suggested bringing it back, and it had been Riku who'd approved it. Then—to escape a Werebeast threat they'd encountered on the way back—they'd sacrificed not one, but two. *Even so*, Simon brightly interjected:

"With this, we won't need to do as much scouting—just think how happy they'll be!"

"…Yeah, that's true."

He was lying. He knew how hard Couron had worked to repair this telescope. But—it was a placebo. No matter how carefully his people proceeded, if *they* wanted to find them, it would take no time at all. Hell, even now, it was highly likely their whole crag could be accidentally annihilated.

—Just as his place of birth had been—and the land where he'd been raised. But seemingly aware of the thoughts plaguing Riku, Couron was chipper.

"It'll be so much easier to detect attacks. If we know in advance there'll be danger, we'll have time to get away, right? We gotta think about how we're gonna use this, you know, man! Come on, let's go!"

They left the workshop. On the way to the personal quarters, Riku asked:

"What about the other expeditions?"

"They're fine. You're the ones who went the farthest. That makes this round almost perfect!"

"Yeah, only that one mistake of mine."

Riku's stolid expression, not particularly self-deprecating, made Couron hesitate. "B—but! You brought back something to show for it, right?"

"We found it in a downed Dwarven airship—we think it's a current world map."

"—! Really?! That's huge, isn't it?"

Riku nodded at Couron's enthusiasm.

"With diagrams of where their forces are camped and their strategies, explained in Dwarven. But some of it's in code. I'm gonna need some time to figure it out—so *leave me alone for a while*."

At these words, Couron's expression contorted in a rather complicated fashion.

"...Mm. But seriously, take your bath, will you? 'Cos you stiiink!"

Holding her nose, Couron turned her back and took her leave. Riku just heaved a sigh.

—Entering his cramped room, Riku shut the door. The space had been tight to begin with, chiseled out of a cave, but it was even more oppressive for the countless books and tools now piled inside. In the center sat a small table for eating. At the end was a mapmaking desk, and beside it a scrappy bed. He put the lantern on the desk, took off his pack, and lined up the various goods he'd procured, the star of the haul being three sheets of parchment—the map the three of them had copied together. He laid them out under the light of the lantern. No omissions, no stains—which meant *Ivan's death had not been in vain*.

...Riku exhaled deeply and looked around. No one was there. The room was somewhat distant from its neighbors', and the door was thick. After finishing his usual check, Riku took in a deep breath, touched his chest—

——and *crnk*—opened his lock.

■■■

"What do you mean, not in vain? You damn hypocriiite!!"

He slammed his fists against the table, excoriating himself. A current world map. The positions of the camps. The strategy of the Dwarves. Sure, it was great! A big find. It might even decide the fate of the village. They now had an idea of where the resources and bases were. They'd be able to avoid stepping onto the battlefield between the other races blindly. Five years of risky expeditions spent just in the hopes of a find like this. Starting by mapping their immediate surroundings. Then a rough sketch of the world. Updating it over and over to reflect danger zones and potential resources. It'd only been recently that the thing had finally become useful. Now, incorporating the information they'd brought home today, the reliability of their maps would be dramatically improved.

—But how many people had died for those maps? Of course, Riku knew the answer to that question. He remembered all their faces. He could even recite their names. If you really wanted to know, he could even tell you when they died, where, and for what. *Forty-seven people*—no, now there was one more, so *forty-eight*.

Riku had given each of them the same order: *Die*. Some directly. Some indirectly. But regardless of who delivered the actual command, Riku'd been the one pulling the strings.

—One for all. Sacrifice one to save two.

—If it endangers others, throw away your life before that happens.

The one who'd set down these rules, shown everyone the way to clamber up (just a rung) from their desperate situation, had been none other than Riku himself—but—

"If we keep on like this…where does it lead?"

Kill one for two. Kill two for four. Stacked up on and on, there were forty-eight. And the current population of the village that had survived by virtue of these sacrifices—was less than two thousand.

—*So, Riku, let's see what you have to say. How far are you planning to take this? Until that day you know will come—when you kill 999 for 1,001? Or—until there's only one left?*

"…Ha—ha, ha-ha-ha-ha-ha-ha-ha-ha——!"

And you have the gall to tell a girl who's lost her father it's a victory for humankind, with that mouth! Fooling everyone into believing that this is all inevitable, that these sacrifices are necessary, dragging them all down! And even you—you cling to those lies, locking away your heart and telling yourself what to believe.

—It made him want to vomit. A self-hatred on the verge of frenzy scorched his throat. *Have you no shame? Or have you forgotten it? Just how low do you have to go—? You damn——*

……

"*Hff!* …*Hff,* hff…"

…Before he knew it, the table was broken. Sharp splinters of wood lodged in the fists he'd used to smash it, blood spilling down. The blood that had rushed to his head immediately subsided. His sober thoughts chided his heart.

Are you happy now? —Yeah, as if I'd be happy.
Are you going to cry? —Yeah, if that would help.
Then are you done? —Yeah, I'm done, asshole.

He had no right to cry. If he was going to spill something—it should be blood. That would suit him better. The bastard, the son of a bitch, the phony fraud.

—Rather than a noble substance like tears, having his hand sullied with blood suited him better. He closed his eyes, put his hand to his chest—and imagined it.

—*Grnk.* With a heavy reverberation, he closed his lock—and that was that. The usual. Expected. Deceptive. Calculating and calm. Reliably encouraging. Riku—the steel-hearted adult—was whole again. Having closed his heart and cooled his head, Riku slowly opened his eyes. And then at sight of the mess before him, the shattered, blood-spattered table—he sighed.

"…Trees don't grow from stone… Ahh, shit… What do I do now?"

Picking the splinters out of his hand, he grumbled. There was no pain, as if his senses had frozen along with his heart.

"…I guess there's no excuse I can make—no, wait. If I use it as firewood, that'll eliminate the evidence and add to our resources; two birds with one stone. I can eat on the floor just fine…"

■ ■ ■

Outside the door. Her back to the wall, Couron, face down, had heard everything.

…As usual. This had been why she'd left him alone. It was his time to collect his heart. So it could accept that he'd sacrificed—killed Ivan. His…necessary ritual. Her brother needed this. Without it, he'd break down.

—Or maybe he was already long broken…

"……"

But Couron couldn't say anything. She could only do this—listen outside the door. To the boy of eighteen—so young he should have been considered a child. This situation, in which he was entrusted with the fate and decision-making for a village of two thousand, was abnormal no matter how you looked at it. But—there was no one else. To lead the defeated two thousand. To make the hard choices required. Who else could take on the resolve of those who'd come before, the wants of those remaining, and still move forward? Who could turn his heart to steel this way? —No one in this world but

Riku. If they lost him, they'd be *reduced* to quivering in fear of inevitable death as prey. Truly worthless, meaningless animals... Even Couron knew this.

—A Great War that raged for eternity. This was no figure of speech. No one remembered when the War had started. Whenever humans established something resembling civilization, it had been erased as though clearing weeds... A pathetic oral tradition absurd to even call history. They simply, calmly, factually, described it as eternity. A world where the sky was closed off and the earth torn asunder, bathed the color of blood, devoid of night or day. No longer having even a common calendar, they had forgotten what it meant for time to pass.

The ages had come to a standstill as the earth and sky, drenched in the ashes of death, were scorched by still more violence—and humans remained powerless. To take a step out of the village was to extend one's neck for the Grim Reaper's sickle. Even an unlucky encounter with a wild animal invited death. The sight of the gods or their relations—the other races—spelled destruction. As little as a stray projectile or the wake of a blast meant annihilated villages, cities, entire civilizations.

...It didn't end. It didn't end, it didn't end. It didn't end, it didn't end, it didn't end, it didn't end—the cycle of death and devastation. *If hell exists, this is it*, thought Couron—yet still people lived.

—For they could not die without a reason.

—For their hearts would not permit their existence to have been in vain.

Staying sane in a world like this—could you even call it sanity?

■■■

Five years earlier. The village that had taken in Riku, Couron's home, had been caught between the Flügel and Dragonias and *erased*. The adults who'd been their leaders had died, and, crushed by despair, weeping and sobbing, the survivors had arrived at a cave. Ignoring those overcome with grief, a child then thirteen scouted out the cave and declared:

"This is a good spot. This could be our next village."

Before a people who had lost everything mere hours before, he said "next," as if it was obvious. A roar of anger.

—*What's the point?* they cried.

—*So far as they're concerned, it's as if we don't even exist,* they wailed.

To these arguments, too logical to sound like hysterical despair, the boy countered without batting an eye:

"That's right. It's not 'as if'—we don't exist. We *won't exist.*"

And the boy explained how they'd go about it.

"We do not exist. We must not exist, and so we shall be imperceptible—we shall be ghosts."

A black gaze, deeper than the darkness of the cave.

"We shall use any means at our disposal to run, to hide, and to survive—until someday, someone—sees the *end of the War.*"

If they couldn't do anything—they might as well carry the hopes of those who had come before them. If they couldn't do anything—they might as well give those who came after them a chance.

"*Achéte*: Those who can say this and follow through—follow me."

—Thirteen years old. The words of the child whose home had been meaninglessly destroyed twice resounded through the cave all too heavily. To those with eyes like ghosts whose lives held no meaning, his words imparted a *reason to live*—and gave *meaning to death.*

■■■

It had been five years since, at the age of thirteen, Riku had assumed headship of a village with a population in excess of a thousand. Those who had died in the intervening years—totaled forty-eight. Couron thought—*that was unbelievably few.* But Riku didn't see that.

Even if he did, the responsibility of ordering their deaths crushed him. The forty-eight casualties had all lost their lives on expeditions. In a village swelled to two thousand, it would have been normal for twice that number to die in a single year just as a consequence of food shortages. And if another race had discovered them, hundreds—thousands—would have died in the blink of an eye. Having kept the casualties to forty-eight in five years spoke to Riku's competence beyond question.

—And that was why they trusted him.

—And that was why they put their lives on his shoulders.

But—sometimes they forgot. And every time they remembered, they felt guilty, offering thanks and apologies. Marta's earlier words had been an acknowledgement, too.

—That the Grim Reaper's sickle hovered over Riku's bared neck *same as the rest of them*. But his neck—hung with the weight of all two thousand of them.

——......

When Riku emerged from his room, Couron tried her best to pretend she didn't notice his injured fist.

"Riku, you're amazing...you're doing all you can. Your sister promises you..."

"—Stop trying to make me feel better. I'll go take that bath."

Riku's eyes were still lightless. Unable to bear it, Couron hugged him. This was the limit. Being the beacon that tethered the sanity of two thousand people in this world—was impossible. At this rate, her brother, Riku, wasn't going to last...!

"Hey—Couron."

"...I keep telling you it's Couronne... What is it?"

"When is it going to end? This age?"

Someone had told him: *Foul weather gives way to fair. Every night gives way to light.* But had any human seen the last time the storm of blue ash settled? Who had seen past the sky, obscured by dust, to the sun? Yes, someday it would end—it couldn't be eternal. But...by

human reckoning, it was impossible to perceive this war...as anything but eternal.

■■■

"So they asked themselves: When— Hey, uh, a-wha-wha-wha...?! Wh-wh-wh-what's wrong?!"

Tet, who'd been narrating through distant eyes as he played, now cried out in panic.

"Y-you bastard, please... You're telling this terrible story, *hkk*, to make me cry so I won't win, please."

"S-s-s-sorry! Maybe it was a bit too heavy!!"

But while Tet apologized to Izuna, her plump tears falling one after the other, it occurred to him: The *empathy to weep openly* upon hearing this tale—something had to be said for it. In point of fact, were he to relate this story to other races, the most he could hope for was to be dismissed with an *Of course*. Even now, over six thousand years later, all the races still despised one another. A girl who could grieve for this and call it terrible—was a child in the truest sense.

"Sorry. But it's a true story... This is how the world was during the Great War."

"...That asshole Ivan...died, please..."

"Yeah, he died. Immanity—without the Ten Covenants—could die at the flick of a Demonia—no."

Lowering his tone slightly, Tet continued.

"Even at a single bite from a Werebeast... They are the weakest creatures on this planet."

"—!! I would never——...!"

Do that—she'd been about to say, but Tet was impressed that she didn't in the end. No...she couldn't say for sure that she wouldn't. This girl was honest, and clever. Was it so different from *what she'd done to Elkia in games*? She saw this. And she felt, correctly, that it was absurd. That it was wrong.

"...That's wrong, please... It's total bullshit, please..."

"Yes—just as you say. The world was nuts."

Truly. Correctly. Properly. Absurdly unreasonable it was. If the feelings of a child could accept that as only natural—that was what would be abhorrent.

"But, hey! No one likes a story that's too heavy, right? Why don't we skip ahead."

Trying to pep up the oppressive atmosphere, Tet wiped Izuna's tears.

"Have you heard of—Ex Machina? ♪"

"…Ixseed Rank Ten…Ex Machina, please… Don't treat me like a dipshit, please."

"You sure are smart! ☆ Studying hard, I see. Good girl, good girl."

Petting Izuna as she took a big snort, Tet deftly continued playing as he talked.

"That's right, Ex Machina…a race of living machines, a race that is itself a machine. Created by an Old Deus 'inactive' since long ago—an Old Deus so ancient as to be forgotten even by the Ex Machinas themselves…"

"…Grampy told me about them, please. He said they'd never fall for the same attack or strategy twice, so during the war, the only ones capable of…'deicide'?…were Flügel and Ex Machina, please. So—"

Right, this is what he said, Izuna continued.

"—'Don't mess with those crazy sons o' bitches,' please."

"You get a perfect flower maaarrrk!! Let me pet you some more!"

Tet plastered a grin across his face and went, *fluff fluff fluff fluff.*

"So, right, Ex Machina—one day, Riku *ran into one of them*—"

YOINK! Izuna jumped up like a cat, distancing herself from Tet in an instant.

"—Yeah, so, that boy Riku, face-to-face with the terrible Ex Machina, was suddenly attacked. At a speed too fast to react with Immanity senses, you understand."

"I—I-I—I thought you said you weren't gonna go on with that terrible shit, please!"

"Whaaat? I just said no one likes stories that are *too* heavy, so I'd skip ahead?"

"I can't hear you, I can't hear you, please!!"

"You can cover your ears if you want, but it won't wooork. —The Ex Machina shot Riku with Lauwapokryphen. It's a weapon designed to reproduce an Elven spell—that fires countless vacuum blades that rip apart everythiiing!"

"Hyuuuuuaaaghh?!"

"The black ash itself was blown away as even the boy Riku's cloak and tools were minced to bits and sent flying through the air—"

"Aaaaah, aaaaah, I can't hear you, please! I can't hear you, pleaaase!"

"And then—she approached the carved-up remains of Riku lying on the ground—"

"Myaaaaaaahhhhhhhaaaaaaaaah!!"

"—and she kissed him and said, 'Big brother, I can't take it anymore. Make me a woman. ☆'"

...

......?

"D-d-didn't you say he was chopped to goddamn pieces, please?"

"Huh? All I said was that his cloak and tools were minced to shreds, right? Riku was ☆ fine. ♥"

Izuna, for the first time in her life...felt the urge to punch someone.

⏻ CHAPTER 2
1 × 1 = RECKLESS

……So, let's review the situation. I'm Riku, eighteen, virgin—…
What? You got a problem—?!

——No. No, no, no, no, the question erupting from my wildly spinning
brain has to…wait, wait—calm down! Get it together. I cannot grasp the
situation, but that means it's worse than anything I anticipated. Assign
priorities to the questions— What happened? What's happening? What's
about to happen? That's all. First, check the lock on your heart.

…It's all right. It's still locked after all these bizarre events—just
barely. Then grasp this situation in a second, no, a ten-thousandth of
a second. If you don't—

"…Assessment… Processing situation…"

No matter what this naked girl straddling you—this *monster in
disguise*—does, you'll be *screwed*! Think faster—stop time—

■■■

From the village, Riku had spurred on his horse to the east, to the
ruins indicated by the Dwarven map. They were supposedly the

remains of an old Elven city, destroyed by a Flügel in a single strike. Information about Elf was very sophisticated, and very valuable. He searched the battlefield, but found nothing useful there, and the intel he managed to gather was full of subtle holes. After all, the bastards didn't use tools. Magic that didn't require catalysts could be swept up clean. But along his way, the black ash grew thick, and he took shelter in a little monument nearby. That was when he spotted one—a member of another race. She had the appearance of a nude young girl with mechanical parts exposed—an Ex Machina. One of the worst races. But it was *fine*. Probably. Riku tried to ignore it and pass on.

—The next instant, he was flat. All of his gear had been eliminated along with the black ash itself, and he'd been thrust to the ground—apparently. He was utterly clueless as to what had just happened...but it seemed he wasn't dead yet. Anyhow, his torso had been stripped bare, and he'd been pushed onto his back, whereupon the Ex Machina, lowering its body over him, spoke.

Big brother, I can't take it anymore. Make me a woman.

——.

...Some sort of memory disorder? He was on the ground. It was perfectly plausible that he'd hit his head. But if his memory was in fact reliable, that line had been delivered in an emotionless monotone, after which, suddenly...

His innocence—his lips were stolen.

...That's all he'd been able to deduce. It answered the first question, "What happened?" Now he was grappling with the second—"What's happening?"—but...

"Error... Comprehension failed."

The Ex Machina, still on top of Riku, muttered this declaration unemotionally, wearing a mechanical non-expression.

...*Hmm, go me*, Riku congratulated himself silently, having successfully suppressed both his mouth and the reflex response prompted by his reason and life experience, both of which were desperate to scream—*I'm the one who fails to understand, you piece of shit!*

* * *

—Ex Machina. A very special race even among all the shits involved in the War. First off, they were a race of machines, *not even living things*, and they operated connected in "clusters." This meant if one found you, the race found you. Confronting one meant confronting the lot. But what made them very special was their manner of fighting. When a unit received an attack, it would analyze it in under a second and immediately design an equivalent armament. Whether it be Elven magic, Dwarven spirit arms, or even Dragonia breath—Ex Machina would *reproduce it and fire it back*. Through the long course of the War, their stockpile of weaponry had continued to grow, and in theory—they'd be able to power up indefinitely: the worst of the races. But they also had another trait.

They didn't attack proactively. If attacked, they would strike back, but as long as you didn't provoke them, they wouldn't engage you. Or so it was said. For this reason, Dwarven writings described them as——"untouchables."

This was the insight that shut Riku up. Were he to say something out of turn, he might be perceived as an enemy—and the entire human race exterminated.

Which brought him to *"What's happening?!"—What the hell is going on here?*

A situation that contradicted his available intel in multiple ways caused Riku to rage at himself. *They didn't attack proactively.* His assumption, then, being that he should be able to ignore it and move on—but now look at this. Riku, having assembled all his information, still found himself unable to grasp the situation or move when—*fwip*, the skin pressed against his receded, though the girl-shaped machine continued straddling him.

"Hypothesis: Values of fantasy parameters invalid?"

At this thoroughly unexpected question—a moment's indecision. Humans were ghosts. They did not exist. They must not exist. They were imperceptible… Should he forgo a reply and remain silent—?

"......It's not even a matter of whether it's my thing or not. Did you get my consent before robbing me of my innocence?"

He decided against it. The thing had clearly spoken using the human tongue. This confirmed that, at the very least, the existence of the human race was recognized. This fact alone chilled him to the core, but to ignore it... Rejection could be interpreted as hostility. Reason demanded: *Just go with the flow for now. Until you can see the situation, you mustn't make a move.*

Seeming uninterested in answering his accusation, the creature continued expressionlessly, its voice flat.

"*Laden:* Preset 072—'I-it's not like I wanted to. It was an accident.' That's right, an accident."

...Its soulless recitation, in conjunction with its initial "Big brother," made Riku's head go blank again.

—Just what the hell is this?

"............Confirmation: No change in subject's body temperature, pulse rate, or reproductive organs."

"Could you please not peep at people's physical reactions?"

Struggling to maintain his composure, Riku inwardly clucked as he discovered another unwelcome fact: *It was measuring his physiological responses.* The probability that a lie would be taken as antagonistic—was significant. Whether or not it was aware of these misgivings on Riku's part, the mechanical girl continued its line of interrogation.

"Doubt: Humans assumed to respond to present values with sexual arousal. Data incorrect?"

"...Well, yeah. I guess I'll just say it depends on the person."

—He couldn't lie. But he couldn't see its aim, either. He couldn't get a handle on the situation. Given that, if it was reading his physiological responses, it should have been well aware how terrified he was, just what did it want...?

"Query: Unit not deemed sexually arousing—or 'attractive'?"

Already struggling with his thoughts, this spectacularly difficult question made Riku feel dizzy. A calamity that spelled annihilation if met with opposition had just asked him something that would be tricky enough just coming from a human—and he couldn't lie.

...Riku steeled himself and took a serious look at the Ex Machina straddling him.

She looked much like a human girl of about ten. Her long black hair contrasted with her white skin and ruby eyes. She was pretty without qualification—or would be, except for the mechanical parts sticking out everywhere and the two taillike cables.

"Objectively, I think you're pretty. But in terms of arousal, I'd prefer someone of my race, and you look a little too young."

...How was that? He hadn't lied or criticized her... Was that not perfect, for a virgin? While Riku congratulated himself for this accomplishment, the Ex Machina girl promptly continued.

"Doubt: User without sexual experience intends to select partner?"

"Are you saying a virgin has no right to choose...?"

——.

In the course of this exchange, Riku's thoughts had gradually settled as he came to see the situation. Their conversation so far had sparked in him a certain suspicion. If he was right—

"So...may I ask by now what it is you want?"

—might as well ask. He was well aware that posing a careless question could be dangerous. However. Based on what he could predict from the information he'd gathered so far, failing to do so could result in *an absolute crisis*. The Ex Machina girl replied promptly and calmly.

"Answer: Analysis of unique language among humans desired."

"...Unique language?"

Riku repeated it—hoping that, somehow, his prediction would prove off the mark. But the Ex Machina girl nodded and informed him mechanically:

"Affirmation: Unique language of 'heart.'"

———.

"Confirmation: 'Becoming one'—*unique language* involving epidermal contact. Act assumed to exchange 'hearts,' which Ex Machina lack. Analysis indicates unit can load 'heart' if act emulated... Data incorrect?"

————————*Good God. Bad feelings sure have a way of proving themselves right*, Riku chortled to himself silently. From the moment he'd been tackled, he'd been strategizing how he might kill himself while it wasn't looking—but here it was speaking the human tongue, making conjectures (albeit inaccurate ones) about human sexual activity, and even gauging his physiological responses. Given what this revealed, Riku laughed at himself for having worried about answering it. Everything about humans was an open secret. It wasn't a matter of whether or not they knew humans existed.

——*They've been watching us. Probably for a long time.*

"—Well, you see, if exchanging 'hearts' was as easy as 'becoming one' physically, we humans would have a lot less trouble with each other."

Watching the Ex Machina as it seemed to deliberate his answer, Riku found his thoughts clearing to the point where it was difficult to believe how out of sorts he'd been. For whatever reason, humans had caught the notice of the worst of races and had been under observation—intense study. While humankind comically deluded itself that they were hiding, they were in reality being stalked. Regardless of the reason they'd been noticed, the situation was *a best-and-worst-case scenario*—right? *A race that all other races feared was watching them.* That was enough to justify humanity's destruction.

—So what to do? Well, just the usual. Maybe not the best move, but certainly the most feasible. That was all.

Putting his hand to his chest, Riku recited his usual incantation. But this time, it was a bit different—— *Seal it off.* Seal it, lock it, and *forget it.* Chase out the recognition that this loathsome machine had murdered humans like it was dusting—stamp it out beyond oblivion. Sacrifice feeling, abandon memory, lose fear, doubt, and panic. Become a ghost. There were two objectives: find the truth and lead the thing.

He took a deep breath. *You and this machine are on friendly terms*—believe it. *Fool your vitals. Deceive your memory. Strap it down, wrap a chain around it*—and lock it.

Can I? *Sure you can, Riku—ya little* bastard.

If it really wants to analyze the "heart," that means it—doesn't have one. *Deceiving someone without a heart should be way easier than fooling humans. And you—you son of a bitch, you're a natural little bastard who's been doing that like breathing. Right…? Then there's no problem*—

——*Grnk.* Several times louder than usual, the sound of the lock closing opened his eyes.

Before him, with her long, long black hair…stood a *girl.* After processing for a long time, *she* finally reached an off-the-mark conclusion.

"Understanding: Interpretation of 'becoming one' as metaphor for reproductive act correct— Request: Engage in reproductive act with—"

"Hmm… I refuse. How's that for an answer?"

A bit of a strong rebuff. Words that could conceivably be interpreted as hostile. But his cool-headed unconscious insisted, *It's fine,* prompting him to add:

"How do you expect me to surrender my virginity to someone who isn't even human? Plus—"

He'd tease out the information he needed.

"—Ex Machinas are all *linked* to their clusters or whatever, right? Sorry, but I'm not an exhibitionist."

Namely…

"Denial: Unit has been *disconnected* from cluster."

That's what he needed to know and just as he'd anticipated. But he couldn't afford to get carried away…

"Huh? Why?"

Respond appropriately. Act confused. Ask why. Even if you can guess.

"Answer: Unit...attempted to analyze whether Ex Machinas have 'hearts,' 'selves,' or 'souls.'"

This was a predictable response. If one was talking about a machine.

"Result: Outbreak of numerous logical inconsistencies led to unit's disconnection and discard."

The self-referential paradox. Finally, Riku had verified why this Ex Machina acted so erratically.

She was *broken.*

That was truly convenient. It was too early to relax, but the worst-case scenario just got a little farther away. *All right, Riku, you guys are on friendly terms, aren't you? This is your cue to get concerned, right?*

"What? But that means...you..."

As Riku knitted his brows and poured on the sympathy, the girl gave an emphatic nod.

"Conclusion: User authorized to defile unit to heart's content. Though unit lacks *hole.*"

"I don't want to! Wait, you don't...?!"

Expressionless as ever, she cocked her head sideways and put forward a suggestion.

"Proposal: User can bring unit to village and defile at leisure."

"That's not the point...come on."

——Investigation complete. She knew about the village—*but never mind that.* Other races could find their village anytime they wanted. They knew that. What he'd wanted to confirm was that she wouldn't hide the fact that she knew about the village. That left two possibilities. But both were fine. Now he had all the data he needed—to create the *character she wanted.* Once more, he imagined hearing that click. This was what he wanted—the Riku who looked like he had a heart though it was actually closed off was all put together. Apparently oblivious of what Riku was thinking, the girl nodded in great earnest, as if she'd understood.

"Understanding: User finds unit unattractive and rejects reproductive act."

"Ahh, you really don't get it at all, ma'am…"

The girl nodded one more time and withdrew from Riku's body. The liberated Riku slowly rose while the girl crouched down in front of him.

"Proposal: Game requested."

"……What?"

"Lösen—Game 001: Chess—"

Then, on the palm the girl extended—no, on the ground beyond it—the silhouette of a chess set seemingly drawn with light on a canvas of air appeared, then solidified.

—*Son of a bitch*, thought Riku, staring at the Ex Machina armament deployment.

"Contest: If unit wins," she proposed, "user requested to bring unit to village and engage in reproductive act."

"—And what if I win?"

"Answer: User permitted to bring unit to village and engage in reproductive act."

"They're the same, aren't they?!"

Riku exploded instinctively as his opponent's inorganic expression tinged with color at her brilliant ploy. At the same time, though, Riku thought—*This is my chance.*

"Well, all right, fine. I'll play your game, but under different conditions."

Maybe not the best move, but the most feasible— Riku's mind, walking hand in hand with death, formulated multiple strategies instantaneously. He'd draw out the maximum information with a minimum of moves. He'd exploit the situation fully with just one. *Now, how far can you go? Let's see those skills—charlatan.*

"If I win, I request you pretend you didn't see me and stay away from my village."

While he said this, Riku knew that, for him, winning this

game was impossible. If Ex Machina were machines of such analytical—computational—power as they were rumored to be, they would own the chessboard. Thus, the girl nodded and responded.

"Acknowledgment: Condition accepted. Condition in case of unit victory unchanged."

Yes, she'd accept it. But that wasn't the issue.

"No, that's gonna change, too."

Because—

"The 'heart' you want to analyze can't be analyzed through the reproductive act."

"......"

Riku considered the dumbstruck girl coolly. There were two conceivable reasons this thing might have mentioned the village. Either it was just indifferently stating fact...or it was trying to *warn* him for some other purpose. He didn't know what that reason might have been, but he could potentially identify it based on *whether or not she swallowed his conditions*. If she had some other aim, she'd accept the change. Otherwise, her plan would fall through. Would it really be possible to get an Ex Machina—a machine—to show her hand by shaking her up? But the machine girl, still without feeling, opened her eyes wide and inquired blankly:

"—Astonishment......Question: What is analysis method?"

......

Could it be...she really had been just stating fact—? The best-case scenario, the most hopeful possibility, felt for that all the more doubtful—but if, hypothetically, everything she'd been saying was true and if he played his cards right, he could *seal the thing off and exploit it.*

"If you win, I'll let you stay with me until you understand the heart."

"......Question: Does staying with user enable analysis of heart?"

Now, time to convince an intelligent machine with the most feasible, the most plausible bullshit logic.

"This 'heart' is not physical."

"......"

"It's *words unspoken*. It's something we feel by understanding each other. If you can get by without revealing that you're an Ex Machina, without leaving my side—in other words, if you can keep communicating without being rejected—it will take time, but you should be able to analyze it."

"…………"

The Ex Machina girl, maintaining her silence, looked into Riku's eyes. Those red eyes made Riku sure she was "analyzing" the veracity of his words. But it was futile. Because he hadn't told a single lie.

…The girl calculated carefully and eventually nodded as if convinced.

"Acceptance: Let us begin—"

It seemed the worst-case scenario had been averted. At the very least, deciding that was likely—

"Oh, before that, let me add just one more condition."

—he grinned audaciously, changing his attitude.

"I'm about to freeze to death. Can you supply me with clothes to replace the ones you cut up?"

Snot freezing from his nose, his teeth chattering, Riku begged.

■■■

The game was one-sided. Without ever seeing a path to victory, Riku lost in just twenty-nine moves. *Exactly as planned.*

"Damn it, you win… Crap, guess I'm gonna have to take you to my village like I promised."

There was no way he could beat a machine that exploited high-level computation to deduce perfect play. And that was why he'd proposed conditions advantageous to the loser.

"……"

With a smile—but not forgetting to feign remorse—Riku stood and considered the Ex Machina girl.

Miraculously, everything had pretty much gone the way he'd intended it to. He still wasn't quite sure what she was really up to, but employing a high-level strategy against the likes of humans would be pointless. If it was just this weirdo who'd taken an interest in humanity—i.e., the other Ex Machinas hadn't—then they shouldn't be receiving any attention from other races. Having said that, this game had no binding force. It was too early to let—

"Question: What is reason for *display of remorse*?"

"—What?"

For an instant, he held his breath. Had she seen through his acting? he wondered... No, she couldn't have. He'd closed off his feelings entirely to play a character. Even Riku could hardly tell it was fake. But if she did see through to the truth within him, then that——

Looking into Riku's wary eyes—black eyes and supposedly incapable of reflecting anything—the machine girl announced nonchalantly:

"Determination: Presence of 'heart' confirmed. Subject judged worthy of further analysis."

Riku didn't know what that meant. But the Ex Machina girl's expression, almost a subtle smiling... Was he just imagining it?

"......Ahh, come to think of it, we haven't introduced ourselves."

The realization came to him a bit late. It had completely slipped his mind given the string of overwhelming events.

"Uh, my name's Riku. And you are—?"

"Answer: Üc207Pr4f57t9."

...

"...Huh? Uh, what? Is that...your name?"

"Affirmation: Unit identification number—synonymous with 'name'?"

"...Look, if you wanna communicate and be understood in the village, you should pick a name that sounds human or—"

The girl mulled his suggestion over a bit, and then:

"Question: 'Name' is arbitrary unit identifier?"

"Well—yeah, I guess."

Next, the girl thought hard enough to make a scratching sound. But then she put her fingers in her long hair and gave her name.

* * *

"Reply: Unit name is Schwarzer."

"That's *not* easy to say, *not* easy to understand, and *not* like a name. I reject it by the three *n*'s—call yourself Schwi."

Riku shot her down. Still, maybe he was imagining it—

"......Enigma: Arbitrary setting corrected... Rebuttal: User able to call freely from start."

—but she somehow looked like she was pouting as she "protested." It must have been his imagination, Riku decided.

"All right, summing up. I'll take you to the village—but a few things before that."

He counted off a finger and said carefully:

"You can't analyze the heart if they find out you're an Ex Machina. They'll all get scared and won't want to communicate with you."

"......Coherence."

With a nod from the Ex Machina girl now called Schwi, Riku continued.

"So, now that we've got your name, can we fix that way of talking you have that screams, 'I'm a machine'?"

"—*Laden:* Virtual personality 1610—"

Schwi looked up, seemingly lost in thought for a moment, and said:

"—Hee-hee-hee, then I'll call you 'big brother'! ♥ How do you like this?"

"Are you messing with me? Denied."

She'd just taken her flat, monotone voice and forced accents onto it. Riku shot it down.

"...Rebuttal: Unit dedicated significant resources to assessment..."

"You think I can just wave my hand and tell everyone I actually had a little sister?"

"...Request: Provide optimal scenario."

Riku thought maybe Schwi was sulking after all, but he set her aside to think seriously. Being straight about it, he'd run off for five days without telling Couron. And now he'd be bringing home a girl.

The most *plausible scenario* was—

"…All right, you're a survivor who lost everything in the flames of war."

"……——"

"You're timid, you don't talk much, and when you do, you mumble little by little. It'll be a pain if they ask about your past. Don't say more than you need to. No more of that stereotypical machine-talk at the beginnings of your sentences—whaddaya say?"

Schwi absorbed Riku's words one by one as if chewing on them.

"………………Mm."

It must have been at least ten full seconds. After deep contemplation, the Ex Machina girl—Schwi—nodded once.

With that, her mechanical expression, previously inorganic and emotionless, assumed a faint shadow. Quietly, she opened her mouth.

"…O-kay… How is…this?"

——. Her unbelievably natural mimicry of a human—even bringing her expression in line—left Riku at a loss for words for a moment.

"…Hey…is this…acting?"

It was as if she'd transformed. Were it not for her exposed mechanical parts, even Riku might've fallen for the illusion she was human. It was so unnaturally natural, it seemed to remind him of something… But Schwi wagged her head from side to side.

"…Acting? No…I traced…emulated…a personality, to support the specified values…"

Riku didn't understand what she meant, but he did recognize that she probably wouldn't be taken for a machine like this. Now there was just—

"Okay, now why don't you put on some clothes. Finally."

Yeah. No matter how well she might maintain appearances

through her words and expressions, human girls didn't walk around naked.

"Cover your mechanical bits. Put a hood over the parts on your head. Listen, don't go showing people your skin, all right?"

Schwi replied with a nod.

"...Mm. I'll, only, show it to you..."

......

"I think the message you're sending is a little off, but...sure. Let's go with that."

Looking at the big picture, he could foresee the commotion awaiting him at home. Still quite uncomfortable with it, Riku decided to give up heading for the city ruins and instead return to the village. Carrying a gift hardly wanted.

"...Riku, we're here...?"

"Yeah. Seriously. Not that I can believe it."

Actually, it was Riku who'd gotten carried. In mere hours, Schwi had zipped Riku a distance that would have taken five days by horse at full speed. When she arrived at the village, she put Riku down. The absurd difference in their races' abilities brought him past astonishment to disgust, and he groaned.

"That movement...are you sure it doesn't use spirits?"

"I'm...sure. I'm a Prüfer... My performance...is below the average, for an Ex Machina..."

This was below average...huh. And without using any arms.

"If I could have used armaments...it would have taken... minutes..."

Setting aside this astronomical assertion... The challenge is from here, Riku reminded Schwi with a look. The mechanical ears and metal piece on her head that said Ex Machina no matter how you looked at them weren't detachable, so they'd somehow managed to cover them up by making a robe with a big, baggy hood. But...

"The challenge is those tails sticking out of your robe..."

"…They're not, tails… They're virtual spirit corridor junction nerves…"

"No, I mean—whatever, but can't you roll them up or something to hide them?"

The two independently gesticulating cables, despite their owner's assertion to the contrary, were obviously tails.

"…I can't… They're…my power source… This is the second time, I've told you…"

Yeah, I got it. Riku sighed. Initially when they were preparing to disguise Schwi as a human, she'd said it would be easy if they used spirits, employing her disguise spell device. But it would be a problem if there was a spirit response from the village. So they had to resort to this desperate nonsense… Apparently, her tails—or in her vernacular, her virtual spirit corridor junction nerves—drew power from the environment. It was like eating for a human. It didn't "use" spirits, but "consumed" them. So there was no spirit response. But according to her, she had no choice but to expose them. Riku tore at his hair and spat in frustration:

"Aah, look… Forget it, we're just gonna claim they're accessories. Let me say this one more time—if they find out you're not human, you're not going to be able to analyze the 'heart,' okay? Keep that in mind and do everything you can to act human."

"…Mm, all right…"

Courage steeled, they entered the cave, passing through the tight tunnel. At the gate, the boy on watch—

"Oh, Ri—"

—started to call to him, but Riku hurriedly extended his index finger to shut the kid up.

"Th-thank you for your work…everyone's worried about…you."

The boy on watch, answering in a whisper, noticed Schwi next to Riku, and his expression clouded. *Shh*, indicated Riku with the same gesture, and he passed through the gate. As Riku tiptoed up the stairs, hiding his presence, Schwi asked:

"…Riku, you're scared… Is it because of me?"

"Yeah, of course, that's one thing. But right now, what really—"

Riku stopped in midsentence. As fast as he turned, he rushed to cover his head—

"Riiiiiiiikuuuuuuuu!"

The very instant the yell rang out, Riku's guarded head—no, his abdomen—took a deep blow as Couron, racing toward him, landed a knee. Unable to even make a noise, he started writhing down to the ground, but Couron, as if unwilling to allow that, grabbed him by the collar and shouted in his face:

"I can't believe you!! You left for five days without telling anyone. What are you trying to—?"

As Couron screamed and shook him violently, Riku, unable to argue, just gurgled.

Then, she abruptly stopped—

"Who's this giiirl? She's so cuuuuute! ♥"

Flinging Riku aside, Couron glomped Schwi, grinning at Riku as he choked.

"Ohh, Rikuuu, if you were going to find a bride, you should've just told uuus! ♪"

"Couron, is your brain all right? What kind of idiot these days goes off for five days to find a—?"

Riku answered squinting, but Couron nudged him with her elbow and went on.

"Come ooon, you don't have to be bashful! ♪ These days, priority one is making babies! Two is eating! Three, four, and five are making babies!"

So what about you? Riku just barely stopped himself from asking out loud.

"But Riku, you never showed any interest. Everyone was worried! I won't get in the way, so you two go get in the bath, and then you can make sweet, sweet—"

"…Stop doing that."

While Couron repeatedly jammed her index finger in the space of a circle she formed with her other hand, Riku held his head.

"Look…shouldn't common sense tell you she's a refugee from a destroyed village?"

As if finally awake, Couron froze with a breath. Adopting a meek expression, she asked:

"…Is she?"

As soon as he said it, Riku thought, *Crap*—but what could be done? Now he'd just have to see it through. He braced himself as he opened his mouth.

"…So I deciphered from the Dwarven map that there was a conflict about two and a half days' ride from here. There was supposed to have been a small village thereabouts—so I went to check."

It wasn't a lie. According to the map, a village had disappeared in a conflict between Dwarf and Demonia. It just happened that had been two years ago. Given that the only one in this village who could read Dwarven was Riku, it was unlikely he'd get caught. But that wouldn't be enough to satisfy Couron…

"All right, but that doesn't mean you had to go by yourself, does it?"

Riku, seeing this coming, shook his head.

"It would have been too dangerous if I had anyone with me. But if I'd told you I was going alone—"

"I would have stopped you, of course!! That's just like you, Riku, but…please think of your sister a little. How many holes do you want to poke in my stomach?"

Couron looked at him pleadingly. Realizing that the corners of her eyes were red and swollen, Riku felt a heavy weight drop on him. He regretted from his heart having made her seriously worry—but still he couldn't tell her the truth. Couron sighed with a vague sense of surrender and turned to inquire gently of the newcomer.

"I'm sorry. You've been through a lot… What's your name?"

"……Schwi…"

Just as specified, just as configured. Schwi behaved timidly as she responded while using Riku as cover. *Mm-hmm, mm-hmm.* Couron smiled and nodded at this before continuing.

"But don't worry, you're safe here. Riku's here for you. I wonder how you and Riku met?!"

Riku thought surely the question had been posed innocently enough. She'd just asked out of curiosity, to advance the conversation. Or it could be that her suspicions were somewhat aroused at how composed Schwi seemed for someone who'd lost her village. Schwi got stuck for words for a moment, and Riku gave her a look to indicate, *Go with the flow.* But—there was no way an Ex Machina like her could grasp what he meant.

"…With…a kiss…and a demand…to reproduce."

Here's the question: Who'd take that statement as "*Schwi* demanding to reproduce *with Riku*"?
And so it was that Couron, with a sharp, heavy stomp forward—
"If you wanna do *that*—"
—unleashed a left that dug into Riku's solar plexus, a shout that shook the cave…
"—at least find sanctuary firrrrst——!"
…and reaped the young man's consciousness.

■■■

He'd discovered a survivor of tender years from a destroyed village and immediately demanded sexual intercourse. The rumor propagated faster than sound, and throughout the village, heated debate flew this way and that.

"No, Mr. Riku was right. You gotta do what you can do when you can do it."
"I disagree. Riku should have obtained her consent first."
"Wait, hold on… You don't even know if there was consent or not, do you?"
"We have her word that he demanded it, don't we? How can you—?"

……

"This is weird."

First of all, the whole subject was weird—mostly in that not one of them brought up Schwi's age. Everything was weird. Or maybe it was just him? They say the chaos of war leads to derangement. After all, it was clearly all the nutjobs in the village who were long gone... Riku traversed a gallery of gazes—some reverent, some spiteful—through the village to his room. Then, in a small voice so as not to be heard, he muttered to Schwi, who walked beside him:

"Look, you, will you give me a break...?"

"...About what?"

Apparently not knowing what she'd done wrong, Schwi eyed him quizzically.

"In the first place, you wanted to learn about my 'heart.' So in a way, *you* were seducing *me*, right?"

He remembered how she'd called him "big brother" when they met.

"Couldn't you have made yourself look a little more mature?"

While Riku complained that if she'd just done that they wouldn't be in this situation, Schwi blinked emptily.

"...I'm supposed to look like...what human men...what you... like."

"Don't you start calling me a pedophile. I like, you know, a more voluptuous—"

"That's not true."

Schwi shot back decisively and went on.

"...If that were true, you'd have no reason, not to engage in the reproductive act...with that human named Couron."

Now, then—Riku debated. He'd just been mechanically judged a pedophile, and Couron had been put forward as evidence of this. At which should he snap?

"...In the first place, all human men prefer...young girls."

"Cut the shit, don't generalize like that. Humans each have their own—"

"...False... Biologically, young individuals...capable of reproduction, have the advantage. No argument."

This chick...... Maybe it was his imagination, but it looked as if the Ex Machina, who wasn't supposed to have feelings, was copping a patronizing attitude with her lecture.

"...I have no fuzzy subjectivity... Humans prefer young women, capable of reproduction... This is a fact."

"—...I don't know what to do with you..."

His face a mask of exhaustion and with all kinds of stares at his back, Riku finally reached his room.

...Was it his imagination that it felt horribly far?

It had been a long day...such a long day. In the end, Riku had failed to find what he'd set out after, despite being half certain it would get him killed, and instead he'd come back with—

"...This is...your room?"

A time bomb of a machine girl, her true intentions unknown, curiously inspected his room.

"Shocked at its shittiness?"

"...I am shocked...at its exceptionalism."

Riku felt a self-deprecating amusement that a machine was capable of irony or flattery. He reached for what must have been Couron's handiwork—a meal sitting on a sheet on the floor. He felt like filling his stomach as quickly as possible and passing out.

"...What are you...doing?"

"I guess you Ex Machinas wouldn't be familiar with this, but humans have to eat or they'll die."

Raising the fork to his mouth, Riku tossed his words out tiredly.

"So I'm just gonna take a few bites and lie down... You do whatever."

"...Mm. Understood... I'll do whatever..."

The girl perused the things in Riku's room—the maps, the measuring tools, and so on—one by one, but suddenly:

"...Riku, let's...play a game."

"...Why?"

Frozen with a fork in his hand, Riku watched Schwi silently point at the bookshelf. There sat…the chessboard he'd been carrying at the start of it all, when his home was destroyed. Looking at it with the dimmest of eyes, Riku spat.

"No, thank you. I played with you that time because I had no choice. Games are a silly pastime for children."

"…? …Why…?"

"Because reality isn't as simple as games."

There were no rules, no victories or losses. You lived or you died. That was all. In this world—

"We don't have the time or resources to waste on pointless child's play like games."

"…What if it's not, pointless?"

While he wasn't looking, the chessboard had been opened, and Schwi began setting up the pieces.

"…If you beat me…I'll disclose…the information you want."

"What?"

"…Such as the reason, the Great War started…the factors required for its termination…et cetera…"

Such was her proposal, but Riku dismissed it.

"Ha…ridiculous."

Why the War started? How it would end? —Who cared.

The War was timeless. Whatever the cause of it, what difference did that make to the fact that it still raged? And how it would end? If anyone had been capable of bringing that about, it would have been done long ago. What would make anyone suppose mere humans could accomplish something that even the bastards ravaging the world could not? Therefore, Riku concluded, *it wasn't worth knowing.* Worthless hope simply invited further despair. Someday… someday it would end. Their hope was baseless—and therefore unrefuted. If you gave them grounds for hope and then somehow it became contested…in this world of degeneration and devastation, wreck and ruin, it would be more than enough to deal the finishing blow to the fragile lives of humans. And so…

"I'm not interested, and I don't need to know. If there's something I do want to know—"

Riku narrowed his eyes as he pointed his fork at Schwi.

"—it's how to survive, and that's all."

One of the vehicles of humans' destruction.

"Ex Machina's knowledge, mathematics, design technology—if I win, you give me that."

He'd use their power in the service of humanity. To survive. For the sake of tomorrow—no, now.

"...Mm...all right..."

As Schwi nodded, somewhat sadly, Riku continued.

"So then, what if I lose?"

Mechanical and calculating, she must have had some demand. Schwi bluntly answered Riku's wry query.

"...'Communication'..."

She peered straight into Riku's black eyes.

"...I want to learn, about your 'heart'...the definition of the 'heart,' as you know it...I request...this information."

"Didn't I tell you it can only be understood by grasping words unspoken?"

"...Mm, so, I request, you try...to communicate, with me...words unspoken..."

"......All right."

Riku set his meal aside, sat before the chessboard, and began. Staring at the board for the first time in how many years, Riku contemplated *seriously*.

......*Beat Ex Machina's computational ability to achieve perfect play*—? Riku thought. It was impossible. But Schwi's behavior, her lacking comprehension of the heart, her failure to read between the lines—these demonstrated definitely that there were factors she couldn't calculate. If he focused solely on the board, he couldn't win. But it was likely that psychological elements—mind games—would work.

"—Check."

As Schwi fell headlong into Riku's simple trap, he now felt confident of his assessment.

"...Check."

But Schwi promptly accounted for it, as if to say, *you won't be able to use the same trick twice.* No. That was simply the nature of her race. So what, then? Simple. *He'd just have to keep changing his strategy without using the same trick twice.* If he was going to incorporate leading, baiting, and manipulation, the number of strategies…was limitless. *If you can count infinity—let's see it, Ex Machina—!!* His fatigue forgotten, Riku's thoughts roaring, suddenly—

"…Riku, you're smiling…"

"———What…?"

Brought back to himself, Riku opened his eyes and touched his mouth.

It was true. The corners of his mouth were upstretched, prompting him to open his eyes wider. Seemingly oblivious of how Riku had frozen, Schwi took her turn, putting down a piece.

"You don't, close it off…during a game…do you?"

—*Stop it. Don't ask, don't find out, brush it off,* something inside him screamed, but—

"…What are you…talking about…?"

"……Your heart…"

———*Grk.*

"…Human survival, in this world…is a biological…abnormality…"

———…………*Pk.*

"…The cause…your 'heart'…is what I…want to—"

"——Hey."

———Inside Riku———

——————something made a noise—————

"Are you messing with me?"

——and broke.

Riku had no memory of it. Before he knew it, his fingers gripped

Schwi's throat with enough force to break them. But this meant nothing to an Ex Machina. Her glassy eyes simply peered into his...

...where she was clearly *reflected*.

"...I didn't think it possible, but do you really *not know where you stand*?"

Riku understood a little late. —*Yeah, now I see.* The countless feelings and memories he'd sealed, chained, and locked away when he'd encountered this *massacre machine*—disgust anger loathing hatred malice grievance grievance grievance grievance grievance grievance grievance pain—had all piled up ad infinitum, straining the lock on his feelings, memories, and heart that had been restrained beyond all reason.

—Until finally, it rattled, cracked, and broke.

His *reason* demanded—*What the* hell *is that thing? Oh, it's one of those bastards who trample humans underfoot.*

His *feelings* wondered—*How the* hell*'d you manage to stay calm in front of* that thing?

Yeah, no kidding—ha-ha—when I think about it "calmly," you're right.

"You kill the shit out of us, take everything we have, do it over and over again for eternity, and then what do you ask...? 'Hey, humans, how's it feel?' Ha-ha! You wanna know what's in our 'hearts'? Sure, I'll tell you.

"FUCK YOU ALL!"

—The bones in his fingers screamed. *Keep it up, and your fingers really will break.* Somewhere in his head, someone asked—*What will this accomplish?* But his reason and feelings both shot back in unison—*Shut up, I don't care!*

"—Ha, ha-ha-ha, ha-ha-ha-ha-ha-ha-ha-ha-ha!"

How could he not laugh? For the first time, his reason and emotions finally agreed on something!! Then there was no need to hold back. Riku told his fingers to break for all he cared and roared at Schwi:

"Do you know how many people have died because of you bastards?! How many people you've killed?! How many—?"

How many you made me kill—?

"...I'm...sorry..."

Schwi mumbled softly as Riku wailed. *Is it something you can just apologize for—?* Riku opened his mouth to scream, but she touched his cheek.

"...I made you, cry...so, I estimate, that what I said, to you, was terrible..."

—...*What...?* At the touch of Schwi's hand, stained by the tears on his cheek, Riku opened his eyes.

"...I have determined...your 'heart'...*wants to kill me...*"

Her next words made his mind go blank.

"...I have been...disconnected..."

Implying that there was no worry of the other Ex Machinas finding out, Schwi calmly opened her chest and, in a maze of complex machinery, pointed out a part glowing faintly.

"...All you need to do is, stick that fork, in here...and I'll...die." As if unsettled by her choice of words, she made a dazed expression and corrected herself. "...? Die...? I'm not, alive... Shut down permanently—fail, irreparably... Be wrecked?"

Entirely too matter-of-factly and all too naturally, she continued.

"...I...want to see your...'heart'...so...it's, okay..."

With this, Schwi, as if it were the only thing to do, faced her reflection in the black eyes of the boy with a heart, Riku—

—and asked:

"...Will you...kill me...as your heart desires?"

————*Ha-ha...*

—*You're joking, Riku. Abdicating responsibility again... Just how low will you go, you worthless scum?*

Sure, if you ask where it all originates, it's this "Great War" the bastards are pulling. But the forty-eight who died—Chad, Anton, Elmer, Cory, Dale, Siris, Ed, Darrell, Dave, Laks, Vin, Eric, Charlie, Thomson, Shinta, Yann, Zaza, Zargo, Clay, Goro, Peter, Arthur, Morg,

*Kimmy, Datt, Ceril, Vigi, Volly, Ken, Savage, Leroy, Popo, Couthon, Lut, Shigure, Shao, Ulf, Balto, Asso, Kenwood, Peyl, Ahad, Hound, Balrof, Masashi, Memegan, Karim...——and Ivan. The one who told them to die, no matter how you spin it...*was you, rodent Riku!!

—Fump... Riku let go, and Schwi dropped to sit on the floor. Unable to bear her eyes, staring vacantly like glass beads, Riku turned his back.

"...I'm going to bed."

With this short statement, he flopped onto his bed, a simple bundle of straw. Softly, he heard Schwi's perplexed voice.

"...Why...won't you, kill me?"

"—I don't know! Why ask me? Shit!! I'm begging ya, just be quiet!!"

Why wouldn't he kill her? He could list any number of reasons.

—Such as, don't think I'm like you bastards.

—Or, would that bring back those who've died?

—Or, what would that solve?

If he just wanted to shift blame and say a bunch of pretty words, he could rattle off any number. But that Riku nauseated him. He had no right to speak for them—the dead. For, little maggot that he was, he could tell people to die *but couldn't kill anyone with his own filthy hands.*

"...I'm...sorry..."

For what—? But it seemed she'd misconstrued Riku's meaning again. Hearing Schwi apologize, her voice tinged with an obscure sense of regret, Riku was once more assaulted by a self-loathing that made him feel as if his guts were spilling out.

I can't take it anymore... I don't know anything... There's just too much...

"Stay where I can see you. If you were to harm anyone in the village..."

"...Mm...all...right."

At her nod, so obedient it gave him pause, Riku felt as though his body had become even heavier.

...What am I trying to do...?

He went ahead and asked himself but had a feeling he already knew the answer.

Riku considered that he must have broken long ago. Whatever calculations might have been involved, facing an Ex Machina—one of the very culprits who were driving humans to destruction—and managing to delude himself into believing they were on friendly terms... If he could do that, he wasn't even human. Compared to this machine, standing confused as if concerned about him, he was by far the more mechanical of the two. And machine that he was, he continued calculating.

—*Looking at it rationally, I should have killed her, here and now.*

—*There are too many uncertainties. There's no proof she's even disconnected.*

—*Could I have even killed her in the first place? Could she have been bluffing? Trying to test something?*

But, Riku asked himself, *did I even consider those factors before I let go?*

No. He'd just...felt *it was wrong*. He didn't even know what was wrong. If he had to say...it was everything. Every damn thing felt wrong.

"The human 'heart'...? I'm the one who wants to know about it... Shit..."

"...? Riku...?"

On the threshold of his closing eyelids, Riku heard Schwi's voice calling out to him in vague confusion. Fatigue and drowsiness seized his consciousness without asking and drowned it in darkness...

■■■

—*Knock, knock.* Prompted by the noise, his consciousness slowly resurfaced.

"Rikuuu... ♪ I know you must be tired, but I've got—" Words followed and the sound of the door opening. "—Oh my! ♥ Excuse me! Your sister can be a bit dense like that. Take your tiiime! ♪"

Footsteps pattered away as the door closed.

—*What?* Deciding he should probably figure out what was going on, Riku drummed up his energy to raise his heavy eyelids—

"......"

"......"

—and made eye contact with Schwi lying on top of him, nestled under the blanket, staring.

"...Might I inquire as to why you are on top of me?"

How long had he been asleep—? Wait, that didn't really matter. After they'd just been discussing whether he'd kill her or not, what the hell was she—?

"...You told me, to stay, where you could...see me...but, then, you closed, your eyes..."

And so. Somehow looking proud (probably just Riku's imagination), she elaborated.

"...I projected, the unspoken meaning...of 'where I can see you'... as 'in the range of my perception.'"

"Huh. And then?"

"...The sense of touch is active...even in sleep... I determined that this would enable perception."

Apparently very confident in her conclusion, she looked at him vaguely as if to say, *Praise me for grasping the abstract meaning of a human.* Riku furrowed his brow intensely.

"I just meant don't leave this room. You see now?"

"............Cannot comprehend."

Schwi opened her eyes to their fullest and muttered, "...Closing eyes...is incompatible...with the parameter...'where I can see you'..."

Schwi seemed perplexed when Couron's voice interjected:

"Oh, come to think of it! Umm, sorry to bother you while you're doing it, buuut..."

"We're not doing it. What do you want?"

"Uh, well, you see...I was thinking maybe you two both ought to take a bath! Especially Schwi, she must have been through a lot. If you want, I was thinking Big Sister could even help wash Schwi! ♪"

At this, Riku shot a look at Schwi.

—*Go with the flow, you. Properly this time.*

As if fully grasping Riku's meaning this time, Schwi nodded firmly and answered:

"...Riku told me...not to show, my body...to anyone else."

...Maybe he should have gone ahead and killed her after all. Riku's head swam, but there was a smirk in the tone of Couron's response.

"Oh, goodness... It seems he's already broken you, hasn't he? My little brother is such a fast worker! ♥"

"Couron...please. I beg you. Just shut up al—"

"So take care of Schwi... I got everyone else away from the bath, so now's your chance!"

"—Stop doing that!"

Couron, poking just her hands through the door and jamming her right index finger through a circle she'd formed with the fingers of her left hand, dashed away like a storm.

......

The exhausted Riku and his rider, Schwi, were left in her wake.

"—You about ready to get off of me?"

"...Mm."

As Schwi obediently disengaged from him, Riku considered his situation.

...There was no point in saying anything anymore. It had now been established that he was a pedophile who had broken a war refugee. *But...* He decided it was better than people knowing he'd brought back an Ex Machina.

"...Are you cool with eating and bathing and stuff?"

To keep her Ex Machina identity a secret, she'd have to go some way toward mimicking a human, but...

"...You mean, can I act, like a...human?"

"—You... How is it you can get what I mean here and not...?"

Riku wondered if she was doing it on purpose, but incapable of determining the thought processes of the Ex Machina, he decided to table the issue for now.

"...I don't require...food. There is no need, to waste...resources, which are valuable to humans..."

Was she weighing their circumstances? Or... No, he didn't know— Tabled.

"But if you don't eat anything, people will suspect you. Let's just say you don't eat much. You can eat, right?"

"...Mm. But only decompose it...no utility..."

"I'll eat less to cover it. Our net food situation won't change—so."

Giving Schwi no time to argue, Riku moved on to the next point.

"What about water?"

"...No issue... I am waterproof, dustproof, frostproof, fireproof, bulletproof, bombproof, spellproof, spiritproof..."

"You damn psychos. So as for the bath, we're just gonna pretend..."

"...But...I am not...stainproof."

"Even though you're bombproof? Isn't that what you'd call a design flaw?"

"...If I could, use spirits, I could use, my self-cleaning device...but you told me, not to..."

Schwi rebutted with a somehow (apparently) sullen expression.

"Damn it, I guess we're gonna have to go whole hog. Let's take advantage of Couron's misunderstanding and the fact no one will be around—"

"...And...you'll wash...me."

Schwi nodding deeply and saying this as a statement, Riku clutched his head.

"Where do you get that...? You're not a kid, right? Get in by yourself."

But Schwi raised fingers to make some very logical points.

"...One, if no one is, around...and I bathe...it is most efficient... for you to bathe as well."

——.

"...Two, I cannot wash, all my parts...without my self-cleaning device... I have never done, so."

And—

"...Three, I can predict...the reason...you reject this. It is because my childish appearance, is not sexually—"

"All right, all right already... Let's go."

Whipping up his heavy body that complained it needed more sleep, Riku stood.

There was no way he could outreason a machine.

■■■

A red-hot stone was dropped into the water-filled cauldron. Immediately, the small bathing room filled with thick, hot steam. The etiquette was to use this steam to elicit a sweat to get the grime off before finally getting in the water to refresh themselves. But sweat wasn't on Schwi's feature list, so Riku used a rag and the tepid water in the cauldron to clean off the mud and dust that caked her mechanical parts. When he studied them up close, their complex intricacy stole his breath. He'd seen some of the tools of Dwarf that manipulated spirits mechanically, but seeing Schwi's exposed insides—equipment—he couldn't even guess what it did. But that was how he knew it was fearsomely sophisticated.

"...Riku...do you have, a machine fetish...?"

"Why is it such a sophisticated piece of machinery only has such off-the-mark assumptions and over-the-line knowledge...?"

Schwi responded to Riku's chagrined tone as if defending herself.

"...I am unable, to project...human thoughts...due to the 'heart'... a computational singularity."

......

Having reached a conversational impasse, the only sound was the dripping water. To break the silence (perhaps), Schwi suddenly suggested:

"...Riku, let's play...a game."

"In the bath? What for?"

"...........Because...I'm 'bored'?"

Schwi mentioning a concept she clearly didn't understand with a question mark after it made Riku chuckle.

"Well, I don't mind...but you can't use spirits, all right? What about the board—?"

As if to say she'd come prepared—well, no, it had probably been her plan all along—Schwi produced the chessboard hidden in her cast-off robe.

"...*Ha*, fine. But we'll be playing while I wash your hair, so no time limits, okay?"

With a sigh, Riku grinned sheepishly and put his hand on a white pawn...

———......

"...Mnghh... Look, you, I'm washing your hair at the same time, so go easy on me."

Scrubbing her hair with his left hand, Riku racked his brain so hard he couldn't believe it and groaned. At this, Schwi slowly and softly whispered:

"I'm, sorry..."

"...For what?" Nah, he knew but still hated himself for it. He joked, "I examined the data after that..."

But Schwi, incapable of understanding such subtleties of the heart, expressed her regret.

"...For an *aggressor*, to ask a *victim*, about the heart...was illogical. No valid data, results..."

Aggressor and victim... Riku was surprised hearing those terms from just a machine. At the same time, for some reason, he felt a strange self-loathing for thinking "just a machine" and tried to paper it over.

"I see...but the real thing is that's what they call being 'insensitive.'"

"...? I am not a human...but I do have...sensory pathways..."

"That's not what I mean..."

Riku sighed with a smile as Schwi continued seriously.

"...But, still...I had no, ulterior motive..."

"......"

"...I really...want to know, about your heart...it's true..."

Just his imagination? It wasn't, Riku decided. Responding to Schwi's downcast, wavering—*sad*—tone, he sighed.

* * *

"Don't worry about it... I was getting a little overemotional myself."

It's weird, but— Riku reviewed the feelings he'd unable to hold in check. What he'd done could never be justified. He knew that all too well. Be that as it may, though, it was a cold, hard fact that she was one of humanity's oppressors... Apologize to her? It was utterly absurd. *But*—he thought. Not apologizing now would be *even more absurd*.

In fact, he had to admit that something had been wrong with him. Normally, he could control himself, but at that moment, suddenly he couldn't. It couldn't have just been something Schwi'd said. *So why*—?

As Riku struggled to make sense of it, Schwi asked blankly:

"Is being emotional...bad?"

"Yeah. Getting emotional—like getting carried away in anger and hitting you—wouldn't solve anything."

"But you want to...hit me..."

"...It's a figure of speech. Wait, is it—? Honestly, I don't even know myself."

Again their conversation broke. The sounds of the water and its fragments, the hot steam, made his head light... The silence continued for a while, until it was broken, again by Schwi.

"...Riku, why...do you close your...'heart'?"

"Look, you, are you actually sorry? You ever heard of tact—?" he started to yell—but as Schwi's red, glass-bead eyes peered into his, he stopped. A machine without a heart (leaving aside the matter as to whether this was the case) wouldn't be malicious.

...Something told him she really just wanted to know about him. Not rational, calculating, cold, fake Riku. But the valuable research subject—the real Riku with a heart.

—*Crnk*. Feeling his lock opening, he sighed.

"...Because that's the only way I can survive this world..."

If he closed his eyes, he could see what lay beyond the cave, as if it were burned into his eyelids.

The sky scorched red, the earth piled with blue death, the sight extending beyond the horizon. Where going outside without a mask was enough to end one's life. A world of death—or perhaps one that had already died.

"...Is it, our, fault...?"

"......I don't know..."

Riku really didn't know anymore. No, actually—

"It doesn't even matter whose fault it is... It's just what we have to face. For a human to exist in this world, we've gotta close our hearts, or else...or else they break. In a world like this... It's just unreasonable."

"...Unreasonable...unreasonable. What's unreasonable...?"

What? Riku almost scoffed at Schwi's soft mumbling, but... Oh, it was true, he realized. If you really looked at it logically, rationally—*there was nothing unreasonable about it.* It was just...

"The strong live, and the weak die. With no meaning or purpose. That's just how the world is made... I think feeling that's unreasonable may be what the 'heart' is... I'm not sure, though."

With a feeling something like resignation, Riku washed Schwi's hair.

"I want to know...about your 'heart'...but...," Schwi muttered, "...I don't want to...*hurt you*... What should I...do?"

——?

The way she put the question to him, making him feel somehow uncertain, Riku asked, "Why are you worrying about me? If you just want to know about the 'heart,' then you can just push ahead like you did—"

"I'm...sor-ry..."

"...Aah, I'm not trying to rehash it all. But it's true, right? Why should you care about—?"

She shouldn't. If it was someone else, she might have to worry about losing communication. But she didn't have to care for him. In fact, pushing him would get his real feelings out—

"........................I don't, know."

Riku furrowed his brow at the machine girl's first ambiguous answer.

"...I don't, know. But I want to avoid, harm to...you..."

"Hmmm. You mean your subject needs to be in as natural a state as possible in order for you to obtain accurate data?"

Half-teasing, Riku delivered this conjecture in his most logical and bureaucratic voice, but—

"......No...I don't, think so... And I don't, know why...but..." For some reason, Schwi lowered her face and answered, her voice subtly tremulous. "...That was...really, unpleasant..."

——. His doubt turned to conviction. Riku's judgment upon first encountering Schwi had been spot-on. This Ex Machina girl, Schwi, was *broken*. Clearly out of order. What she'd just said, whether she knew it or not, was a clear assertion that she'd been hurt.

—A machine? One who herself claimed she didn't know the "heart"?

"Hey, to begin with, your cluster disconnected you...and discarded you, right?"

"...Mm."

He'd even heard why, the details. She'd caused a self-referential paradox, a breakdown of logic. Was she really herself? What made her herself? Without the fuzzy "heart" of a human, the problem would be difficult to avoid. That she'd be discarded—it was harsh to say, but—it was no wonder. Still...

"So you want to analyze the 'heart,' whatever it takes, so you can get back to your cluster. But what difference does it make if you harm—?"

"...? I'm not, trying to go...back?"

——*Hng?*

"Uh, wait... But then, *who ordered you to analyze the 'heart'*?"

"...? I was just, interested...and decided, myself..."

"'Interested'... Hey, that feeling—that's the 'heart,' isn't it?"

Schwi froze at Riku's puzzled mumbling.

"......? ....? ...I don't know."

"Pardon? What?"

"...I don't, know... You make, sense. But, it doesn't, seem, important, to me... Why is it?"

"Y-you're asking me?"

Schwi's deadpan query made Riku's face contort involuntarily.
Suddenly, Schwi—

"List, of possible answers..."

—began positing.

"...I don't care; all I need is you; I'm not interested; it's meaningless; it doesn't matter; I reject synchronization; I prioritize
analysis; I prioritize understanding over analysis—Error—Error—
Error—Error—Error——"

"H-hey. Hey, hey, hey! You've got smoke coming out—hey!" Seeing Schwi venting exhaust with a hiss, Riku lost his cool.

It lasted for only a few seconds, though. Schwi swung around,
looked at Riku, and nodded once.

"Conclusion: I don't want to go back...*apparently*."

"Wishy-washy, aren't you?"

"...Cannot...identify basis...but *apparently*, I don't."

"Wishy-washy, aren't you..."

Finding it funnier and funnier, Riku smirked and repeated himself, only to hear:

"...That, aside...checkmate."

——*Oh*.

"Damn you... I was totally distracted by that conversation. One
more time."

"......Mm."

After all that, the Ex Machina's nodding face made Riku wonder.

*Is it possible to create a smile so innocent through calculation and
mimicry—?*

"...By the way."

Moving on. Riku sighed tiredly.

"Your hair...it's too damn long. This takes forever. My head's
going mushy from the heat."

"...If you'd prefer it, short...I'll cut it...?"

"No, it's fine, really... Seriously, you are so out there..."

Grumbling, Riku rebuked himself. —*I know.* She was, after all, an Ex Machina, capable of killing a human without even thinking about it. Just like the other races, she'd trampled his kind any number of times. He could by no means let down his guard. His reason screamed this at him. *But—then why?* The girl who kept considering the length of her hair didn't look logical at all. Spontaneously, he smiled faintly...

■■■

How long had it been since Schwi entered the village? It was impossible to say precisely since they didn't have an exact calendar, but according to Schwi, it had been "approximately one year." Riku thought it had gone by too fast. Considering that just surviving a few days felt like eternity......

"...Hey, how many Old Dei are there?"

Playing chess with Schwi in his cramped room, Riku rested his cheek in his hand crossly.

"Theoretically, they are infinite...proportional, to the number of concepts...but in many cases...their activation conditions, have not been satisfied..."

Riku frowned at the murky answer—and at Schwi's move. With a sigh at her single gambit that countered and crushed the orthodox strategy he'd envisioned, he began concocting his new plan and continued.

"So the Old Dei... There's the god of war and the god of the forest and stuff, right?"

As Riku remarked to himself—*Not that they're actually doing anything different. It's all just war*—Schwi nodded.

"...The former is Artosh...the creator, of the Flügel... The latter is Kainas...the creator, of the Elves."

But Riku interrupted her. A repartee of words and moves. As the pedestrian move he'd come up with next was immediately overturned, Riku remembered something: the feeling of trying over and over, making what seemed like the best moves again and again—and *being surpassed.*

...The boy with the bold grin, whom he'd seen in the darkness as a child, the one he could never beat—

"Hey, there isn't a *god of games*, is there?"

It was just a passing thought. It wasn't like there was anything to do about it, but Schwi answered seriously.

"...*There is*. But...ether not found... Activation conditions assumed, not satisfied..."

In this approximate year, he'd sure come a long way in getting used to talking to Schwi. Riku chuckled to himself. He didn't know the details, but basically, it was like this: Old Dei were "concepts." As long as the concept of games existed, the god of games *definitely existed*. But the presence of the activation conditions—of this "ether"—determined whether or not the god was "real."

"So basically...you're saying he's not around. At least, not now—"

Checkmate. Adding yet another mark to his loss tally, Riku sighed and stood.

"You know, I've been thinking of saying this for a while, but you don't have to talk like that when we're alone."

"...Mm...but it's as if...my thought vocalization core, has been modified irreversibly...apparently."

"Hmm. And in words a human can understand?"

"...I can't go back, *apparently*."

Wishy-washy, aren't you? He teased as usual, offhandedly and grinning, and Riku and Schwi left the room together.

The atmosphere of the village they saw as they walked had changed. Looking at Schwi walking beside him, Riku had to admit it. Since she'd joined them, the means at their disposal had expanded greatly. Thanks to her help with calculation and design, which they hadn't even asked for, the precision of their measurements and reconnaissance had improved. The performance of Couron's telescope had been further enhanced, and their inefficient dairy farming had progressed somewhat. The need for scouting had dramatically lessened, and stockpiling food had become feasible. Because of that—

"Hey, Riku! You spending the day all sweet and slippery in your room with your wife again?"

"I told you she's not my wife, baldy. Go spend the rest of your life squinting into that telescope."

"Schwiii! Thank you so much for the other day when you played with my children!"

Clearly, the village had more smiles. As long as she was here, they could live without fearing death. But this sight cast a faint shadow over Riku's expression.

He knew this was only a temporary peace, the calm before the storm. This ephemeral "interval" would vanish like dust with a single unconscious fancy from one of the so-called gods above them. Perhaps forgetting this fact was a blessing, to live bathed in temporary tranquility. But it would *disappear*. Maybe tomorrow, maybe today—maybe even now. Were he and Schwi giving them too much hope? Riku frowned. But what were they supposed to do? Pretend they didn't see the despair, believe that *they were safe here*, and live until someday the War ended? Riku wondered. At the very least, it was impossible for him…

"Ho, General! Take a break from playing with your wife's crotch for a second and give me a hand with this water leak I've got!"

"—Hmmm, if you want me to hit you, just say so. I'll lend you my *fist* all you want."

As Riku rolled up his sleeve with a strained smile, turning to the origin of this hail, Schwi stood alone, left behind, awaiting Riku's return as if she'd taken root.

"Schhhwiiiii! ♪"

Finding herself abruptly embraced, Schwi turned wordlessly. There was Couron, smiling.

"What are you doiiing all alooone? You're not gonna stay with Riku?"

"…He didn't tell me…to come, with him…"

"Waaa-ha! Schwi, why don't you ditch that no-good husband of yours and marry me?! Forget about that stupid man who'd leave a wife as faithful as youuu! Wuzza wuzza wuzza—"

"…Riku's not…stupid…"

Couron narrowed her eyes at Schwi's little pout.

"Hey, Schwi. I know this is weird for me to ask as his sister, but—"

"…Riku said…'She's not really my sister, so ignore her'…"

"Ah-ha-haaa! ♪ …I'm gonna have to sock him a good one later! ♪ But anyway!"

Clearing her throat loudly as a diversion, Couron asked bluntly:

"Schwi, what attracted you to Riku?"

"…Attract…?"

"Oh, you! I'm asking what made you like him! Come on, you know! ♥"

Suddenly, Schwi became aware that she was "tense." She didn't know why. She'd thought she'd gotten accustomed to acting human. But now, behind Couron's sunny attitude, she sensed that she was being *tested somehow*. She thought hard. To begin with, she'd still hardly managed to analyze the "heart" at all. Consequently, her analysis of the feeling of "liking" was also incomplete, undefined, so—

"…I don't, know…"

—Schwi decided to answer frankly.

"…I was interested…in Riku's…'heart'…his 'feelings'…"

The *day she'd first met* Riku passed through Schwi's memory core. Something deep in Riku's eyes…generated in her a thought no Ex Machina should have had. A "logical error threatening cluster integrity" that prompted her disconnection. *That* was—

"…Huuh, huh-huuh. ♪ I see how it is. ♪" Couron, as if piecing something together, casually defined it. "You're talking about *love at first sight*, aren't you?"

——*What?*

"Mm-hmm! ♪ That Riku. It's not like he's that smart, and his personality *comes off* like, you know…"

Couron nodded at Schwi, wide-eyed and frozen, then announced with a smile:

"If you saw through to his *real heart* to fall in love with him—yep, I can trust you with my brother. ♪"

"……"

Love at first sight. Another concept to analyze, Schwi thought with fatigue. Love. Liking. Affection. None of these had been fully analyzed, and now there was the entry "love at first sight," which implied *instantaneous occurrence*. Could it be that she'd never in her existence be able to analyze the "heart"?

"Hey, Couron, are you filling her head with some kind of nonsense again?" Returning from his chore, Riku confronted Couron.

"You're such a cheeky little brother. Cheeky and disrespectful, I declare!! When have I ever—?"

"You told her I was a boob guy and got her to stick two precious loaves of bread to her chest... Is something wrong with your brain, Couron?"

"What cheek! I could not be more right! This girl's going to be my sister one day, you know? So I've gotta help you enjoy a varied and fulfilled sex—"

"Let's go. Her stupidity's gonna rub off on us. Don't get too involved with that chick."

"...IQ is...transmissible...?"

Schwi's eyes bulged at this new data while Riku pulled her hand to urge her along.

"Oh, Riku...where are you going?"

"It's about time I taught her how to gather food, isn't it? I'm gonna show her how to use the scouting equipment and stuff."

Of course, this was a lie. An Ex Machina could knock down a Demonia with her bare hands. Moreover, Schwi's age—the number of years since her manufacture—was, according to her, *211*. There was something he needed Schwi's mobility to check out. He just couldn't tell Couron that.

"I might be out pretty late, but anyway, we're not going far."

Couron clapped her hands together with a knowing smile.

"Ohh—you're 'banging under the blue'? ♥"

"Couron, you really should get those brains replaced."

"Oh, but these days, I guess you'll have to 'bang under the red'?! Anyway, it'll be cold, so make sure you—"

"Shut the hell up. We're going, Schwi…"

Riku peevishly turned away… He probably didn't realize. Only Schwi and Couron noticed. Especially Schwi…

It was the first time Riku had *called her by her name.* Her thoughts were filled with undefined errors. She detected a rise in her chassis temperature… But Schwi tagged the memory "top priority" and—without knowing why—saved and protected its contents.

■■■

Standing on the ground for the first time in hours, Riku thought: *How much easier it is with Schwi.* The distance he would have covered in five days by horse, fearing death the entire time (or after several months of careful crawling), Schwi had carried him in *half a day.*

"…So this is the fallen Elf metropolis…"

It was the place that, a year ago, Riku had been trying to reach by himself. The unique structures woven of trees had been smashed down the line. The ugly scars of char still remained, yet the ruins were blanketed in brilliant flowering plants, as if it were all a graceful garden. The sky was stained the color of blood, and the earth was sullied by the poison of the black ash. Yet in this world of death, it appeared that the fallen metropolis still enjoyed the protection of an Old Deus. One could expect no less of a metropolis built by the great Elves, created of Kainas. Riku smirked ironically. It seemed that, after turning the planet into hell, they still wanted to preserve their abode as a paradise. After walking together for a while, they stopped at their destination. Amid the charred ruins, before the one building that still held its original form, Riku asked:

"Is this…a library?"

"…Probably… The building, would correspond… Relative to the damage, to the city…the damage is minor…"

So—it was a building that had been given defensive priority in the

Flügel attack. That could mean it was a shelter, some kind of research institution, or—a storage facility.

"...I see. This is definitely *probably* a library or something."

Not recognizing anything that looked like a door, they squeezed between interlocked trees to get inside, where they found— The innards of this bizarre architecture were still stuffed with things whose usage wasn't immediately discernable. One such item just barely suggested...a bookshelf? But it was spectacularly empty. It seemed more or less everything had been carried away...but that was fine.

"After all, information they don't need is still gonna be useful to us..."

With this, Riku began rummaging through the few leftover scraps of paper and damaged books.

"...Riku, can you read...Elven?"

Schwi asked as he flipped and scanned pages.

"Dwarven, Elven, Fairy, Demonia, Werebeast—which tongue do you want me to answer in?"

Schwi stared at Riku's nonchalant reply.

"...How do you, know so, many...?"

"That's what it takes to survive. The information I suffer to get is worthless if I can't read it."

Riku's expression was strangely severe, neither angry nor hateful.

Schwi knew that expression—those eyes. That was the demeanor Riku adopted when bent on beating her at chess.

"All evidence to the contrary, it's not as if humans have just been continuously getting destroyed for eternity. We've used any means we could think of—oral or written—to pass on the traits, tongues, and customs of other races, all the way down to today."

Within those unreflective black eyes, which spoke of humans' weakness, frailty, inability to do anything but run—*deeper, beyond that*—was the very thing Schwi wanted to know, the quality that contradicted appearances.

The essence that demanded, *Don't underestimate humanity*: the "heart."

"...Oh...Riku, Riku..."

Riku, who had apparently been literally scanning the area, looked up at Schwi's prodding.

The sway and roar of bedrock peeling. The screech of thick iron being wrenched apart overwhelmed the place. As Riku stood stupefied, Schwi reassured him.

"...Underground, under a...composite concealment rite...it's hollow... There's a basement...see?"

Watching her casually cock her head as she lifted an iron door ten times her height, Riku's face fell...

———......

After Schwi scanned for signs of life, the two descended the stairs. Then—

"...The hell's this?"

Riku couldn't help but voice his dubiousness at the inscrutable sight sweeping beyond the end of the long underground stairwell: an expansive hall, its center lined by a number of giant columns. The pillars were bizarrely warped, and countless red patterns were etched into their surfaces.

"...One hundred eighty-six columns... The patterns are, the seal of protection, of the Old Deus Kainas......? No."

Instantly tallying the number, then attempting to identify the markings, Schwi tilted her head.

"...No match, with my data...on seal, rites, used by Elf...at all?"

"Well, they must have been making some kind of new bullshit even you don't know, or they've made it. Nothing they did at this point would surprise me, even if they split the damn planet—but before that..."

From the perspective of humans, splitting the earth or the planet itself were hardly different. "Before that..." Riku dusted off the pedestal under one of the bizarre columns and read off a placard.

"—Áka Si Anse Proof of Concept Reactor... Schwi, does this mean anything to you?"

"......No data... No data on Elves, using tools...or catalysts, for magic...at all."

I see. Riku didn't understand, but his gut was speaking to him.

"In any case, we can't stay here too long. I don't know if there are any, but we'll scout around for any records that may be left and then get out of here."

Schwi nodded and deftly collected the remaining documents. Riku's gaze fell on one of them.

"...They even write the names of the 'Development Staff' in code for this thing? The hell...?"

Looking at the coded register, Riku felt his body jump.

■■■

Riku and Schwi's intention had been to stay only briefly and get out fast, but...

"What can I say...? I guess there's no way we can move in the middle of this."

No sooner had they left the library (or rather secret research base) and departed the ruins, than they encountered a "death storm." It was a phenomenon during which an unusually high precipitation of black ash caused a reaction among the ashes to create a whirling funnel of blue light. If you ran into this, no matter what you did, the dead spirits in the ash would penetrate your gear and taint you. The two hurried back into the ruins.

"...Riku, what do you usually...do, in this situation...?" Schwi asked as they took shelter in a small room on the ground level of the research facility.

"There's nothing to do. You get in a cave, in ruins, or dig a hole if you need to, and you wait it out."

Riku sighed. Death storms weren't that uncommon. In his experience, they usually lasted a few hours. A day at most. He'd curled into a small hole and waited a day more than once or twice. The question was—was this place *safer than a hole*?

"What about you, Schwi? Can you scan for life?"

"…Dead spirits interfere… My long-range observation equipment is almost…totally ineffective…"

"Hmm… But on the other hand, that means we're kind of safe ourselves."

In short, the death storm *helped* conceal them. They couldn't go outside anyway, and it wouldn't be safe to use Schwi's high speed without her long-range scouting functions. *So*, Riku asked:

"Hey, Schwi, I bet you brought the chessboard, huh?"

"………………………"

Having been instructed to "travel light," Schwi might have thought he was rebuking her.

"……I'm sorry…"

Apologizing with her face hidden, she timidly produced the chessboard from her backpack. This sight—*an Ex Machina fearful of a human's wrath*—was strangely amusing, and Riku chuckled.

"I'm not complaining… It's not like we have anything else to do until the storm passes, so why don't we play?"

"…? Really…?"

Sounding both surprised and secretly delighted, Schwi set up the pieces. Squinting at the board, Riku considered the record he'd built up against Schwi after almost a year.

—Out of 182 matches, he'd never won. Never mind checkmate, he'd never even stalemated Schwi. But a few times, he had managed to get her on her toes with tactics that startled her. *Which means*, he thought, *it's not impossible.*

At Riku's unknowingly bold grin, Schwi suddenly inquired:

"Riku, why…do you keep playing, even though…you can't beat me?"

"Huh—? That's a weird thing to ask! Aren't you the one who said she'd give me the information I want if I win?"

"…You're lying… There's no way…you haven't…realized…"

No, he had to have. Riku, of all people, must have realized.

"…I've already…given you, all my…information…you want…"

……

A heavy silence fell under the bluster of the wind.

"…Riku…you're amazing…you're doing all, you can…"

"—Stop trying to make me feel better."

Reacting to a statement strangely reminiscent of one Couron had once made, Riku employed the same response.

That was it. The conversation was finished. Or so Riku thought, but—

"…Make you feel better…? No… It's just, a fact…"

Schwi blankly *countered*. And then Riku saw something unusual, his eyes widening. Her expression clearly conflicted, uncertain whether she should go on or not, Schwi proceeded.

"…The current environment, of the planet…is lethal, for humans… For you, to be alive is a, biological…*abnormality*."

These had been Schwi's words a year ago, when Riku lost control and grabbed her. Even knowing that they had *hurt Riku*, she continued.

"What makes this ab—correction: *achievement*…possible is… your 'heart'…your will." She looked straight into those black eyes that reflected nothing. "—No matter…what you think…it's an objective fact…"

"Huh—so in other words, what? I'm losing pathetically every time, but I have the great machine's assurance that I'm helping humanity in doing so?"

"…I'm not…'the great machine'…but that's what I've determined. But—"

In dead earnest, Schwi's red glass-bead eyes locked with Riku's.

"—you won't accept it…"

"Of course I won't. What's so great about surviving in a—?"

"…No."

She'd reached her conclusion and interrupted him to make her point.

"…I didn't…know before…but…"

Now I do, Schwi declared, gazing into Riku's eyes.

"...Riku, you don't want...*anyone*...to die...*no matter who*. Even if it's someone...who destroys humans—like me."

"_____!!"

Riku's face contorted severely. Schwi still didn't know the reason Riku hadn't killed her, then. The criteria Riku himself had said he didn't understand could not, therefore, be grasped by Schwi. And that was how...how she could be certain.

"...That is the 'heart'... That's my projection...definition."

"......"

As Riku sat silently, his eyes downcast, Schwi went further.

"...I am certain...you are amazing...but you *will not accept it*."

Yes, the reason being...

"...Because *you don't want, to be accepted...Because you can't, acknowledge yourself...*"

——...

————...

In the room where only the wind resounded, a smile spilled out. Riku sluggishly lifted his face, putting his chin in his hand.

With eyes clearly reflecting Schwi, he said:

"You *really* piss me off... I never realized how annoying it would be to have someone around who only says what's logical..."

"I'm, sorry..."

"Don't apologize... I'm just a bonehead getting pissed when I get called out."

Yes, Riku acknowledged, with a sigh as if blowing out his soul. Ahh—in the truest sense of the word, this was checkmate. This was what it meant to have no room for argument, no room even for complaint. The lock on his heart had been pried open. Even if he tried to act strong now, it would only look pathetic.

"Yeah, you're right—I don't want anyone to accept me as the bastard I am..."

Running and running off, living and living on... What was the point? But. Then. In that case. Just. What else could he do...?! Riku looked to the ceiling, leaned back against the wall, and mumbled as if in penitence, "...Hey, but then what should I do? What can I do... to forgive myself?"

He'd abandoned lives that were irreplaceable, *stepped down from the game*, every time. He'd killed one to save two, killed two to save four. Fooling even himself into thinking that that was the only way.

Having carried that on—on and on—how now could he acknowledge himself? Riku asked her shamelessly, pleading, but she met his gaze and put the question back to him.

"*That's what I want to know...* What about your 'heart'? ...What does it say?"

"——Ha-ha, I asked you because I don't know. How can you do that...?"

But—Schwi persisted despite Riku dropping her gaze with a dry smile.

"Whatever it says...I will...help you..."

"...Why...?"

Schwi's response was blank, as if the answer was obvious.

"I told you...I'd stay with you...until I understood...the 'heart'..."

—*Ha-ha... So reassuring...*

"In, any case..."

Schwi thunked a piece on the board.

"...Checkmate."

"Schwi...... Isn't this the scene where I at least get a stalemate? Read the atmosphere."

"...? ...Has there been...an atmospheric event?"

Riku smirked at her typical answer and looked out the window. At some point, the storm had abated. From the window, perhaps thanks to the protection of Kainas, all one could see were flowers and trees blooming brilliantly, with no sign of the death storm that had passed. Rather, the brightly colored petals swept up to dance in the wind—though one hated to admit it—looked...

"......Beautiful..."

Riku turned to stare at the one who'd stolen his line, the machine girl with feelings far more human than his own. Her eyes sparkled in fascination, following the fluttering petals. Those clear red eyes reflecting everything exactly as it was...

"—Schwi."

As she turned slowly, Riku asked for the story he'd once dismissed as meaningless.

"The reason for the War and the conditions for its conclusion—tell me."

■■■

Together, Riku and Schwi walked through the ruined Elven metropolis amid blossoms falling, as if in a garden. The black ash had been washed away by the death storm, but it was just a matter of time before it started falling again. They couldn't take too long...but Riku reflected on the story he'd heard from Schwi.

"The *throne* of the One True God...the Suniaster...hmm."

A War to determine the greatest of the gods, who would rule over all gods and spirits—the One True God. A *conceptual device said to grant absolute dominion*—the Suniaster, or "Astral Grail." These were the purposes and objectives of this War. And the means......for heaven's sake......

"Hey, Schwi, can I ask you just one more question?"

—*It couldn't be, it couldn't be*, Riku thought, but he asked anyway.

"That is...is it possible no one's noticed that there's *another way*?"

"...Another...way...?"

Seeing Schwi's eyes widen at this, Riku could only groan to himself.

—*I see. So even Schwi doesn't get that you could do it that way, huh. No, maybe it's because she's Schwi—because she's strong—that she can't see something so simple?*

* * *

"…Hey, Schwi—it's good not to be by yourself, right?"

"…? Riku, haven't you always been…by yourself?"

"No…I was struggling like an idiot to put on a front by myself, but…"

Riku smiled and put on his particle mask. Now his expression was obscured. Through the goggles, though, Schwi could clearly see his dark eyes sparkling powerfully.

"I'm starting to get a feeling that, with you, we could do some amusing things in this world."

"…Amusing? I…don't understand jokes…"

Stroking Schwi's head as she looked down apologetically, Riku smiled wryly.

"That's what's so amusing about you… What about you, Schwi? Do you get bored being with me?"

"No."

She answered immediately with a straight face.

"Really? Not to brag, but I'm a jackass, you know? Maybe you haven't learned what it means to feel—"

"If I weren't interested, in you…I wouldn't have gotten myself disconnected…to be here."

Again, her answer was immediate and deadpan, though this time more aggressively so, making Riku think:

—Schwi says to ask my "heart" what to do. And whatever it is, she'll help… Then actually, I could ask—What do I want to do?—and just follow whatever I come up with faithfully… Could I?

"…Yes, that's…it…"

Schwi peered into Riku's eyes as he weighed his options.

"…I was…interested…in those eyes…"

"Really? What I'm thinking about right now is grandly delusional even by kids' standards, you know?"

"…That's fine…no—correction…"

Cocking her head several times as if thinking hard, and then, as if finally reaching a conclusion, Schwi nodded broadly, having successfully defined one feeling. As if quite pleased with herself, she smiled so brightly as to make one forget she was a machine.

* * *

"That's what I—yes...*like*...about you, I think?"

Even Riku wasn't sure why.

"Wishy-washy as ever!"

Nevertheless, unable to remember the last time he'd done so to such an extent, he clutched his gut, laughing so hard tears formed from his heart...

■■■

And then, not long after, the time came.

"Riku!! This is bad. The telescope's caught six Dragonias and several Dwarven battleships headed this way!!"

As Simon descended from his post as white as a sheet, Couron elaborated, instruments in hand.

"Respective headings north-northwest and east-northeast! If they collide on this course, there will be a battlefield nine leagues to the east!!"

These screams resounding throughout the village proclaimed the end of the transitory peace.

Riku efficiently directed the withdrawal of all the villagers and the selection of foodstuffs and equipment to carry. In parallel, Riku, Schwi, and Couron together deduced the range that would be affected by the battle in a quarter of an hour. Of the two options they had scoped out in five years of investigation, they selected the more suitable evacuation site. Eight hours before combat was predicted to commence, they finished preparing for evacuation, began moving, and...

......nigh unto two thousand villagers watched their home engulfed in a flash and blown away. The dead were those who had directed the evacuation to the very end, fewer than two hundred. For combat of such scale to break out so close to their village, the losses were inconceivably small. But looking down from the plateau at their village, vaporized with the entire crag, the people sobbed.

—*As they well might.* Couron's fist trembled. If one lost a house, another could be built... Logically, it held. The telescope they'd gone to such pains to restore had also been lost, but what could be done? It could be argued that it had all been for this day. They had rescued their most important documents, maps, instruments, and so on— But.

But—so what? Material goods weren't the only things that held value. The countless labors and sacrifices that had been piled up to maintain that village, the feelings of the people who had lived there, the wishes and prayers with which the place had been entrusted...

The whole of it had disappeared in an instant, destroyed by what most likely had been a stray shot. No malice, no meaning. It would be wrong *not* to cry. It would be unsound *not* to be heartbroken. It was true that their lives had been saved—but what would they do with them? Repeat the cycle? Sacrifice more, swallow bitter tears, bite their lips in pathetic frustration—only to once more have everything blown away like rubbish? Just before her tears exceeded her ability to hold them back, the sight of her brother's back caught Couron's eye.

"Riku...? R-Riku!!"

Sitting with Schwi, Riku's shoulders trembled as he hugged his knees, and Couron ran to him.

"Riku, please, hold it together! Look how many of us survived—you did as much as you possibly could!"

—*No more of this. No more. Stop making excuses*, Couron told herself, bracing for what she knew she needed to do. She couldn't keep leaning on her little brother, making him carry the weight...from here on—!

"Riku, you've done your part—right? From now on, your big sister's gonna take care of things, so—"

...but then...

"—Schwi, you got her on record, right?"

"...Loud and...clear..."

Riku, lifting his head easily, beamed with an incredibly disconcerting smile.

"—Uh, wh-wha? R-Ri...ku?"

Call it feminine intuition or what have you, Couron instinctively stepped back at his sudden transformation. *You won't escape!* Riku snatched her arm, and without intending to, she squeaked out an "Eegh!"

"Sooo, with that, Couron, from today, you're the head of the village. Live it up! ♥"

"Huh, uh, uh...?"

Grinning ear to ear, Riku pressed a map into Couron's hands, stretching as he rose.

"Here's the position of our *new village.* Go through that underground tunnel there, and you should get there safely. It's a little messy, but I've got it ready for you to live in. *I picked what to bring with this in mind.*"

Riku exchanged a glance with Schwi, who stood next to him. Then Couron, watching her little brother stroll off frivolously in the opposite direction, finally recovered enough from her stunned distraction to shout:

"H—! Wait a second, Riku! How am I—? How will we—?"

For all her bravado, without Riku—without her little brother—Couron couldn't fill his shoes. She cried out to him, but...

"Nah, you'll do fine, Couron. After all—*no one's gonna die* now."

"......What?"

"Ahh, relax. I'll be in touch. And I can rest easy knowing I can entrust everyone to you."

As he said this, Couron, dazed, watched his back recede.

"—Hey, Riku..."

She called his name, but the one who turned wasn't the Riku she knew.

—No, that wasn't true. She did know him. He was...the Riku from the very first time they met. The young boy with eyes blazing bottomless fire but who'd firmly closed off his heart. The one who'd pried open the lock was the girl who journeyed beside him—Schwi, Couron was suddenly certain. She heaved a deep, gentle sigh and asked anyway, though she expected an answer that would undoubtedly confound her:

"Hey…what are you up to——?"

His response was exactly as she'd anticipated. No, no…even more than that… The original Riku's reply—wide-eyed, bold, outrageous, and full of burning determination.

"—A game. We're up to…mere child's play!"

⏻ CHAPTER 3
1 + 1 = DEATHLESS

A cavern far removed from the new village indicated on the map given to Couron. In this ramshackle hideout, those who'd held the reins of the evacuation to the very end, *supposedly* giving their lives—179 "ghosts," including Riku and Schwi—surrounded a round table. Looking them over one by one, Riku, the head of these ghosts, slowly declared:

"We're done waiting for the War to end someday—for a future that will never come."

Before the stupefied assemblage, Riku continued his speech, which grew increasingly impassioned.

"Are we going to spend our lives scampering to survive in this shit world, praying for the War to end? *Praying to whom?*"

As if vomiting out all the things he'd always wanted to say but never could...

"Those destroyers who call themselves gods?! The asses in the heavens who can't stop them?! Enduring and enduring this shithole of a world—*and then*?! *What do we do then*?!"

Brandishing his hand furiously, Riku howled as if pounding out his feelings.

"I understand that the bastards are fighting for the throne of the One True God. But no matter who ekes out some bullshit victory among these bloodthirsty pricks, can we expect we'll be any better off than the shit we're in right now—huh?!"

Then Riku lowered his voice precipitously and announced in a voice devoid of temperature:

"It's time we admitted it. In this world…hope exists—not."

——.

They'd all sensed it. But the fact that admitting it would break their hearts made the ghosts hang their heads. As their faces grew pensive, he resolved himself. *So—*

"All we can do is *create* it with our own hands."

At Riku's powerful assertion, their gazes lifted.

"There's one chance. A truly warped-in-the-brain, questionably sane, common-sense-defying fool's venture."

It was a seat-of-the-pants plan at which even he could only smirk.

"We are ghosts—noted and noticed by no one."

Riku looked at the girl standing beside him…

"We are ghosts—but unseen, we carry the will of those who came before us."

…at the red eyes that told him they still *could*.

"That is the proof of our *existence*—that the world *still exists*."

Riku once more steeled his resolve and tightened his expression.

"Let us cast aside our pretense of wisdom. We humans are fools."

—And he said it.

"Therefore—we shall *fight*."

They would fight. Not run, but fight.

One hundred and seventy-seven gazes locked on Riku, who had undeniably made this assertion, and he smiled thinly.

"Yes, we shall fight. Every enemy looming over us, no matter who they are, by our own power—that is, our foolishness. Deceiving all, outstripping all, like ghosts. Like the weak. We'll devise every kind of plot, with no regard for shame or reputation. Fanned by cowardice. Extolled as base. Celebrated as the lowest of the low—!!"

—And then—

"And that's how we'll win."

—Yes, they could lay claim to one and only one victory.

"A victory built of endless defeats, piled one atop another, *converted into meaningful losses and canceled out."*

In the silence that followed, everyone—including Riku—pictured *them.* The opponents Riku said they'd face, those *things* that had countless times consigned people, whole civilizations, to nothingness. Those *things* that on a whim could turn mountains into craters, sea into land, shatter the very planet. Titters pervaded the room. Everyone was so shocked, they couldn't help but laugh, and Riku laughed, too.

"Yes, we shall challenge *them*—and emerge victorious. It's so foolish, so preposterous, you can only laugh, right?"

Indeed. How could one help but laugh? —And that…

"That is the proof we are human. *The proof of our folly.* The final culmination…of our existence."

With these words, Riku surveyed the faces of the 177 and assured them:

"—The conclusion of the Great War. That is the victory we shall claim."

……The eternal War among the gods. They would end it. As mere humans. Hearing Riku's assertion, the 177—no, even Schwi beside him—widened their eyes.

"Well, as for the conditions for victory… Even looking at it generously, they're tough enough to make you dizzy, but…"

But Riku faced them with the smile of a child who'd successfully pulled off a prank…and remembered.

—When he was a child, he'd thought the world simpler. That there was no contest you couldn't win, that hard work would be rewarded, that anything was possible. What he'd believed as a child, still foolish and ignorant, seeing the world through cloudless eyes—

* * *

"This world... All along, it's just been a simple game."

All along... It wasn't wrong.

"It's just been the gods enjoying a game for the Suniaster, playing *vale tudo* as they like."

Riku thought, *It is simple, isn't it?*

"That being the case, all we have to do is create the rules *we want to play by.*"

With that, Riku fiddled with a chess piece in his hand and turned to Schwi. The Ex Machina had said she wanted to know the secret Riku's heart revealed. *Then here's your answer,* Riku thought, and seeing Schwi nod, he grinned boldly—and laid out his rules.

"One: No one may kill."

—The premise: that to kill another was to die oneself. The heart of it: *he didn't want to kill anyone.*

"Two: No one may die."

—The premise: that to let another die was to die oneself. The heart of it: *he didn't want to let anyone die.*

"Three: No one must know."

—The premise: that discovery meant death.

"Four: All means are fair."

—The heart of it: *it wasn't cheating if you didn't get caught.*

"Five: We don't give a shit for their rules."

—The premise: that they were doomed on an even playing field. The heart of it: *a fight to the death is for dumb shits.*

"Six: Any act that deviates from the above shall constitute loss."

—The premise: that inconsistent rules were meaningless.

—The heart of it: any victory violating these rules was meaningless.

So Riku would *play by his own rules...* His heart having dictated the terms, Riku once more surveyed the 177 gathered around the table.

"We are ghosts. We won't kill anyone—not other races, not the Old Dei. No one will know we exist. We will simply *lead the front by the nose* to end this war."

Emotional rules, tantamount to a child's tantrum. But at the same time, if mere humans were to end the Great War, there was no other Way.

"It hardly bears mentioning, but if we fail, we'll be wiped out. Our backup plan...? Well, it probably doesn't exist. 'Hey, some talking monkeys are directing the course of the War'—if they notice, we're dead."

So basically... Riku summed it up.

"Win or lose. All or nothing. When our chips are in, it'll be too late to back out."

Then Riku showed a glimpse of his true self, which no one there had seen before.

"Our enemy is the gods, those forces that scorch heaven and earth, those manifestations of despair. Our odds are infinitesimal. Since doing everything in secret is one of the conditions for victory, even if we win, there won't be any memories or records, and there won't be any songs about our exploits. We're ghosts, and ghosts don't sing. Still, if by some stroke of luck—"

This impulse to write off an insane world as a "game" and take it on... The huge smile stretched across his face—

"If somehow we do manage to succeed in this game...if we *win*—"

—served as affirmation.

"Don't you think we'll be able to brag to ourselves that we led the most *awesome* lives before we die?"

......And so.

"That's the game. Stay only if you want to play."

Having put it all out there, Riku closed his eyes and waited for them to leave. Silently, he chuckled. *Fools hardy enough to play this game would be hard to come by*, he thought. The people Riku had selected, without exception, were possessed of superior intellect and skill, having faced death any number of times and survived just as often. From the perspective of other races, they were mere dirt and dust, unworthy of touching. But among the dirt and dust, these motes stood above in ability—and that very fact was what made Riku laugh inwardly.

Surely none would stay. It was insane. One fool was enough. That was that. It couldn't be helped. In the worst case, he and Schwi would go it alone—show them all. It would mean the difference of odds beyond the void and odds past the quiet reaches of nirvana.

…To be completely honest, he could hardly think of any strategies he and Schwi could pull off by themselves. But still—

……

Kept company by these thoughts, Riku counted out a full ten minutes, then opened his eyes.

"……Uh, let me be honest here, all right?"

Surrounded by 177 faces (in other words, there'd been *no deserters*) all looking perplexed and seemingly wondering, *Just how long are you gonna keep your eyes closed?* Riku couldn't help but remark—

"I thought you guys were a little smarter than that."

Riku's 177 "ghosts" chuckled at this, and each said their piece:

"Come on, General. Don't misread the first move. How we gonna win at this rate?"

"Riku, you think anyone with any brains…would still be living in this world?"

"Questionably sane? What do you think could be less sane than the world we live in?"

"The wise would choose death over this world. The wiser would choose not to be born…"

"Look at us, the ones who survived to be here… Riku, we're the ones you chose, you little bastard."

That's just how it is. Everyone laughed and nodded.

"Doesn't that make us the appointed representatives of the fools?"

Riku grinned—and laughed. Yeah, it was exactly as they said.

Humans were foolish. Because they were foolish, they honed their wit and wisdom so as not to be done in by their foolishness. They'd survived this long... In a world not worth living in, they'd survived despite it. The ones who'd staked all their wit, wisdom, and artifice to accomplish it.

If not the proud fools—the great weak—what would you call them?

"We were born to this world with no purpose."

"We've survived eating dirt for nothing."

"But now we'll die significant and awesome. What more could we ask for?"

"Is there any greater freedom, Boss?"

"In your hands, we'll strike a stunning pose to the end. We're ready to live—tell us how, General."

Riku lowered his face as if scoffing from his very core, but...

"...Every one of you guys is a crazy son of a bitch. It's good to know. So..."

Muttering sincerely, he spread out the map. For five years—no, even longer—they'd revised it so humanity could survive. The *game board*. Woven of countless corpses, the game board fell under the scrutiny of 179 ghosts (including Riku and Schwi), and Riku prepared to unfold his concrete plans...

"Come. Let the game begin."

"—*Achéte*."

They all answered in unison with the usual response, but Riku corrected them.

"...That word is banned from now on. Our moves won't be dictated by convention, but by the rules to which we have assented."

And so...yes.

"It's...'*Aschent*.'"

Thus began the quiet maneuverings of those who did not exist. Bereft of a future, of hope, despairing even of despair, they'd finally grown tired of being fed up. Waiting no longer but seeking, the ghost ship of 179 set sail...

■■■

"...Riku, I really...don't understand...the 'heart'...after all..."

Schwi muttered this after the meeting while playing a card game with Riku at the entrance to their hideout. Schwi had seen it. Everyone in that room had touched Riku's "heart" and resonated with it. All but one. Her. Schwi looked down. Her isolating inability to understand aggrieving her fiercely, she continued.

"...The probabilities of...success, of your plans...are all...less than one percent..."

Not to mention the probability that they would all survive, which was logically equivalent to ze—

"Mmm. Look, Schwi."

Riku cut her thoughts short.

"You're talking about probability? Is this pretty much it?"

Lacking the mathematical prowess of an Ex Machina, Riku interpreted Schwi's attitude with his own spin and asked:

"You roll a die, and the probability of a six is one in six. You roll it two times in a row, and the probability goes from one in six to one in thirty-six—percentages are beyond me, but that's pretty much how you're figuring it?"

"......Y-yes...so......"

Schwi was certain she'd never underestimated Riku. Unable to hide her surprise at his ability to unpack Ex Machina extrapolations so easily, she tried to explain the probability of—

"Then let me teach you something useful. The way you're calculating that—is wrong."

—She froze.

"When you roll a die, the probability of a six is one in six. But that methodology doesn't apply in *this game*."

The reason being... Riku chuckled as he shuffled the cards.

"If it's six we win, and if it's not we lose. So—it's one in two."

—That was absurd. But it was accurate that perspective and conditions were important factors in probability. *All or nothing*—calculating it from Riku's point of view, even this absurdity was logically consistent.

"............"

An Ex Machina—Schwi of all Ex Machinas—being outreasoned by a human. And by emotions. While Schwi's thoughts tripped at the shock of it, Riku went on.

"And here's your second mistake. If a die can come up six once, then it can come up six ten thousand times in a row...so I definitely think your calculation is wrong."

"...No...accounting, for variables...if you roll it, ten thousand times, the distribution error converges..."

Strictly speaking, the probability that a die would come up six was not one in six. There were many variables. But the more that trials were undergone, the more the probability would converge, making it, on the contrary, easier to calculate. Which would make the result just as— This was Schwi's argument, but Riku grinned broadly.

"Can you account for everything? Even what you don't know and have no way of predicting? For example—"

Yes, for example, Riku thought.

"—even if we slip in a *die that only comes up six*?"

She couldn't. At least, not the first time. But if it continued, she would detect an abnormality and identify the cause of the error— Having thought this far, Schwi froze. At last—Riku's words and strategy came together for her. *No one must know. No one must even notice.* What this actually *meant*. What he *planned*.

"...*Deliberate manipulation*, of the variables...inconspicuous— within the range of error..."

They would keep them predictable—*deliberate variables*. There could be no greater impediment to mathematical calculation. Riku nodded, seeing that she'd caught on.

"This is what you call cheating. Fun, huh?"

Even so, she still couldn't fully grasp it. Probability theory wouldn't explain this game. That much she'd understood. But be that as it may, how—?

"…How can you…treat the lowest-probability outcome…as the *expected value*?"

Schwi posed her question, her gaze boring into Riku, who paused to consider it. *Hmm.* He could say anything—like, because we can't keep going unless we have faith? Like, because we don't need any evidence to believe, to have hope?

But Riku decided that those weren't the kinds of answers Schwi was looking for. Looking out their hideout at a world transforming into a planet of death, Riku gave his reply.

"Schwi, the probability of humanity having survived in this world…what's the percentage?"

"…………I have understood."

Riku's ironic quip earned Schwi's acknowledgment. Probability was a matter of statistics. Confronted by results, with a "miracle," all calculations went out the window. Then, paradoxically—

"…If you perform…'miracles'…probability theory, itself, becomes a false…justification."

Riku grinned and nodded at Schwi's assessment.

"To put it your way, we're gonna operate as a computational singularity. All kinds of expectations, strategies, calculations… With just a little manipulation, we'll lay them all to waste and make them converge in the direction we want."

Even as he said this, Riku thought, *But it's impossible to predict everything…* His own words came *right back at him*. He knew this. But if he could pull it off…now that would be a divine feat, wouldn't it? *Then all the more reason…* Riku's smile deepened.

"Ain't it amusing? We're gonna take the doings of those pompous pricks in the heavens and *bring them down with simple, human handiwork*. If everything works out—don't you think that'll be the *sweetest* irony?"

Listening to Riku's naïve fantasy—watching those clear, dark eyes of his—Schwi finally…got it.

This was it. What she'd seen *the first time she met Riku*. She could finally identify it conclusively. It was the "source of the heart"—the "soul." That quality in which she had taken an illogical interest, which she had come to admire. That which one who was only what she was required to be—an "adapter" such as herself—lacked. That which inspired *wishing, standing, struggling, and seeking* what they wanted to be... *Ideals*.

"And, anyway...fundamentally, probability is all a bunch of empty theory, you know?"

She had indeed been refuted, but hearing it described as "empty theory" left Schwi floundering.

"Here's the proof—Question: What's the probability I'll propose to you?"

Unable to grasp the purpose of the question, Schwi ran some rough numbers.

".........? Cannot identify purpose of query... I estimate... approximately zero."

"See, you were *wrong*—marry me, Schwi."

Riku proffered a small ring to the stunned Ex Machina.

"There's no such thing as zero in probability. No one can say we don't have any chance of winning this game, right?"

Schwi looked up with eyes round as could be at Riku holding out the delicate ring and gave her answer.

"...Cannot understand... Request denied."

■■■

Prone on the cold ground, Riku—virgin, nineteen—drowned in tears.

"Hee, hee-hee, eh-hee-hee-hee-hee-hee-hee..."

His all-out proposal, sliced down with a single stroke. The end of the world had arrived a bit early. *Come on, Riku... Why don't you just forget about it? Silly old world... A twit who messes up the first move is gonna make all kinds of mistakes and lose anyway. Who gives a crap already? To hell with humans and the world. Ahh...Couron, I'm exhausted...ah-ha-ha, hee-hee, ee-hee-hee-hee.*

"...Riku, I request...an explanation..."

"Well, you know...I'm sorry, I got carried away. I'm just a damn virgin... Please don't rub salt in my—"

Riku rolled laughing on the ground as if broken.

"...Denied... Please...explain." Schwi came across unnaturally inexpressive given the topic. "...'Marriage'—a contract formed between mating pairs of humans..."

As if pulling her reference information from a dictionary (and not even appropriately) she projected:

"...You have evaluated my utility...and wish to lock me, for exclusive use?"

"Noooo! I just want to be by your side forever!"

"...Why? I'm by your side...right now."

"That's not what I mean... Look, see, as a life partner!"

"...Partner—One who accompanies. Ally. Or—spouse...?"

"Yes! That one, that one! As a spouse!"

But as Riku nodded desperately, Schwi remained impassive.

"...Spouse... Husband, wife. I am an Ex Machina. I am incapable of reproduction."

"That doesn't matter!!"

"...Incapable of...the reproductive act... Riku, you'll be a virgin... forever...?"

——.

"That doesn't matter!!"

"...A momentary...delay..."

"Ahh, come ooon... I don't caaaare... Detaiiils!!"

Despite Riku's disruptive wailing, Schwi went on, now *unnaturally* deadpan, even for her.

"...An interracial...marriage, would be...unprecedented."

"Then we'll be the first! The pioneers—go us! Yahoo, goddamn it!!"

His shrieks now positively desperate, Riku pounced with cryptic conviction. If he backed down now, he'd lose. He was convinced of this despite any evidence supporting his position. But as if overwhelmed by the force he was emitting, Schwi's expression gradually crumbled.

"…I can't… Because—"

"……Schwi?"

Schwi was bewildered, confused, and for some reason—sad. Responding to her trembling voice, Riku, concerned, called her name. He didn't understand…

But hearing him say her name like that landed the coup de grâce on Schwi's mental processing, which spit out errors one after the other. Her thoughts broke down at an accelerating clip—failures and conflicts and inconsistencies multiplying to infinity. Logical inconsistencies and conflicts in an endless loop. But a sentiment greater than that logic began overwriting her restrictions.

"…Because…I—"

As she opened her mouth to speak, Schwi's logic, her protocols, screamed: *Don't say it!* But the *error*—which she could identify as nothing else—howled: *Say it. Turmoil* the likes of which an Ex Machina was never designed to experience. Prioritize logic or the error? But in her mind, video of her initial encounter with Riku kept looping. The associated errors—undefined errors such as "fear" and "guilt"—collided.

And Schwi's thoughts betrayed her as, with a trembling voice—

"…Because, I'm the one…who destroyed…your homeland…"

—they…prioritized the error.

■■■

Twelve years earlier in a rare circumstance, Ex Machina had engaged in a large-scale conflict. The enemy was one of the three Rulers of Dragonia—Aranleif the Ultimate and his seven Followers. The forces on the Ex Machina side were organized as a mittel-cluster of eight überclusters, including the Quelle. Each cluster contained 437 units, totaling 3,496. A full fourth of Ex Machina's resources had been dedicated to this truly epic battle. The result of the conflict: a strategic victory for Ex Machina. The losses on each side were as follows:

Enemy: Aranleif the Ultimate and 7 Followers terminated.

Friendly: 1,468 units lost (42 percent of dedicated troops). Forces effectively devastated.

Almost all the losses were attributable to Aranleif the Ultimate's dying blow—his ultimate roar, which cost him his life—his Far Cry. Zero-point-zero-zero-seven seconds after the Far Cry of the Ultimate One was initiated, approximately 20 percent of the Ex Machinas involved in the conflict were *vaporized*. Zero-point-zero-one-eight seconds later, the Prüfer made a quick judgment based on the information from the Seher: No armament capable of adequate defense against Ultimate Far Cry could be found in the Ex Machina arsenal. They transmitted the results of their analysis to the Befehler and estimated the damage that would occur in the 0.4 seconds it would take for the Zeichner to develop a new armament. Estimated damage: 90 percent casualty rate. Strategically equivalent to annihilation, it would spell defeat. However, one Prüfer proposed not blocking the Far Cry—but deflecting it. Ex Machina possessed an armament capable of bending the orientation of energy: Org. 2807—Umweg. They estimated that deploying multiple instances of this armament would mitigate the damage an additional 20 percent. The proposal was immediately approved by the Befehler. The Far Cry's trajectory was bent, and it skewed off far beyond the battlefield. The Ex Machina losses—severe as they were—fell short of "devastation." The Prüfer that formulated this proposal deemed it necessary to reanalyze the deflected Far Cry based on the damage. She investigated some ruins far from ground zero that appeared to have been the lair of a pack of beasts called humans. And then—

"......——"

The Prüfer detected a young human clutching a tiled board, glaring at her. Hostility radiated in the human's eyes, but—he simply turned his back and left.

To the Prüfer—the unit tasked with analyzing the situation—his actions were inexplicable. Though in a dire situation, the human assessed the enemy calmly and dispassionately. And it chose to live.

This clearly did not correspond with the instincts of a beast. The gaze it had leveled at the Prüfer held neither fear nor emptiness, but a bottomless—deeper than the Far Cry of the Ultimate One—heat. The Prüfer produced an error—*Astonishment.* The child had been convinced he could win—*just not yet.* Hypothesis: Could that have been something Ex Machina lacked—heart, or life? Something enabling conclusion without evidence, bestowing certainty beyond calculation?

The Prüfer determined that humans—particularly this specimen—required further analysis.

However, her subsequent study generated an abundance of errors, necessitating that she be disconnected—and discarded. Übercluster 207: Prüfer 4f57t9—Üc207Pr4f57t9.

The unit later renamed by that same specimen.

Schwi.

■■■

"...Now, after that...can you still...say those things?"

After Schwi's confession, she found herself unable to meet his gaze, just mumbling shakily, her face down.

—Error—Error—Error—Error—Error—Error—Error—Error—

The same old chain of errors raged through her mind.

—Interrogative: *Why did unit speak? Action lacks rational or irrational gains.*

—Rational answer: *Benefit—None. Cost—Loss of observation subject due to hostility.*

—Irrational answer: *Benefit—None. Cost—Riku won't, like me...anymore?*

Cost? Being disliked? Previously cited consequence? Error, error, error...

"...Schwi, you know—"

At the sound of Riku's voice, Schwi noted that her shoulders jumped to an extent that surprised even her.

The storm of errors shouted at high decibels: *Flee*.

—Flee? Why?

The storm of errors answered at the same pitch: *Because I'm scared*.

Scared. Afraid. No such concepts existed in Ex Machina. Yet she couldn't deny the errors. She was looking down now. Why? *Because—to look—at Riku's face—was so* scary— These were just a sampling of the new errors swirling in the maelstrom of her mind.

"...I knew. Just vaguely, but..."

His words silenced the errors all at once as her thoughts converged on just one question:

"...How...?"

"Hmm... It's embarrassing to say, but I first sensed something was funny—"

Riku bashfully scratched his head.

"—when we met the first time and wondered, *How does she know I'm a virgin?*"

"_____."

Riku chuckled as Schwi apparently froze.

"Well, there were other things, too—like how you said you'd 'confirmed' I had a heart, how you took for granted that my heart was the reason humans had survived in this world, how you were waiting for me somewhere far away from the village, how Game Number One is chess... So, yeah."

Schwi could only stare as Riku sheepishly smiled as if to say: *Your defenses aren't as good as they look, are they?* At a loss for words, her thoughts awash with errors, spinning idly, she nevertheless managed to spit out a question:

"...If that's the case...then...why...?"

"Hmm... Why? Ha-ha, I don't know."

Riku laughed as if genuinely uncertain.

"Maybe because I'd already taken all that into account when I fell in love with you."

——.

"…You'll forget, the past…?"

"No. You ended up destroying my homeland… That is confirmed as the past."

His words brought Schwi to the verge of collapsing under the weight of a pain she shouldn't have been able to experience, but—

"Mmm… Well, I guess I just really am an idiot. 'Cos, see, I see it this way, too." Whether trying to hide his embarrassment or sincerely self-recriminating, he scratched his head. "If we denied the past—that you destroyed my homeland—we wouldn't have met, would we?"

"——……!"

She felt suffocated. A machine with no respiratory organs.

"What happened, happened. No matter how you try to twist it, it's not gonna change anything. That's not what humans are about."

Riku slowly walked up to her, knelt—

"We gnash our teeth at what happened, cry, wail…then say, 'next time, next time,' and move on. But…"

—and touched her cheek with his hand, gently cupping her chin, lifting it up—

"…that's why…you got interested in me, right?"

—and there he was, smiling like a child. Seeing her frightened expression reflected deep in Riku's eyes, Schwi herself was shocked. Riku continued quietly, as if to soothe her.

"I'll never deny the past."

——.

"Your past, your present by my side, your future, which I want to share… I love them all."

———.

"And your guilt? Just throw it away, *whoosh*. Unfortunately, humans—well, maybe just I'm an idiot. In any case, we don't have room to look anywhere but now. Waiting for tomorrow, hoping for next time. Taking the past into account, you know."

So... Riku took Schwi's left hand—

"If you'll be there for me, I'll be able to want to keep going in this world."

—gently placed the ring on her finger—

"If you'll be there for me, I'll make it through, my heart whole."

—showed it to her, its stone red, just like her eyes.

"If you'll be there for me, I'll never lose my smile again."

And then, as if somehow vexed—

"So please. If you don't hate me—"

"I don't...hate you—! That's not true, at all—"

—Riku held out his hand to Schwi as she shook her head as if to cut him off, and he made a wish. *Then...*

"Will you ignore all logic...and walk the same path as me? As my wife."

...

......Suddenly, Schwi noticed. At some point, the error storm that had been cluttering her thoughts had stopped.

"......I see..."

Ex Machina was a race of adapters. If required, they could rebuild themselves as needed. When an unknown function was added— But a tear running down her cheek made her realize. The storm of errors. The logical inconsistencies had finally been processed together under a single designation: *feelings.*

"...Riku."

"Uh-huh."

"...I'm literally...just as you see...not worthy of you—but."

"I think you're way too good for a moron like me, personally."

Riku smirked, but Schwi, overwhelmed by feelings she still didn't know how to properly express, sank to her knees and with a damp voice squeezed out:

"...Let me stay, by your side—forever and ever and ever..."

■■■

"...Look at this. I ended up having to peep all the way to the end...
You stupid brother, you..."

Outside the entrance to the hideout, Couron gave a begrudging
sigh. Having set out early after learning its location, she'd chanced
across their exchange, spying on them the whole time.

I mean, what could I do? I missed the timing for my entrance.

Watching from the shadows as Riku stroked the back of the
still-sobbing Schwi, Couron remembered: The day Riku, having
outlived his village, was taken in by the grown-ups in Couron's—

———......

"Hello, hellooo... I'm talking to youuu! What's wrooong?"

Their reasoning had been that while Riku had thus far refrained
from speaking to anyone, maybe Couron, being the same age, would
have some luck. The once-hopeful adults covered their faces. *There's
nothing* wrong. *He's just a survivor from a village that was destroyed.*

"Okaaay, if you have something you want to say, Big Sister will
listen! ♪ Come on, come on—let's hear it! ☆"

As Couron tickled him, Riku opened his mouth for a single word:
"...Dork."

"Eh-heeeh, Big Sister isn't gonna get hurt by words in an age like
this! Yeah, yeah, now you can't use the excuse you can't talk anymore, riiight? I wonder what happeeened?"

Riku mumbled, little by little. A light had come from the south.
His village had burned. He'd pushed aside the charcoal that had
been his parents and headed east—

"Didn't you look for survivors? Why'd you go east if the light
came from the south?"

Ignoring the gasps of the grown-ups, Riku kept answering flatly.

—Even if there'd been survivors, he couldn't heal them. If any had
been sound enough to walk, they'd have evacuated, just like him.

—He'd gone east because that was the wasteland...where black
ash doesn't pile up.

—Farther east, there was supposed to be a river. If he got that far,
he figured he could survive...

While the grown-ups were speechless at his remarkable composure for a child, Couron asked:

"…What did you want to do after you made it out?"

"…Win next time… To do that, I had to survive…"

—*Next time*…he'd said *next time*. And—he was talking about winning. The adults were dumbfounded, but Couron rubbed her cheek against his and yelped.

"Ohhhh myyyy! This kid, he's gotta be my brotherrr!"

Couron had noticed. His eyes when he'd said *Win next time*—those bottomless eyes. But then it occurred to her. She couldn't leave him alone. She had to be by his side. She'd decided then to keep Riku from flying out of control, from rushing to his death…but really…

——……

"I knew…a big sister wasn't what he needed for that. He needed *someone who'd walk the same path*."

He, Riku, would go far. Far, far away—somewhere she'd never be able to keep up…

…But even so…for now…

■■■

"How long are you gonna let Schwi cry?! You useless excuse for a husbaaaaand!!"

Suddenly, someone popped out of the shadows, driving her fist into his abdomen. Riku groaned.

What just happened? he wondered, and as he lifted his head, there loomed Couron, beaming:

"Anyway, as your big sister, let me congratulate you on your marriage! ♥"

Hmm, gimme a minute here. Riku held his gut and got up.

"Couron—uh, sorry… How'd you…? I mean, why are you here?"

"Huh? I came to visit your hideout. You had a bit of an atmosphere going—so I had to peek, right?"

Couron said that without an ounce of shame, her face asking, *What other choice did I have?*

His so-called sister... *How the hell—?* But Riku just scratched his head.

"Uh, so, I guess I can't keep hiding it from you—"

"Oh, I know *Schwi isn't human.* That's what you mean, right?"

......

————*What?*

"H—wait... Wha—? When did you...?"

"*The first time you brought her to the village.* When I hugged her, she totally didn't feel like a human."

Couron cast shade at him like, *How could you think I didn't know?*

Then Schwi remembered and understood.

The feeling she'd had that day Couron asked her what attracted her to Riku.

She... Couron must have been trying to ask her this:

—*What attracted you to Riku?*

And that was why she'd felt that strange tension.

"...If you knew, why didn't you say anything?"

If Couron had known she wasn't human from their first meeting, then what was the point of all that fuss about him being a pedophile? Shouldn't she have said, "He's brought another race into the village"—been on guard, given a warning—? Riku was flabbergasted, but Couron smiled casually—just like a real sister.

"After all, she's the one you chose, isn't she?"

"———."

"There was something going on at the beginning, right? Riku, when you first brought Schwi home, you were so tense, you seemed like you were gonna snap any minute... So I tried to *play along...*"

That made sense. If she'd read that far into it—if she was gonna keep up the charade—that was all she could do. More than that, though, it was all motivated by her faith in him.

"But look—it all worked out so fast, didn't it?! And now I'll have suuuch a cute little sister!! Come on, it doesn't really matter whether she's human or not, does it?! You know, Schwi, humans have a tradition that says when you get married you have to kiss the fam—"

"No, we don't! Don't listen to her, Schwi—stay away!"

"Oh, hey, Riku! Now that you've brought us new family, at least have a wedding, will you?!"

"Couron, I appreciate the sentiment, but we don't exi—"

—That was what he started to say, but he stopped short when he noticed the seriousness of Couron's expression.

Neither Riku nor Couron had anyone else they could call family. Not…anymore. And on top of that, Riku and Schwi were supposed to be dead. So…

"I'll be the go-between, so let's make it official, all right? How about a wedding with just us three?"

Unexpectedly, Schwi jumped in.

"…Yes…"

She looked up at Riku and muttered:

"I want us to be…officially married…"

——……

It was simple. Hardly a ceremony. They exchanged their vows, the three of them wrote their names on a document, and it was over. Normally, they'd have gathered the whole village—but Riku and Schwi were "dead." *And so*, Couron insisted they'd do it then and there.

"Riku, do you swear to walk together with Schwi, support her, love her, and survive as husband and wife?"

Riku chuckled to himself. What a fitting vow for this age, for that village. A liturgy that, every time the village hosted a wedding, forced him to lower his eyes. But now……

"Sure. I do."

"Come on, Riku! You say *achéte*—"

"Sorry, we just abolished that. Now it's *aschent*."

Puffing out her cheeks, Couron groused.

"You certainly get on when I'm not around. Can't say it sits well…"

"Heyyy, officiator. Aren't your personal asides a bit much?"

Glaring at her brother as he heckled her as if from the audience, Couron cleared her throat. She turned to Schwi and prompted her vow.

"Schwi. Do you swear to walk together with Riku, support him, love him, and survi—"

"...I do..."

An answer quicker than immediate. Couron's shoulders slumped at the persistent disregard for form—but Schwi continued.

"...Riku gave me a meaning, a reason to have been born...a heart. I swear by him—I'll never let him die...I'll survive, and stay with him...to the end... *Aschent*..."

——.

Mm-hmmm. Couron glanced at Riku and saw something precious. She never thought the day would come—that she'd see her little brother blush.

"Now, continuing, Schwi. Do you swear to be Riku's—'beautiful bride'?"

"...Beautiful...bride...?"

Riku sighed, *Here it comes*, while Schwi gaped at the undefined term, but...

"To never make Riku sad. To never take the smile...from this boy who lost it for so long..."

Schwi silently and seriously contemplated Couron's question.

"...Can you?"

——.

Honestly, she wasn't confident. She didn't know how she could— but she answered anyway.

"...I do... I swear I'll be...his...'beautiful bride'..."

...*Okay.* Couron nodded broadly once, as if relieved, and then—

"Oh, also...it's a requirement that you be a beautiful bride in bed, too, you know? Totally skilled in—"

She doubled down on the teasing, but...

"Uh, Couron. Schwi can't do that kind of stuff. See, it's a race—"

Hearing her brother's explanation, Couron's face fell with regret. She'd just been trying to lighten the mood, but she'd put her foot in her mouth. That was when Schwi raised her hand.

"...If I understand, the structure...I can modify my hardware——I can make, a 'hole.'"

"You—what?!"

"Oh my! ♪ Aren't you lucky, Riku! Congratulations on losing—"

"...So, Couron...please show me, your reproductive—"

————*The world is absurd*, thought Riku as his brain rattled from the fist launched into his cheek.

"—What? Why'd you punch me?"

"'Cos all you have to do is stay a virgin forever! Now then..."

Couron retrieved the stone she routinely wore at her hip.

"That done, we just have to carve our names into this, and you'll be officially married." She knew what Riku was thinking before he even said anything. "You two supposedly don't exist, so we can't leave documentation, right? This stone is a precious heirloom from my grandfather. We can just decorate over the area where we engrave our names, right?"

So no one would be able to see it. She was a clever one, Riku observed in silent admiration. He'd been right—he could entrust everyone to Couron. The reason being that the stone was already *engraved with Couron's full name*. Neither Riku nor Schwi had a family name. So her true intent—

"...This will make you husband and wife. And my official brother and sister."

She said this with an expression that was a mixture of delight and melancholy. Smirking, both Riku and Schwi each took blade in hand, inscribing Couron's family name after their own, though the combination sounded a bit funny... After the stone had been fully engraved, Couron in particular seemed dazzled by it, and she put it away as if it was truly precious. Then, with an expression more sisterly than if she'd been their real sister:

"...Hey, Riku. Schwi."

She wanted to stop them but couldn't. She understood that, and forced a smile despite that.

"I don't know what you'll...you'll all be doing from here on. You're no longer part of this world, but..."

She embraced them both. Her brother and sister.

"I know...that I have a precious brother and an adorable sister. So please... I'm begging you..."

"—I don't want to lose any more family. Don't go crazy..."

They couldn't see her face, but responding to her trembling whisper, her siblings nodded.

"Sure. No one will die. No one can die. Because this is one game—we're gonna win."

"...Leave it, to us...Sister..."

■■■

——......

At the round table surrounded by ghosts, their leader spread his hands over the board.

"We do not exist.

"We kill none, and we do not die. We exploit all means at our disposal to direct the course of the War. With information, with scheming, with sheer guile... There are rules and conditions for victory, so this is clearly a game...

"And all will be decided on this map—this board. As such...let us select our pieces."

Summoning the gazes of the ghosts to himself, their leader produced a white piece.

"This is us."

A white king.

"The weakest piece. The piece that can never become anything. But the most important. If this is taken, the game is over."

He placed it off the map—correction, the board—at the edge of the table and continued.

"We are the king. But at the same time—we are ghosts."

Those who did not exist. Who must not exist. And who were therefore invisible.

"We are nowhere, and we are everywhere. We manipulate everything from beyond the board."

And then, producing several more pieces—all white—

"We shall not take a single piece, and yet we will win the game. Therefore, all races—are white."

With this, the piece displayed—a white pawn—

"This—is Werebeast."

On the board, he placed the white pawn in the territory belonging to Werebeast.

......—

■■■

Three Werebeasts roamed the forest, keeping low, searching for prey. In this world, this age, securing food was not easy, even for Werebeasts. First off, there were hardly any worthwhile animals left. What's more, there were few other races they could hunt without risk. Sharpening their senses, they followed a scent—and at last found a stray to take.

It was a human. Not a very tasty animal, but it would at least appease their hunger. They coordinated their attack in voices only Werebeast could hear. Even against a human, they couldn't be careless. They surrounded it and pounced as one, sinking their fangs in—

"——?!"

—nothing, for at the very last moment, they leaped back.

"You Werebeasts are sharp. If you wanna eat me, go right ahead—but I *promise you I taste bad.*"

"...Who the hell are you?"

The three Werebeasts interrogated the *thing that resembled a human and spoke in the Werebeast tongue*, making no attempt to conceal their wariness. It reeked, this *thing* that had ingested a heavy dose of poison and answered flawlessly in their native language.

"You know that forest you're camped in? To the west, by the bay…? The Dwarves are planning a bomb test there."

"—The hell are you talking about?"

Simultaneously, all three were sizing up the thing with every sense available to them, from the beat of his heart to the sound of the blood coursing through his veins.

His body temperature was abnormal as was his heart rate, both owing to the poison. His pupils—

"If you don't believe me, go check out this point on the map. You, you're a *bloodbreaker*, right? You should be able to slip into a Dwarven facility no sweat and find out what they're doing. Let me just give you a tip…"

—Signs of lying—none. Just as they reached this conclusion, the human delivered the punch line.

"They call it the E-bomb, and it can even kill an Old Deus—a *weapon of mass destruction*."

""""—?!"""""

Once more, they checked his heartbeat, his pupils, the flow in his capillaries—he…wasn't lying?!

"Go look. Steal it away somewhere or destroy their records and equipment. But be sure you don't try to destroy the weapon itself, all right? 'Cos in that moment, there's a chance you might blow everything away—I mean the whole western half of the continent of Lucia."

With that, the mysterious *thing*, having said his piece, casually strode away.

——……

"—Schwi, anything?"

"...No...it's okay..."

In response to Riku's query, Schwi used the spirit compass—or pretended to need it—to scan for signs of life. As soon as it was confirmed that no one was there, the ghosts infiltrated the Dwarven facility.

"Seriously, though...please don't ask me to 'chat' with crackpots capable of shit like this again, General."

The ghost formerly known as Alei took in his surroundings and gasped. The steel structure, *formerly* a Dwarven facility, had been rent and warped by claws. Blows pockmarked the ground as deep as a man was tall, but even so—

"I'll make you do it as many times as I have to. You're the only one who can speak Werebeast perfectly. The serum worked, didn't it?"

"That it did. I got off with just two days of spasms."

The ghost returned Riku's chide with an ironic smile.

There'd been nothing to it. With a little strategic "application" of the map Ivan had left behind, they'd slipped into the wreckage of the Dwarven battleship that had blown away their village and exchanged a few "communiqués." All that was left after that was to leak the news to Werebeast—that *their home had been designated a bomb-testing site.*

"Just how many of those 'bloodbreaks' did they come with? Busting it up this good...were there really no casualties, General?"

"Nope, no casualties. I don't see any blood... Those Werebeasts, they're cagey."

The literally inhuman senses of Werebeasts were capable of deducing the number of Dwarves in the facility from a distance.

Then they just had to raid it with enough bloodbreakers.

The Dwarves weren't stupid, either. They couldn't carelessly employ magic next to a bomb capable of wiping out everything. So if a bunch of bloodbreaking Werebeasts turned up? What choice did they have but to run?

And the Werebeasts weren't stupid, either. The fleeing Dwarves couldn't be as high a priority as—

"Looks like the E-bomb's gone, General. Either the Werebeasts or the Dwarves must've taken it."

"The Werebeasts. Who else could leave footprints on steel floors and walls?"

They must have dragged it out by force. But better than anyone, Werebeast intuition would have sensed the danger of that bomb. So the best they could have done was snuff it out and then—run.

"That's why I'm telling you. This is a game."

Under the right conditions, any given race was helpless against another. That was why the battles continued.

"But the Dwarves aren't gonna abandon this place. We have fifteen minutes to move. We'll collect our information and disappear. Ghosts—"

"Exist nowhere—*aschent*—"

As the ghosts dispersed to dig up intel, Schwi asked:

"...Is this...what you call...promoting...a piece?"

"We haven't gone that far. Still..."

The reason he'd assigned Werebeast the pawn— It was because a pawn, advanced deep into enemy territory, could *be promoted to a queen. Still*, Riku snickered.

"Even a pawn can take a bishop. That's all it is."

■■■

——......

Once more, at the round table surrounded by ghosts, their leader spread his hands over the board.

And he produced—a white rook.

"This—is Elf."

With that, the rook was placed on the board. The coordinates— the Elven capital.

——......

■■■

The Elven capital. A mansion at its outskirts. The Elf who'd just returned, Nina Clive—

"—?! ...Who's there?"

—sensing the presence of an intruder, immediately cast spells of detection and illumination, and put up her guard. Deep in the fringe's darkness, as if melting into the shadows, a figure in a robe sat at a table. Covered in rags and pelt, with a fur robe and a hood low over its eyes, this shade spoke.

"...How do you do? I'm afraid I've made myself at home."

Despite the shadow's fluent Elven and sociable air, the Elf quickly wove an attack spell—but did not fire. This was due to the results of the second rite she'd simultaneously deployed—an analysis spell.

—*Identification impossible: identity unknown...* The shade sneered. *You must be surprised.* Though her visitor might well disguise his appearance, the Elf could not have foreseen that magic would be unable even to reveal his true form. Thus, she had to ask:

"May I inquire who you are?"

She couldn't make any rash moves against an unknown adversary. The shadow smiled.

"Let me introduce myself simply as a ghost. And I'll also volunteer that I am neither your enemy nor your friend."

Of course, the Elf used her magic to determine the veracity of his words—but the ghost already *knew* what that would yield.

That he was a ghost was *false*, and the rest was *true*—that's what her magic would tell her. *It is indeed the case that I'm neither your friend nor enemy.* The ghost smiled thinly.

"Your circumstances must be quite pressing to invite yourself into another's home, I presume?" asked the Elf, unable to grasp his purpose.

Most pressing indeed. Otherwise—would a *mere human* dare sneak into the city of Elf?

"—I was hoping we could play a simple game."

"...Come again?"

"The chips we shall bet are *information*... If you win, I shall provide mine, and if you lose, I shall receive yours."

Nina remained wary, but the ghost sneered to himself and said that was fine. The Elf called Nina Clive was a keen thinker and the finest mage of her generation.

It was *for that very reason* he'd chosen her as his contact. Her visitor voiced her concerns for her before she'd even had a chance to formulate them.

"Chips without collateral—like unverified information—don't make much of a wager, you say?"

"————Yes, I suppose I do."

Nina treaded lightly, fearing that her visitor might have *read her mind*—naturally. A keen thinker, when faced with an unknown opponent, will consider the worst possible scenario first. In this case—a race above her own. But she was also too clever to humbly withdraw. Three possibilities still coexisted: that he was of a higher, a lower, or the same race. Given this, the ghost smirked, thinking—*She'll definitely accept the game.*

"Then let me offer you one *on the house.* I shall prove to you that the game's stakes, regardless of veracity, hinge on information you cannot afford to ignore."

Yes, at the mere mention of this term...she would definitely play the game.

"'*Áka Si Anse* has been discovered by Dwarf.' ...What would you say to that?"

"——?!"

The ghost couldn't sense it, but she must've used her magic to check for a lie again... But it was *futile.*

"...Are you convinced? It is not a matter of whether the information is valid. As the conceptual originator and rite compiler of Áka Si Anse, surely you have the pull to verify the fine points yourself—am I correct?"

The Elf feigned composure, but her thoughts were panicked. The ghost saw that clear as day.

—Áka Si Anse, the "Devoid Zeroth Guard," was such a vital secret that even the identity of its conceptual originator was kept under wraps. The names of those involved in its development had been recorded in code, even on documents that were themselves confidential—such as that *handful of documents* that Schwi had found abandoned in the basement of the ruined Elven metropolis. In the Elf's eyes, not privy to this detail, the ghost must have appeared positively omniscient. Yes, regardless of his identity—*rash moves against him would clearly be ill advised.*

"……——"

Though undetectable to a human, the Elf must have been employing multiple spells to check what he was saying—but it was futile. There was no falsehood to find. The information had indeed been leaked. Indeed, by none other than the ghost himself…

"…Very well. Whoever you are, I see I shall have to deal with you."

With that, she squared off against the ghost and folded her hands.

"Now, as for the game—as you mentioned chips, I suppose you have in mind a card game?"

"No, speed chess. That should make it easy for both of us to see that there is no cheating, yes?"

The Elf considered the chessboard on the table.

"—Very well, then let us begin."

"All right, but first…" The ghost's tone was mocking.

"…*would you mind terribly putting that piece back?* White makes the opening move. My apologies."

"————Oh, excuse me. I am afraid I am not very well-versed in the game."

Putting on airs while clucking to herself, *He caught me,* her expression warped ever-so-slightly. Her ruse, probably covered with her full might—an octa-cast—had been seen through. The Elf called Nina wondered—was testing her enigmatic guest too risky? She returned her piece to the board, undoubtedly intending—

"Then, as for my chip… The conceptual originator of Áka Si Anse is actually—"

"Not you. I have that information."

—to test him with a bluff. As the Elf cursed inwardly, her opponent's next statement—

"As well as the information that *that's a lie*, and the information that you'd use magic to convince me of it."

—made her visibly blanche.

"Now, will that satisfy your prodding as to whether lies will work on me? Can we begin the game?"

Merrily taunting her, the ghost could see her thoughts clearly, wholly without need of magic. Her expression broadcast—*Who in blazes is this fellow?*

It made the ghost—Riku—smirk.

As long as he knew her race, there was nothing to it. Riku was human. He couldn't detect magic. He'd been unable to sense that the piece had been moved. But he could predict what the sharpest wit and finest mage in a generation of Elves would do when presented with a prearranged chessboard by a stranger. So. He'd refrained from mentioning which piece had been tampered with and disinclined her from using a spell to make him believe her.

It had been a bluff, of course, but it didn't look that way to her—it couldn't. He was bluffing a lot—*and if he flubbed even one, it would be over.* The notion of walking such a tightrope…to her, it was inconceivable. The *human weakness* that demanded such things? …Inconceivable. And thus her inevitable conclusion—

She could not detect a hint of magic, such as a disguise, from the ghost. Neither could she tell if he was lying. That required magic that not even she—an octa-caster unparalleled in the present, legendary by measure of the past—could pierce. With such might at his disposal, she would be helpless to resist her guest in any case. He'd even seized the upper hand in their psychological battle, allowing her a glimpse of information she could not ignore. That he was neither enemy nor friend… She had no choice but to trust those words and try to extract his information. Just as the ghost had said, she could verify it after the fact herself. But having collected her thoughts to this point, suddenly—

"You can decide for yourself the information you wish to wager.

Should it be deemed that said information holds no value, though, an alternate demand may be made. How is that?"

—she found herself at risk of being forced to disclose secrets that were too compromising. The ghost's tone gave the impression he'd been waiting for her to catch up, and the Elf clucked.

Why had Riku targeted this Elf? She was the compiler of Áka Si Anse, thought to be Elf's ultimate weapon, and possessed vast knowledge. Further, she was an exceedingly accomplished mage with a sharp wit—an outstanding intellect. That was why he had chosen her—because *that's all she had*. Intellect underscored by the power to destroy everything if it fell short. Versus intellect honed to walk the tightrope of human frailty and foolishness. For her to contend with humans—with the weakest—on intellect was a futile endeavor. All of which led to her current predicament.

"In other words—if I demand your identity..."

"Then I shall demand that you wager information that is exceedingly inconvenient for you."

Yes, thought the Elf. In the end, that was what he was after. She should abandon optimism and assume the enemy would reveal all her lies. Then she should draw out whatever information she could, using it to ferret out the identity and purpose of this so-called ghost.

"Very well, let us begin the game. Neither friend nor foe, I posit that you *mean no harm*."

Riku cackled to himself at these words. He knew it. Because she had an outstanding intellect. Because she was strong. Because she was proud...

For all these reasons—*she was easy to read. She was easy to lead.* And smiling as if he did, in fact, see through everything, Riku gestured with this hand.

"In that case, let us declare an affirmation. In the tradition of ghosts, to begin the game, will you repeat after me?"

This.

"—*Aschent...*"

——......

*　*　*

"...With that, first, regarding the intel you so kindly provided...

"...I will demand you furnish me with details of how the Dwarves came to know of Áka Si Anse and proof, if possible."

"That chip was a *gift*... I'll provide what you request, no wager required."

So saying, he held out the sound stone that had recorded the communication from the crashed Dwarven battleship. Riku couldn't wager information that would give him away, and that was why it was on the house...

"Let me offer you...something better..."

And he flicked a more attractive hook and bait before her.

"I shall wager the reason Dwarf learned of Áka Si Anse and yet decided that it was *of no consequence.*"

"——They—what?"

Áka Si Anse had been classified as being *inconsequential.* There were only three conceivable things that could mean: They had underestimated it; they had a means to defend against it; or, of all things—

"—Yes, of all things."

After waiting for the Elf called Nina to reach that point—Riku said it. He was reading her mind—that was the illusion he meant to deepen. So she responded again:

"...I demand your information about that. *Which you say you know.*"

She'd come back with a bluff, not specifying what "of all things" was—but Riku laughed.

"I know...of the weapon Dwarf believes to be at least as powerful as Áka Si Anse."

Such was Riku's rebuttal. Finding it the very "of all things" she dreaded, the Elf ground her teeth.

But...you fell for such a childish trick again. Riku chuckled to himself. If her ultimate weapon had been deemed "inconsequential," the

possible reasons for such an assessment were limited. But she didn't
realize the significance of her phrasing—"information about that."
If she, convinced as she was that there could be no defense, was asking him for detailed information about something...

...by process of elimination, "of all things" could only mean an
even greater weapon.

She was enraged. Her thoughts were being read somehow. The finest mage of her generation, acclaimed for her sharp wit, was being
toyed with in a battle of wits. It wounded her pride—and gradually
robbed her of her ability to think calmly...

Riku formed an opinion of her then: *You half-assed half-wit.* Had
her strength been unconditional, she would have struck him dead
the moment she encountered him. *If your power's so half-assed you
need to prod your enemy to decide whether you can—don't boast
of wit.* If you can't boast of *folly and weakness*, then when that
half-assed power is stifled—

—you may try to contend with humans on intellect alone, but you
won't stand a chance.

"I honor your pride as one who has taken a magical system lost
to the Flügel and woven from it a new form you feel surpasses the
original. Should you defeat me, I shall tell you the details. What do
you wager?"

With a sigh, Riku recited the information the ghosts and Schwi
had collected, maintaining his composure all the while. The Elf
called Nina bit her nails and racked her brains.

"—How about the number of Áka Si Anse units currently available for deployment and information on the carriers upon which
they can be mounted?"

"Your quick understanding delights me. You live up to your reputation as the most sharp-witted of Elves."

A weapon that surpassed Áka Si Anse. Its very existence was a
startling piece of information. To reveal the details—she understood that he could hardly agree but for a considerable price.

What a dangerous gamble that would be. Riku could only imagine. Still, utilizing the advantage he'd already seized—and making a point of using it to shake her as well—he asked:

"By the way, could you tell me exactly what will happen to you if the fact that you leaked this information came to light?"

"…I'll be convicted of treason on grounds of leaking critical national secrets and executed without so much as a summary trial, I imagine."

The Elf glared at Riku, interpreting his question (the answer to which struck her as obvious) as an attempt to steal her concentration from the game. But Riku gaped inwardly, *Wooow*, shocked by this revelation beyond his expectations. The thing was, the details of Áka Si Anse *were a complete mystery to him*. He knew the name and developers…and the Dwarves' reaction to the line of bullshit he'd tossed to them about a "weapon of mass destruction." But now—her reaction finally started bringing the bigger picture into focus. Defiantly, the Elf went even farther, feeding him nice information.

"Despite that, all of my—all of Elf's—spirit has gone into making Áka Si Anse the most powerful *rite of spirit-breaking*. If it's true those grubby moles have built something beyond it, I will sacrifice my life to obtain your information…"

—*Well, whaddaya know?* It seemed Áka Si Anse was something called a rite of spirit-breaking. Positively rolling with laughter in his mind, Riku pulled himself together.

"Well, then—shall we begin the game?"

■■■

Their chess match consisted of twelve games. The Elf won five, lost four, and drew three. In the end, she took the win. So Riku provided her with all of the information she wanted—*correction: the information he wanted to give her while obtaining much of the information he wanted*. But the Elf, supported by the table, put her head in her hands and groaned.

"Detonate the ether of deactivated Old Dei…? Those filthy moles, they're unhinged…"

Meanwhile, Riku, lowering his face, couldn't help but think, *Who are you to talk?*

Keeping up the pretense that he knew what Áka Si Anse was, he'd collated the intel she'd revealed to arrive at the rite's principle.

(The one who'd come up with a way to make a Phantasma self-destruct *calls someone else unhinged—it's not even funny.)*

This world has reached a point where everyone and anyone in it is insane. Complaining to himself as he rose to slip past the head-clutching Elf—

"Hold it, you."

—Riku was brought up short.

"By now, I've no inclination to pry into who you are or how you came upon such information. And until I verify it, I can only treat it as suspect."

"That's fine. A wise decision."

"But there's just one thing."

Sharp eyes. Were it not for "certain circumstances," even Riku's poker face would most certainly have buckled. Facing her visitor with a look to kill sharpened like a knife, the Elf made her point.

"There were moments in our matches when you *moved as if trying to lose*— Let me ask you just one more time."

Depending on his answer, regardless of who he might be, she would attack unconditionally with every means of injury known to her. Even if it might sail back on her, her gaze indicated she was prepared to do so.

"—Are you an enemy? Are you a friend?"

But unfortunately…

"This marks my second time informing you that I am neither your enemy nor your friend, but…" Riku smiled. To him at this point, a look as murderous as hers was less than a gentle breeze. To those who lived hand in hand with death, a *look* to kill was nothing more than an adorable little wish. "…if this answer fails to satisfy you, I shall add this."

Having lived through the aforementioned adversity, Riku spoke from his "heart."

"I wish for as few of you to die as possible."

——.

"...All right, Mr. Ghost. So you mean to ask me and no one else what I will do with this information."

She must once more have checked his truthfulness, using all eight threads of her magic.

There could be no falsehood, for these were Riku's true feelings. That being the case, even if she could not grasp his purpose, even if he was neither friend nor foe...

"—I'll just conclude that you bear us no ill will. *Which is exactly what you want*, yes?"

So with a smirk, the Elf called Nina—no...

"—By the waaaay."

Suddenly, she changed her tone—no, her very personality—

"I know a few things, Mr. Ghoooost...that even you do not knooow."

As if an entirely different person, the Elf—

"Nina Clive is an alias. My real naaame..."

—confided with a soft smile that suggested the warmth of a hearth:

"...Why, it's Think Nirvalen! ♪"

And she tittered, *hee-hee.*

"This is my truuue seeelf. Did you see through my aaact?"

At Nina's—no, Think Nirvalen's—playful grin, unleashed seamlessly as if by an entirely different person, Riku kept his face down but answered with a chuckle:

"Yes, I did."

"......"

"Did you ever hear me call you Nina?"

The documents written in code down to the developers and the conceptual originator. So thorough that doubting the veracity of the names—was only natural. But now that Riku had learned the principle of Áka Si Anse, it made even more intuitive sense.

Think Nirvalen wasn't stupid enough to publish such an insane scheme under her real name.

"Hee-hee… If I may speak plainlyyy, right nooow, why, my insides are boiliiing!"

The greatest mage among Elf—who had also fancied herself an actress—laughed in annoyance. Having failed even once to rattle him, Think seethed, but Riku—

"Sorry, but acting is a ghost's stock-in-trade… I know what it looks like."

—Yes.

"*That's why* you were the one I chose."

The final reason he'd settled on Think was this: She would cover up her contact with the ghost completely, dig up the proof of his information, and then—lead Elf on the most appropriate course. As Riku took his leave, Think did not look at him.

"By the way, Mr. Ghost…have you heard what they saaay? That Elves never forgive and never forgeeet?"

"Yes, I've heard that a number of times. They say they'll take out their grudges even if it takes scores of generations."

Think giggled softly like a flower.

"I shall humbly accept the informatiooon and your wish that we not diiie…*but that asiiide*…"

Smiling, Think Nirvalen turned a specter's glare on Riku's back.

"I shall find out who you are, Mr. Ghost—and steal ahead and kill you. Why, I promise I wiiill. To think you played with *meee*, of all Elves, in the palm of your hand… Why, I'll make you regret iiit— For the rumor that Elves never forget a grudge…originates with none other—than the Nirvalen familyyy! ♪"

—Hmm.

"I admit this is the first I've heard of this, and I already regret provoking a rather troublesome opponent."

With these words, Riku took his leave, and Think watched him the entire way, wearing a smile that could kill...

■■■

"...Riku—hurry! Drink...this...!"

In a shack some distance from Think's mansion, Schwi desperately rushed to cure Riku, who writhed in agony, feeling as though he might lose his consciousness and his life any moment. The hallucinatory feeling that someone had poured molten iron into all his blood vessels prevented him from even screaming. *No, maybe it's not a hallucination.* He laughed to himself. Pretending to be a ghost before Elf, the race with the highest magical aptitude of them all—and, of all Elves, their very finest mage. Under normal circumstances, the spirits in his body would have been, and he'd have been laid bare in a blink. So what could he do? It was simple. *Become unidentifiable.*

"We have to, get the dead spirits out, fast...or you'll die, Riku!"

Schwi fed Riku her decontamination fluid, the Ex Machina equivalent of blood, and squealed.

Yes, he could just ingest the black ash, intentionally contaminating himself with dead spirits. Broken spirits—dead spirits upsetting his own, inside and out, devouring him, destroying him. Even the finest of mages would be unable to identify a body beset by spiritual contamination. One with a fine wit would have been that much harder pressed to imagine it—such a *suicidal act.*

"...Riku...you liar! You said...one hour...it was over two...!"

Riku had swallowed and coated himself with a *barely nonlethal dose* of black ash, as calculated by Schwi. But she'd calculated its lethality—assuming one hour. Riku's body, ravaged by dead spirits for over two, was being mercilessly corroded, destroyed. If he wasn't decontaminated fast, just as Schwi had said, it would kill him, but—

"What could I...do...? That bitch...was tougher...than I thought..."

Riku struggled to reply. He hadn't thought it possible that some-one could be better at chess than Schwi. Think Nirvalen might not be able to beat her, but she'd put up a good fight. He thought back sardonically, *"Trying to lose"? How nice of her— What an overesti-mation.* He'd gotten the information he needed, but otherwise, *he'd fought for real and lost.* It was all thanks to his successful bluffing. One wrong step, and he'd have been dead—

"...Rikuuu...! Just a little, more...so—! Hold on...!"

If Schwi's decontamination failed... In any case, it didn't look like he'd have to wait long.

At the very least, his skin would probably never be the same. He'd seen many times how people ended up when they came into direct contact with the ash. Burned and befouled, those scars—were for life. However many more years he might live, however things might go, Riku would spend the rest of his life wrapped in bandages. It wasn't just on the surface. His innards must have been likewise affected. The only idiot Riku had ever heard of who'd orally ingested a large dose of black ash was himself. A historical first in idiocy. If his skin looked like this, one could expect his organs were charred and necrotized. He'd prob-ably never be able to eat a proper meal again. At least he hadn't taken it in nasally. His cardiopulmonary functions should have been fine.

Unless the dead spirits had gotten into his blood, but—

"...Riku...you said, no one will die...no one shall die...!"

Schwi was still fighting desperately to decontaminate him. *Yet,* Riku thought...

It had been worth it. He'd uncovered the secrets of Elf's "Áka Si Anse"—and even how it was to be implemented—from what Think had let slip. *"Carriers upon which they can be mounted."* Meanwhile, he'd discovered Dwarf's "E-bomb" from the strategic map Ivan had given his life for. Now finally, in cooperation with the ghosts lurking in each territory, *he could accomplish their first objective.* To lead the front away from where the humans lived. *And then...* Riku laughed to himself. The final move almost seemed within reach—but.

"Hey, Schwi...how much longer...you think I've got to live?"

The point of his question had been whether or not he could make it to that last move, but Schwi turned on him atypically—with a glare full of rage.

"…You shall not, die… You shall…live, until I…die…Riku!"

"—Huh… Hey, how long do…Ex Machinas live?"

"…There are, approximately, eight hundred and ninety-two years…left, in my service life…"

This answer, despite his being assailed by pain that made it feel as if his whole body might crumble, made Riku smile.

"Ha-ha—guess I'll have to grit my teeth, huh…"

This really…isn't the place…for me to kick the bucket…anyhow…

■■■

——……

Once more as his ghosts surrounded the round table, their leader spread his hands over the board. Most of the races' pieces had already been situated, with over ten arrayed.

Now—this time he produced the white queen—

"This is Flügel."

And with that, he placed the queen on the board. The coordinates—Avant Heim.

The queen. The strongest piece. The ghosts raised an eyebrow at his assignment of it—not to Phantasma or Old Deus—but Flügel.

"…Because, they're strong?"

The ghosts' leader just chuckled.

"There is that, but it's because they don't grow."

No one was sure what he really meant, but then one of the ghosts commented on the fact that the board had been set with white pieces only.

"But look—you've made them all white. They're all on our side?"

"That's right. We shall win…without taking a single piece. We have no enemies."

"Hey, but then how will you know that we've won?"

Hearing this, the head of the ghosts smugly displayed—the black king.

"If we get this guy...we win."

"...You say we're gonna win without taking a single piece—but then we *do* have to kill someone?"

With this question, the ghosts bathed their leader with puzzled stares. However, seemingly suppressing a grin, he held out the black king...

"Did you not hear me? The rules are absolute. No one will die. Because the black king—"

...and emphatically slamming it onto the board, he declared:

"—is this guy."

Of all the ghosts assembled there, only their leader—with his conviction—smiled.

————......

◉ CHAPTER 4
1 ÷ 2 = HELPLESS

The ghosts, scattered throughout the world, had been quietly orchestrating the War from behind the scenes for close to a year. Today, sitting in their hideout and playing chess across the table from Schwi, Riku once more studied the strategy board…

Just as expected, Elf had brought Fairy to their side. They'd increased their contacts with Dragonias who could combat Dwarf's airships, uniting against the common hypothetical enemy of Dwarf with an "Elven Alliance."

Meanwhile, Dwarf had built on their healthy relationship with Gigant by bringing a number of Phantasmas to their side. Certain ghostly whisperings that the Elves had created a "Phantasma killer" had resulted in the explosive birth of a rock-solid "Dwarven Alliance."

But there was no forgetting the most powerful force of all, over on the next continent, which included the Flügel: the camp of Artosh.

With these two alliances concealing their own weapons of mass destruction, even his almighty lordship Artosh—hand clenched and shaking furiously behind his back—could not afford to make any hasty moves against either of these "Unions," and the front ground to a standstill. Demonia relocated to profit from the struggle that kept the big players busy, while Werebeast, wary of the E-bomb, moved to the archipelago to the west. The world was on a hair trigger, bracing for Armageddon with nothing left for the combatants to do but stare one another down!!

This was the state of the board that our smart little ridiculous bozos had worked so hard to construct. The continent of Lucia, comically, had left Immanity "home alone" for the first time. The setup was perfect, the plot ripe for a once-in-a-lifetime showdown... All that was left was the endgame.

——......

"Hey, Schwi, I asked you before if there was a god of games, right?"
"...Uh-huh..."
"You said a concept becomes an Old Deus when the activation conditions are satisfied... What activation conditions?"
"...Acquisition of ether...strength of feelings, prayers...cannot produce strict definition... *Flow...?*"
When he'd asked before, she'd said there was no ether and therefore no such god, but—
"Well, actually, if I said *I've seen the god of games*—would you believe me?"
"...What you believe...I'll believe..."
Moving a piece with a serious expression, Schwi continued.
"...Riku, you overturn...all my projections... If you say, there is one, then there *is*... If you say, the sky isn't red, it's not red...I won't give it, a second thought..."
——.
——*Ahhhhhh, daaaaaamn!*
"Whoa, make sure you share that line with somebody! My wife is so, so into meeeee!!"
"...That...aside..."

Her face looked slightly flushed, but it wasn't just his imagination. Schwi announced timidly:

"…Checkmate."

"—Come on, god of gaaames… Let me win at least ooonce…"

Schwi gave a little smile as Riku, grinning, tore at his hair.

"Ummm, pardon the interruption while you're having a conversation more embarrassing to listen to than to have, but do you mind?" asked Couron, diffidently popping in.

"Oh, great timing, Couron," said Riku. "Wait, wait, did you—?"

"Yeah, yeah, thanks for the yums, but aren't you the one who called me here? Can I make my report now?"

Couron flipped through her papers on the state of the village—no, of humanity—and began.

"I can't believe it…but just like you said, there haven't been any more sightings of other races."

Couron, ignorant of the reason, furrowed her brow at Riku as he laughed, as if to say, *Shocking!* and went on.

"…And so we lit beacons and sent out scouts and found a number of villages in the northern part of Lucia. It won't be easy to integrate them, since their combined population totals almost eight thousand, with the village we—"

"Relax, Couron. Pretty soon, we'll be able to live wherever we want without fearing death."

"……"

Couron's fists trembled at Riku's flippant response, his attention seemingly more focused on his chess match with Schwi.

"Everything's going fine. Schwi and I just have to pull off the last move—*and we win.*"

"…Come on, stop joking around, Riku… Do you realize the shape you're in…?"

Couron had been struggling to bear her feelings without showing them—but Riku's attitude pushed her beyond her limit.

"*I can't even believe you're still alive in that state!!* If you make a long trip like that, you're gonna die!"

Despite Couron's tearful outburst, Riku grinned.

"I ain't gonna die. I still gotta live another eight hundred and ninety-one years."

"—Look, Riku, I'm begging you. Quit fooling around and take a good hard look at yourself—!"

Given his big sister's heartfelt plea, Riku had no choice but to concede and do a self-inventory. First—he was covered in bandages. The burns on his skin from the dead spirits had never healed after all. His entire body's skin was contaminated, but it was what it was. Then there were his internal organs... Schwi had saved them from necrosis—just barely—so they were all right, more or less. He'd never been able to take what one would think of as a meal since then, but he could handle soup at least. The dead spirits had gotten into his blood a little bit, so there was some damage to his bones and respiratory tract, but it wasn't too bad.

"Otherwise...I'm down one arm, and my vision's been impaired— Well, I guess I'm blind in one eye. No big deal."

"—It's a helluva big deal! You—!"

"The other ghosts are like this or worse."

Couron started to argue, but Riku's icy voice stopped her short.

"...It's a *miracle* that no one's died, but we've all been beaten to a pulp."

To a pulp. Literally, just as he said, they'd been beaten to a pulp. It was true that not a single crewmember of the ghost ship, 179 strong, had died—

—yet. It was just a question of *yet.* Guzzling poison, contamination by spirits, lost limbs... The ghosts cooked up any means they could to deceive other races. From tossing away a left arm for the sake of one trick, to eating the flesh of a corpse to hoodwink a Demonia, to willfully submitting to a Dhampir to lead them on, they'd exploited every asset at their disposal—

—every one but their lives... So Riku pleaded:

"Just one more move, Couron. Look the other way. Then the War will end, and I'll—"

*—Finally be able to forgive myself—*is what he started to say, but he swallowed it.

"In that case, at least tell me…"

Couron looked down, shaking.

"I still can't believe you manipulated the other races—even the Old Dei—to get them all off Lucia. I do think it's amazing…but end the War? Even after all that, I still can't believe this!!"

"……"

"If you want me to look the other way, then tell me! Or do you not trust me—your own sister?!"

——……

As Riku and Schwi exchanged glances, Couron's heartbroken tears stained the ground one after another.

"…Couron, if I didn't trust you— If it wasn't you, there's no one I could entrust with everyone."

"Then why—?"

"You know, right? What the gods are fighting over?"

Thrown for a moment by Riku's sudden change of subject, Couron answered. "…The throne of the One True God, isn't it? They say…"

"Yes. The throne of the One True God—specifically, an artifact called the Suniaster, apparently."

Relating what Schwi had told him in the ruins of the Elven city, Riku stood.

"Old Dei—are born of the planet."

By wishes or by prayers, they obtained "ether" and were born. That's what Schwi had told him.

"But *too many were born*. The Suniaster is a 'conceptual device' instituted by the Old Dei in order to determine a single god—a single being with magical power on a level capable of creating races."

"……"

"But for the Old Dei to create a device able to encompass the power of all the Old Dei is *impossible*, right?"

"——Well, yeah. 'Cos that—"

Though this was her first time hearing all of this, Couron understood immediately and bluntly broke it down.

"—would mean using the power of ten to create the power of eleven...right?"

"I knew it, Couron. You got it right. Yes, it's a story so asinine, one can only marvel."

It should have been self-evident: One True God would rule over everything, including the Old Dei. If you supposed that there were ten Old Dei who pooled all their power, it would only equal ten. But the Suniaster—was supposed to produce power that would bring all ten to heel. But it was fundamentally insufficient. It was impossible.

"So, here's what you can do..."

His eyes alight with a notion unfathomably fatuous, Riku spelled it out.

"If there are ten gods, you just *kill nine, which leaves you* the One True God—right?"

Yes, summarizing what Schwi had told him that day boiled down to this: They'd destroy the ether of all the other Old Dei and absorb the power generated. In this way, they'd boost their own strength to obtain the power necessary to manifest the Suniaster. But as it happened, there were as many Old Dei as there were wishes. Even if you slaughtered the big guys, you'd still have to worry about some upstart surpassing you. So if you just conquered the throne of the One True God—the Suniaster—there you were, the only god.

"That's the truth behind this ridiculous Great War."

......

"That's...idiotic— You're saying that's why we've endured this whole waaar—?!"

Couron shook with rage, shouting as if spitting in his eye.

"Couron...watch your mouth. That's an insult to idiots. 'Cos, you know—"

Speaking languidly, Riku touched the map, the board, and said disgustedly:

"—*you can manifest the Suniaster even without any of that.*"

*   *   *

"——Huh?"

Ignoring Couron's blank look, Riku toyed with the black king in his palm.

"Hey, Couron, did I mention what gives birth to the Old Dei?"

"—The planet, right?"

"Yes, the spirit corridors. The source of all things. The stream of all life: the planet itself."

Schwi picked up where he left off.

"…Their creations…the races…are also created, through the Old Dei's ether…through spirit corridors."

"Yeah…so you know?"

With a sigh, Riku came back to the same thought he'd had that day—the day he'd heard this story in the Elven ruins. What had occurred to him before anything else, when Schwi had told him the cause of the gods' strife and the story of the Suniaster… How could no one have noticed something this obvious? He uttered a conclusion so self-evident it had surprised even Schwi.

"All the Old Dei on the planet in total—couldn't be as powerful as their source, if you give it any thought."

Couron's eyes opened wide. *So…* Black king in hand, Riku turned the map—the board—and put it *right in the middle.* With that, he bluntly announced their, the ghosts', victory conditions. That is—their final move.

"If you destroy the planet, the Suniaster will manifest itself."

—…

Ignoring Couron's stupefaction, Riku and Schwi pointed to the floor and continued.

"If you pierce the core of the planet—*the source of the spirit corridors*—the power discharged will surpass that of all the Old Deus."

"…The manifestation will occur, in 10^{-46} seconds…destruction, power discharge, manifestation, and then…"

"Right there—we seize the Suniaster and rebuild the world…"

Riku and Schwi announced simultaneously to the still dumbfounded Couron:

""…Checkmate.""

"B-but that—where are you going to get the power to impale—?"

By the time Couron had recovered enough from her trance to stammer this, the strategic map on the wall jumped out at her.

—*It couldn't be. It couldn't be, it couldn't be, it couldn't be!!*

"*You're going to make them do it themselves?!* You're not aiming for a deadlock—*but an all-out collision of all the factions*?!"

Riku gave a giddy, thin smile at Couron's shriek.

"Artosh's camp and the Unions—*aren't deadlocked.*"

"—Huh?"

Mutually assured destruction—a deadlock based on the assurance of the destruction of both parties if one made a move—only worked when there was an *option not to make a move.*

"Their *objective* is the Suniaster—is death—so the spark's gonna go off soon no matter what."

It meant a battle of a scale never seen before in the eternal Great War—

—It meant Armageddon. As Couron blanched at the image, Riku spoke.

"But the firepower—*won't be aimed at anyone.*"

Once more, Couron was at a loss for words.

"On the stage *we've designated* for the final battle, Schwi and I are installing Umwege—devices that will bend the orientation of the blast so all the force will point straight down. Yes, just like a telescope lens."

According to all the information they'd gathered on the weapons that would be used in this confrontation (which the ghosts had staked everything but their lives to collect), as quantified and number-crunched by Schwi, the number of Umwege they'd need to achieve convergence—was thirty-two.

"The goons will *pierce the planet themselves*, the spirit corridors will be destroyed, the Suniaster will manifest itself, and once we snatch it—we win. And one of the main reasons no one's gonna die is because, when it's all over, I have something I want to ask those gods…"

Riku's face beamed with an enormously ironic smile. One might even have called it sadistic.

"'Hey, hey, how's it feel—you know?'"

For real. The eternal Great War was coming to a close, for real. At the hands of Riku and Schwi, her wonderful brother and sister, and fewer than two hundred others. Moreover—it would be accomplished without killing anyone. To do that, just creating the situation… He could have wanted to slaughter the gods and their creations— No, if he was normal, he must've wanted to. Her brother had lost his skin, his viscera, an eye, an arm, but despite all that, he still smiled impudently. Couron shivered. *To end the War without killing anyone*—to accomplish that, he'd done all this—

"…So, Couron, please. Look the other way just a little longer. And take care of everyone."

But even as Riku grinned boldly, it was already becoming painful for him to breathe, though only Schwi noticed.

■■■

"…Riku… Go to sleep…"

"…I can't… We've got to go install the Umwege right away…"

Schwi nursed Riku as he squirmed on the bed. Though Riku had put on a brave face for Couron, everything she'd said had been true.

The spiritual burns spreading across his skin from the dead spirits alone would invite significant long-term health problems. As if that wasn't enough, having taken them into his organs, Riku couldn't absorb nutrients adequately. No human could be expected to recover from that… That he'd survived at all was abnormal.

"…It's all right…your projections are, never, wrong. The attacks won't start, right away…"

"……But…"

"...You can rest...a little... You can do it... Just a day."

My wife is crazy calm as usual. Riku chuckled to himself, but—

"...I guess...then we'll go to install them tomorrow, and today I'll concentrate on getting better."

"...Mm."

"Hey, Schwi... Sorry for always dragging you down."

"...You're lying down... You can't drag me."

Riku let out a laugh, but even that sent pain searing through his body.

"Then let me ask one more thing. Today I'm gonna sleep and work on recovering—so can you hold my hand?"

She understood the request was intended to help him bear the pain. At the same time, Schwi now understood that he was warning her not to try going by herself.

"...Mm. I'll stay, holding your hand. Don't worry... Rest... Riku."

——.

"Hey, Schwi."

Presumably unable to sleep, Riku spoke up again.

"...Mm."

"...Thank you. I'd never have been able to do this without you."

"...It's not...over yet."

"That's true...but I'd never even have been able to make it this far without you."

—*So.* Riku closed his eyes.

"Thank you for coming for me...and also..." As if he was dozing off, Riku's breath softened as he mumbled, "I really love you...and I always...will..."

...Just what agonies had the corrosion of Riku's spirits ravaged him with? Despite them, Schwi's hand holding his was enough to allow his breath to descend into the peaceful solace of sleep.

Schwi sat thinking to herself. She...liked Riku. But her definition of the feeling known as "love" was still incomplete. It was deeply frustrating to her not to be able to answer his words. Even so, she knew what she had to do. She couldn't let Riku die. Riku had to live another 891 years. If he got the Suniaster, *that could be reality.*

——*So.*

"......I'm sorry...Riku... I'll be...right back."

For now—she let go of his hand.

■■■

Twenty-four installed. Another eight Umweg stations, and it would be done. Schwi once more came to the same conclusion—she'd been right not to bring Riku. She was operating covertly on the site of the final battle, where the greatest forces in the world were currently arrayed. She had detected opponents on several occasions already who would end the game if they caught her, and each time, she'd done everything in her power to hide. Be that as it may, if they by some chance noticed, Riku's presence would have increased the probability of instantaneous death significantly.

...It's all right... I just have to install...eight more, and I'll come back... Riku, wait for me...

Once that was over, she was prepared to endure however much scolding came of it. She couldn't let Riku die. Eight more—finding next coordinates—

"Oh my? I was just drifting about—and such an unexpected find presents itself at my feet! ♪"

Schwi turned to the voice suddenly above her. Prismatic hair and amber eyes. Wings woven of light, and the signature of Flügel—a geometric halo. *Referencing data—* Schwi suppressed the voice in her heart saying this could not be worse and looked at the Flügel's serene face.

"—Good day, scrap heap. Have you decided to take a walk by yourself today?"

Flügel—Close Number: Jibril...

■■■

She never thought the day would come when she, an Ex Machina, would be telling herself to calm down. Attacking an Ex Machina was a sort of taboo. *Act like just a machine, just a counterattacker—*

"Question: Does Flügel have a task involving Ex Machina?"

Activating language circuits long gone idle, she barely managed to act the part. But seemingly oblivious, Jibril continued.

"I do! ♪ It seems Ex Machina heads are—my, my, my!!—now as valuable as Dragonia heads—Rarity Five! ♪"

Bending her body as if vexed, Jibril went on.

"You see, following the defeat of Aranleif, even those in Avant Heim have reached a consensus that it shall be taboo to lay hands upon Ex Machina, whereby the rarity of their heads has soared and soared, to the point that they are now platinum!"

"Warning: Validity of consensus confirmed. Hostility to unit will result in significant consequences."

At her words, though, Jibril hiked up the corners of her mouth in reply.

"From a single Prüfer, you say? ♪"

————Had she managed to keep her panic off her face? That was all Schwi worried about, but Jibril continued without regard.

"I have confirmed no sign of Ex Machina in a one-hundred-meter radius! ♪ Which raises the terribly interesting question of just why a single unit of Ex Machina, which normally operates in clusters, would be operating alone. ♪ Also," Jibril continued with a devilish smile, "as an isolated unit should be unable to perform your race's famous copycatting, I take this to be a *bonne occasion* chance to seize a super-rare, *merveilleuse tête*. Might I be correct? ♥"

Schwi considered once again, without saying it…that this was the worst. Finding herself discovered by, of all races, the most outlandish—and of those most outlandish, the wildest and most overpowered of them all—she could only conclude that Riku had been right when he'd said that probability was nonsense.

To think that the very first card she'd draw would be the joker, the "old maid."

"Now—I'll be chopping through your neck, so please don't move.

♪ There is no use resisting, so your cooperation will make this go more smoothly for the both of us. It's not as if Ex Machina have a concept of death, after—"

"......I refuse..."

"...—Pardon? Did I mishear you?"

—*Death*— The word suddenly motivated Schwi's mouth. Riku's Rule 2: None may die—so she couldn't die. What's more, the fear that *death* inspired—that *she'd never see Riku again*—denied the request.

"...I don't want, to die...I can't—die..."

As Jibril's eyes stretched ever wider, Schwi continued.

"...Unit...disconnected... Scrap... No value, as Ex Machina."

—*So.*

"...I beg you... Please, look the other way..."

But Schwi didn't realize she'd made the worst possible choice. She did not adequately grasp what hovered before her—the wildest member of an already outlandish race.

"What...a machine that fears death?! Not only that, but an Ex Machina *begging*?! And further, you say you are disconnected—a defective item?! R-R-R-Rarity Five doesn't begin to cover this!"

"......——"

"Geh-heh, gweh-heh-heh-heh-heeeeh... E-everyone will be so envious, the duels will be endless!!"

Watching Jibril drool while radiating a lethal hostility, Schwi had to admit failure. *Diplomacy* was something Riku could have pulled off. She shouldn't have let go of his hand—but.

"...Final, warning..."

"Yes, please proceed as you like. Though the outcome will remain the same. ♪"

Schwi's eyes locked on Jibril, who materialized a sword woven of light and looked prepared to set upon her anytime.

"...I don't want, to die... I can't die... If you're, still, going to kill me..."

Little by little...Schwi murmured as resolution:

Analysis of respective forces:

Enemy: Flügel Jibril. Capacity unknown—estimated double average Flügel.

Friendly: Ex Machina Prüfer. Power level less than 32 percent output of Kämpfer (dedicated combat unit).

In addition, friendly unit lacks Ex Machina's greatest weapon, cluster—supporting units. Armaments available are limited due to disconnection: 47 of 27,451. Probability of success: nonexistent.

Nevertheless, Riku's words came back to her:

There's no such thing as zero when it comes to probability.

"*Laden:* Launching code 1673B743E1F255, script E—Lösen—"

Loosing all the armaments she could at once, Schwi declared:

"—All armaments...forces, tactics, strategies online... Initiating supplication for life with maximum output."

"Oh my! I understand that Ex Machina is a race that analyzes and imitates the factors by which it is damaged—"

In response to Schwi's declaration of war, Jibril replied with an expression that seemed to deride the gods themselves.

"—but did one of your kind ever *die of laughter*? Now that is a new one on me! ♥"

Interrupt—short-term battle—only possible victory, Schwi concluded. She discharged all the armaments she'd prepped at once, compressing spirits into an ultra-enriched particle. A spirit particle so dense, any reasonable living thing—even an Elf—would die instantly on contact.

"—Over-Boost—!"

Schwi volatilized it—and in that instant, she disappeared from Jibril's vision. Ultra-enriched spirits, given directionality and volatilized for ultra-rapid acceleration. The volatilized spirits coughed out blue masses of dead spirits, sowing pollution in their wake—as they shattered the bounds of physics. That was how Ex Machina, a race incapable of utilizing magic, managed to use "magic" through the brute-force employment of technology. Though Schwi moved at speeds approaching teleportation—still.

"...Surely you don't really think that's enough to escape me?"

Jibril scoffed, having shifted past *distance itself* to cut her off. As if mocking, toying with her, Jibril brought down her mountain-cleaving blade of light, but... Internally, Schwi answered her assailant's question:

—*Why would I?*

"—Asyut-Armor—!"

As the unblockable blade of light cleaved toward her, Schwi volatilized the ultra-enriched spirits that had just produced her acceleration—meaning she hyper-charged a force beyond physics *without directionality*, producing an "offensive barrier." Killing the ultra-enriched spirits en masse—turning them into dead spirits—she unleashed a blue, spherical particle membrane. That moment, the shock and energy exploded into the earth.

It would have been enough force to wipe out a small city, but—

"How inconsiderate... With a weapon that spews dead spirits, the environmental standards of this machine are rather questionable..."

Asyut-Armor, Schwi's barrier that annihilated most living things through shock and acute dead spirit pollution—Jibril shrugged it off by covering her face with a grimace as if brushing away so much dust. Schwi silently concluded that it was just as she'd projected. Whatever Flügel might have been, as magic woven by Artosh, a Flügel could not have the maintenance of her substantiation poisoned by the obstacle to magic that were dead spirits—!

"Still, do you think this will be enough to———what's this?"

Jibril was confused to find that, beyond the shock membrane of blue light that she'd just pierced, Schwi wasn't there. Once more, Schwi inwardly answered her opponent's query:

—*Why would I be?*

At the same instant she'd launched Asyut-Armor, Schwi had used Over-Boost again to gain some distance, and now she had her sights locked.

For an individual Ex Machina to destroy a Flügel was all but impossible. The probability was astronomically low—and even if by some miracle she succeeded, it would violate the Rules Riku had laid down. Victory in a short-term battle. There was only one route: escape.

"—Lösen: **Enderpokryphen—!**"

A weapon loathsome to Schwi who, by employing it in one of Ex Machina's conflicts, had robbed Riku of his home. The greatest force in Schwi's arsenal, which replicated the Far Cry of Aranleif the Ultimate, fired at Jibril. A storm of dead spirits to defile the world vented as light erupted from her muzzle. Jibril stared into the radiance barreling toward her and was seared—

——.

Schwi made a silent apology to Riku. He'd have to revise the map again.

The single blast of Enderpokryphen, at the same instant it landed on Jibril, rewrote the terrain. The blast of blue light ripped up the landscape's crust, instantly vaporizing it, the reddened earth *gas* it became forming a small-scale tsunami, and the ultrahot sediment—reaching temperatures in the thousands of degrees—sailed in a blink to the stratosphere... A direct hit of that magnitude, sufficient to alter the shape of the planet, would leave not even a Dragonia unscathed. But Schwi *was under no illusions that this would be sufficient to put down her adversary.*

"—Einweg—!"

At the precise moment she confirmed the hit, Schwi launched her last armament. A "space crusher" designed by Ex Machina to counter the shifting abilities of races such as Flügel and Elf. Just as its name suggested, the smashed space would create a unidirectional hole enveloping Schwi's body, closing behind her.

If she leaped to a distance outside the Flügel's detection range, even Jibril should have been unable to pursue her. But the farthest distance Schwi could leap using Einweg was one hundred kilometers—the same distance in which Jibril had claimed to be clear of Ex Machina, so it was impossible to predict Jibril's scanning range. Schwi would have to engage her again when she arri—

"Oh myyy! Where do you think you're going?"

Schwi's mind froze. In the time before the smashed space closed—0.000046 seconds, not even a fraction of a second—Jibril had extended a hand, prying open the wormhole with brute force to peek inside. Hell's voice rang out of a mask of a face plastered with a smile...

"If your intent was escape, a more prudent move would have been to use the light and dust to obscure my vision rather than attempt a long-distance leap... Oh, or, could it be—?"

Seeing the space she'd rent torn open once more by an even greater force allowed Schwi to define a feeling previously unknown to her, as she transitioned from her firing position to a posterior-plant.

"Did you expect your little attack would injure me?"

Definition: This is a nightmare.

It can't be. It can't, it can't, it is impossible! Granted, Enderpokryphen is an imperfect reproduction of the power of Aranleif's Far Cry. It reproduces only 43.7 percent—per the Zeichner's report. But the Ultimate One was one of the Rulers, the three greatest of all Dragonias. A Far Cry unleashed by such an individual at the cost of his life—even 43 percent—

"...It seems you have underestimated me...you silly bit of scrap, you... ♪"

A direct hit—couldn't leave her without a scratch—

—That—that couldn't———!

"However, I commend you—for at least forcing me to erect a *defense spell*."

Jibril's words made Schwi doubt the functioning of her hearing apparatus. Flügel themselves were a kind of magic, woven by Artosh. Therefore, a rite to maintain themselves, which might be called a defense spell, was *always active*. In fact, it was because of this that Schwi had calculated she could breach it with Ender-pokryphen. But this Flügel—no. *Redefinition: This individual no longer fits in the Flügel category.* This anomaly, Jibril, must have doubted the defenses granted by her creator Artosh—and deployed an even stronger defense. It wasn't the work of a Flügel. It was inconceivable. This individual—was already beyond all—

"I had struggled to stay my hand so as to bring your head home safe and sound—but I have changed my mind."

——.

What did the anomaly just say? That she'd stayed *her hand?*

"It is beyond my ken whether you have something that can be called a brain..."

The anomaly faced the wide-eyed Schwi, hiking up her skirt and lowering her body in a graceful curtsy, her face pealing like a bell, like an angel, but so much like a devil.

"...but it seems that whatever you may have which could be likened to one has become appallingly swollen with pride. Allow me to cool it down a bit for you—*forever.*"

The bit of input Schwi was capable of processing was that her right arm had been detached.

■■■

Correction. That was inaccurate. Even Schwi, a Prüfer—one of the units most specialized in processing power—was *utterly incapable of assimilating this.* At best, she could read the damage report: Right arm lost. What had happened was beyond her ability to grasp; her combat power had been annihilated—but.

"...Oh my. I meant to strike your torso... Did my aim waver?"

Was this what Riku—what humans—called intuition? Despite a bit of a lag, she realized that she had escaped critical failure by an abrupt evasive action that bypassed logic.

"......What is it? Something feels amiss..."

Though Schwi had no way of knowing, Jibril was experiencing a strange conviction.

A mere Ex Machina—just a lone Prüfer, in fact—had survived her attack. Why was she operating alone? How had the unit survived her strike? So many interesting questions, but Jibril growled in a low voice that Schwi could nevertheless hear:

"I have an *unpleasant presentiment*. I think it time that you hush now and be buried in the earth like the metal refuse you are."

Hearing these words, issued with a malice infused with mass—Schwi understood again. There was no such thing as zero in probability. She'd trusted in Riku, fought and fled betting on odds from the quiet of nirvana. But at this point, it wasn't even a question of probability anymore. Against this monstrosity, all further attempts at flight, at survival, using any manner of logic or absurdity, were futile. This was the assessment of her irrational thoughts, otherwise known as intuition.

—But—*Even so*, Schwi shook off her misgivings.

—*Even so*—she had to win. Schwi, purportedly just a bundle of logic, admitted it clearly:

...I don't want, to die... I'm afraid...to die... Rikuuu...

She'd never see Riku again. At this prospect, she experienced a sensation of her thought circuits freezing over—*but, more than that*. What Riku—her husband and his comrades, the ghosts—had burned their skin and viscera for, had staked everything on: that singular victory.

...It'll turn to...defeat...because of me—

She couldn't accept it. She could never—never acknowledge it!

Then what to do? In this situation, how could she prevail...? She processed fast enough to stop time—

—until finally—

—Schwi arrived at a move. If she thought of Riku, it was the basest of all solutions. The worst possible idea, which threatened to crush her with self-hatred. Even so, she—who had invited this hopeless situation—could only map out this one route to victory...

So—

`<Unit identification number Üc207Pr4f57t9—d Re-`
`questing reconnection to Übercluster Befehler 1.>`

Communication—she transmitted to the Ex Machina cluster that once had discarded her.

—No response.

Jibril was once more compressing light with eyes that conveyed she would not miss this time.

<Retrying request! Analysis of "life" complete; no time—synchronize—reconnect!>

—After a seemingly eternal short time—she received a response.

<Üc207Pr4f57t9 unit has been permanently disconnected. Request denied.>

At the sound of approaching death, Schwi broadcast in what could best be described as a howl:

<Request denial rejected! Urgent request for data synchronization, forwarding to Einzig! Über-Eins, I know you lack permission to reject forwarding requests from Prüfer to Einzig!>

Schwi contradicted—and ultimately outreasoned—the Befehler of her cluster...but there was no response. Undeterred and irrepressibly provoked, Schwi continued transmitting, as if screaming:

<Über-Eins...no, correction...you unreasonable ass! <——.

<...Really! I don't want to give it to anyone! ... This feeling...belongs, to me!>

The error she'd received from Riku—so great that she couldn't contain it: the one that said she adored him, that she never wanted to leave him. A heart she'd decided she'd never share. Because—it was embarrassing... It belonged to her and no one else—! And yet—!

<...And yet...I'm saying, I'll give it to you! Please get, what that means...you jerk!!>

Because there was no other path. Schwi could think of no other way to atone for her mistake and allow Riku to win. *So...* Forgetting it was a transmission, Schwi screamed aloud:

"**...Stop giving me shit! Just take this feeling—and *pass it ooon*!!**"

......——

```
<Üc207Pr4f57t9. You are indeed broken.>
<...I know!>
<You are inconsistent. You are incoherent. And
yet you function. This is abnormal. Invalid.>
<...I know that, too!>
<Therefore—you have been determined to represent
valuable sample data.>
```

That instant, Schwi felt her severed connection—*reconnected to the cluster*. A feeling she hadn't experienced in years—a sharing of sensations among 437 units, including herself—rushed back to her.

```
<You meet the conditions for a special exception.
Data synchronization—Initiating.>
```

The sensation of being a real Ex Machina—unity. Many as one cluster. One thought entity. Now that sensation—of having the inside of her head peered into unreservedly—felt abominable to her. Even so, for now, it was necessary—that was what she'd decided. Schwi shook her head.

```
<Caution: Until synchronization completes, do not
perform any actions which could damage—>
```

You— The transmission had been about to continue, but a sudden cognizance stopped it short. Now that she was reconnected, all the units in Schwi's übercluster grasped the situation.

The enemy she confronted. The most powerful of the Flügel—Jibril. She felt all the units throw an error at the fact that Schwi had faced the creature alone and was still operating. Schwi laughed at their reaction. *I can't wait until synchronization completes.* Because the error they threw—was a feeling: *Astonishment.* Wouldn't they be, though? *Considering it logically,* even if you discounted the fact that her opponent was the exceptional Jibril, a single Prüfer engaging a Flügel should have been *impossible*—shouldn't it?

But this was reality. Made possible by the "heart" she'd received from Riku—*the ability to make the impossible possible.* An incontrovertible fact, the tip of the iceberg.

```
<—Situation assessed. Üc207Pr4f57t9—unrestricted
```

access granted to all armaments possessed by Ex Machina.>

The deployment network for all armaments possessed by Ex Machina—all 27,451 of them—was unlocked.

<Use all arms and firepower necessary to prevent destruction before synchronization completes.>

Schwi responded with a smirk.

In this scenario, her response was something humans—things with souls—would have said.

<...Can't you say..."stay alive"...?>

Über-Eins didn't know. The conceptual difference between destruction and death—but—

<"Stay alive" until all data is shared. This is a command. Rejection will not be accepted. *Aus.*>

Feeling something in that response, Schwi thought: *They must understand now.* She raised her face to see the onrushing reaper, Jibril—

"......Huh?"

—and the display, Time until synchronization completion: 4 minutes, 11 seconds.

Can that be right? No data has ever taken more than three seconds to— This was Schwi's immediate reaction, but then she shook her head and got it. Of course it would take longer—she was synchronizing her soul. The sentiments, feelings, emotions, memories she'd received from Riku were more than she could hold. It stood to reason that, compared to any armaments, weapons, or information, they'd be far—far, far larger. Riku's face flitted through Schwi's mind, and she smiled sadly... This was a game. She had to survive four minutes and eleven seconds—that is, 251 seconds—against death incarnate, Jibril. If she ran down the clock, she won, and if she died, she lost. Riku's...least favorite game.

"...All these feelings, this heart...everything of the life, I've gained...born, a machine..."

—*I stake them all—on these 251 seconds—!!*

"—*Alles lösen—!*"

She unleashed all the arms, all the firepower, all the equipment possessed by Ex Machina simultaneously to the best of her ability, spreading foolish wings woven of tools built for no purpose other than slaughter and destruction—giant wings of iron.

"—Oh my! You intend to vent your frustration? …By all means! ♥"

So saying, Jibril, too, spread giant wings, as if ejecting light—and sneered. The Irregular Number, Jibril. Her power level yet unknown. Even with all the armaments of Ex Machina at her disposal, it would be impossible for Schwi alone to destroy her. Such was her *assessment*. Maximum possible duration of survival: Cannot estimate.

But Schwi nodded. *No problem.*

"—Forme… *Combat algorithm for unknown*—Launch."

As they bore witness to what she constructed, Schwi felt the cluster panting and gasping with errors. Schwi wondered, *What's the surprise? If the enemy is unknown, all you have to do is anticipate everything you can't anticipate. Don't try to understand. Don't try to calculate. Just believe what you feel and move—that's all.*

Survive the death before you for 251 seconds.

Her logic queried—*Can I?*

The error replied—*Why ask?*

Humans have survived under these conditions—for almost eternity. At this point, of what consequence is another four or five minutes—?!

"…Schwi…"

"Pardon?"

"I didn't, tell you…my name…"

That's me…what Riku gave me: my precious, precious…self.

Jibril peered back dubiously for a moment, then responded with a slight bow.

"Is that so? I am Jibril. Pleased to make your acquaintance. And with that—

"—I bid you farewell."

■■■

Standing atop a landscape savaged cataclysmically.

"......To think the likes of a puppet such as yourself should vex me so... You have quite the nerve."

Jibril complained through thick rage at her inability to destroy a mere Ex Machina, a single Prüfer.

"......I can't, die—not yet...I still can't...diiie—!"

Schwi moved beyond her limits. Plasmifying her joints, which melted with a white glow. In the storm of Jibril's attacks, which she could neither detect nor react to, she barely stood. She whipped out all the armaments of Ex Machina, everything she'd learned from Riku, writhing as if her life depended on it.

—Stay off your opponent's stage; never let them take control.

—Get your opponent to drop their guard; make them think you're theirs.

—Rattle your opponent's nerves; shake them by taking risks.

—Don't read your opponent's moves; lead them where you want them to go—

Can't react to her attacks? Anticipate them.

Can't anticipate them? Dictate them.

So, at a hairsbreadth, Schwi dodged, parried, and canceled—Jibril shook beyond amazement, on to anger. The Ex Machinas in the cluster had strayed from the tracks of understanding and just chanted *Error*. But—all the pulped Schwi saw was the number displayed in her vision.

—Seventy-two seconds.

...Hey...Riku... Why is it...?

When she held Riku's hand, an entire hour felt like an instant—

Unable to ward off one of Jibril's attack, her right side flew away.

—Fifty-one seconds.

...Rikuuu...now, a second feels, like...eternity...

The latest wave of light Jibril released was about to strike Schwi's left hand.

"—?! Lösen—Umweg!"

The "detour" Schwi summoned with a reaction speed even she could hardly believe diverted the wave. From her right arm—into her chest.

"—At last you have fouled up properly... How you have troubled me."

Hearing Jibril crow, Schwi just asked absently—

—Twenty-four seconds.

"...Fouled up...? ...*What do, you mean...?*"

It was true that, now immobilized, she'd entirely sacrificed her ability to dodge. *But...* Schwi smiled, shifting her gaze. On her left hand—its fourth finger—the faintly glowing ring she'd protected......

——.

"...Is that...? So—I 'apologize' for calling you scrap."

What Jibril felt just then, Schwi had no way of knowing. But *thump.* Spirits throbbed as if that apology itself were an attack. High above the helplessly splayed Schwi, her halo tracing a complex—giant—pattern, Jibril spread her arms and declared:

"*Madam*, I hereby acknowledge you as a threat that must be eliminated—an enemy worthy of sure measures."

Beyond comparison with the concentrated spirits used by the weapons of Ex Machina, spirits forcefully culled from the atmosphere—from the planet—were compressed, condensed, compacted and, glowing, manifested themselves in Jibril's hands as a swaying, amorphous lance.

——A Heavenly Smite.

There was no mistaking it. The Flügel transubstantiated the entire structure of her body into *pure spirit corridor junction nerves*, scooping up power from the source of the spirit corridors for one shot—the Flügel's literal most powerful smite. Ex Machina had a weapon that emulated the Heavenly Smite. And this was not Schwi's first time witnessing one. But Jibril's—her whirling power, compared to the Heavenly Smite as recorded in the data, in Schwi's memory—differed by too many orders of magnitude. Schwi's expression fell, remorseful, sad.

The Irregular Number, Jibril—was indeed beyond—

<Syn-chronization...com-plete.>

The network notified her despite the interference, possibly from the massive power whirling overhead.

—*...Oh...*

I didn't see it—until now.

<Üc207Pr4f57t9, renamed—Preier Schwi...>

The numbers displayed in her vision—changing to Synchronization complete—

<Task reassigned to us. Access granted to *rest*— sweet dreams.>

As the Heavenly Smite rained down, Schwi looked into Jibril's face—and grinned.

—*This game's victory—belongs, to me...*

"___?"

Ignoring Jibril's uneasy frown, Schwi said her last words:

"—Lösen: Kein-Eintrag!"

It was impossible to block that Heavenly Smite. Just as Jibril had promised, Schwi would be rendered voiceless scrap... She had no means of overturning that. But if she focused the full output of "No Entry" into a twelve-millimeter radius—she should be able to protect it.

...Just this gift, from Riku...this ring...

An absolute force, one the "heart" she'd received from Riku labeled *absurd and unreasonable*, rained down. Its direct impact would—in deciseconds—erase her, body and mind, from this world...

......But why was it? The Heavenly Smite unleashed by Jibril felt terribly slow. She detected an abnormal acceleration of her thoughts—perhaps what the humans called "flashing lights." Schwi wondered, *How did it get this to happen?* Her enhanced thoughts provided the answer immediately. There was nothing to it. It was simple.

...Riku...I knew it...I can't do anything...without you...

Still, she'd thought she could install the Umweg stations herself, that there was no need to expose Riku to danger. It was her pride that had invited this outcome. Riku had been right all along. Riku would probably—definitely—have been able to pull the wool over even Jibril's eyes and avert this battle; she was sure. Why had she let go of Riku's hand? After she'd decided to trust him without a second thought. He'd told her to stay with him forever. She shouldn't have left him for a second…

…*I'm sorry…Riku… Even so, I leave you…the* last move…

She knew Riku would never accept it.
But she also knew he couldn't refuse.
She knew how hard it would be for him.
She also knew all too well he couldn't deny it.
—*I'm sorry, Sister— I—never did—manage to become—that "beautiful bride"—*
—*Even, so—*
"…Riku… Hey, Rikuuu…"
She called the name of her husband, though he could never hear her. Her voice output apparatus had long since been destroyed. She didn't make a sound. There was no way he could hear her, but even so, she had to say it.
"…I…finally, figured it, out…?"
Because she remembered there were words she'd never said to him.
"…I'm…really—glad…I met you…"

Because now—she understood them clearly.
"…*Next time*…I'll never leave you…again."

"…I, really…love…you———……"

The Heavenly Smite, which bored through the mountain, capping the sky with dust, ended.
"…Hff…hff………hffffff—!"
Having overexerted herself and now nearly exhausted of spirits,

Jibril, unable to maintain her usual form, had become a small child. Out of breath, she lit to the spot where her enemy had been, but no sign or trace of the Ex Machina remained.

"…Ahh…look… What part of this was worth it…?"

The whole battle had started because she'd wanted the head of the Ex Machina operating as a solo unit. Given the machine's singular behavior, Jibril's desire for the head had swelled—until it became a Heavenly Smite. The Flügel bemoaned the fact that even she had no idea what it had all been about—*but her instincts had screamed that the machine was an enemy she had to destroy.* Looking back at it objectively, though—was that really true?

"…I failed to secure her head, blew away every bit of her, and on top of that, look at me…"

Considering her diminutive, cherubic appearance, Jibril heaved a deep sigh. She'd gained nothing, lost all her power, and wouldn't be able to move properly for at least five years—that was her prize.

"Hff… I suppose I shall at least report to Elder Azril that there was a strange Ex Machina… I hope even that mush-head will be able to grasp the significance of the creature making me employ my Heavenly Smite…"

But… Considering her childish appearance again, Jibril muttered pensively:

"If I engage my elder in this state…I can hardly see her letting me go…"

Little Jibril unenthusiastically flapped her wings into the distant sky.

—Small. The glint of the silver ring was too small to attract her notice…

■■■

The game was over. Schwi had died. Receiving the ghost's report, it was all Riku could do to put on a brave face and return to his room. At the table, across from an empty chair, he went through the motions of the game of chess he'd played so many times with Schwi.

Alone. Just as he had once upon a faraway time, when he was a child. The game he could never win— Moving the pieces, he looked at the empty seat in front of him. His sanity suspect, he saw just what he'd seen back then: The boy with the bold grin. The presence Schwi had promised to believe in without question. The god of games.

"Hey… Why can't I ever win…?"

The boy would never answer, but Riku still asked.

"I thought that this time I'd beat the odds…with Schwi—with everyone. I thought I could win."

—Rule 2: No one may die.

—Rule 6: Any act which deviates from the above shall constitute loss.

"Why can't I ever—win…!"

Yes, the minute they broke the rules, the game was over—and they'd *lost*. What was worse was that it was Schwi—

"What…am I missing…? Tell me, please—! Come on, you're there, aren't you?!"

The sight would have convinced anyone who might have been watching to think that he'd finally lost his marbles. Riku screaming at nothing. At the boy sitting across from him—the god of games. The boy didn't answer. By all appearances, he simply…dropped his smile and lowered his face.

"Come on, all right… Can't I win just once? If not—

"Then why—? Why did you give me a 'heaaart'?!"

The "heart" Schwi'd admired and had opened for him. It now meant nothing to him as his body ached. All he could do was scream.

"I don't know what damn god created humans! But if we're gonna live in this world just to lose and lose and lose some more and get the shit kicked out of us and lose everything and do it again—then why do we have hearts?! Answer me!!"

He screamed as if grappling with his crippled body—

"Come on, I know you're there! I don't know who you are, but answer me—I'm begging you......!"

No answer. Not that he'd expected one to begin with, but he was spent. Dejected, raving indiscriminately, he leaned heavily on the back of his chair and gazed at the strategy map.

Vaguely, he put the pieces together. They'd succeeded in pitting all the races against one another and laying the groundwork for the conflict of Camp Artosh versus Everyone Else. But it was as he'd anticipated all along—one side would definitely launch the first strike.

If it was to be the Union, there would be a deadlock until the Elven Alliance and the Dwarven Alliance could figure out how to neutralize their rivals' trump cards, Áka Si Anse and the E-bomb. All-out assault would commence in ten years at the latest, and Artosh's forces would probably lose. Then Dwarf and Elf would spring straight back at each other—until every damn body was dead.

And if Artosh's side struck first? Right now, the Artosh camp had the upper hand—because of the Godly Smite. But the Union wouldn't form their lines so as to be annihilated by a single Smite. Then, once Artosh had used up his power and was temporarily weakened, they'd turn the power of Avant Heim against him. That was the Union's goal.

However powerful Avant Heim might have been, Áka Si Anse would kill any Phantasma, and the E-bomb would kill any Old Deus. There was no victory to be had for Artosh in a preemptive attack.

—Was what the Union *had been led to believe*, but that wasn't reality. Artosh's Godly Smite *was of such a scale that it would trigger the collective firepower of every faction*. So the result—both for Camp Artosh and the Union—would be mutual destruction. In the end, Artosh's forces were unlikely to win by attacking preemptively. At the outside, ten years—before the War went into sudden death.

Ten years. Yes, ten years. One hundred and seventy-nine ghosts had staked everything, thrown away everything but their lives—and he had lost Schwi—to gain, at most, a deadlock of just ten years. That was when Riku could have sworn he heard a voice.

—Ten years of peace. Isn't that enough? Isn't that pretty good?
"......"
—Mere humans managing to arrest the war of gods for ten years?
"......"
—That's plenty. It's more than enough. It's an amazing feat.
——Don't you think that's worthy of being called vic—

"—...Are you messing with me?"

Was this someone's voice or the excuses in his heart? Riku didn't care. He howled as if intent on ripping open his throat:

"Humans waged everything! I lost Schwi! Just ten years of some temporary sham peace is worthy of being called victory?! And *what then*?! We'll be back to the world of cowering in fear of death! Are you dreaming, asshole?!! That's not even a goddamn draw! What makes you think the scales are anywhere close to even?"

......

Silence was the sole reply, and the boy Riku'd seen up until a moment ago was gone...

"...Ha-ha, I'm really beyond hope now..."

That being the case—there was no more need to act tough. So he chuckled and acknowledged it: *Yeah, it's true. I hurt all over. Contaminated by dead spirits, my skin's in constant agony. I can't even remember the last time I got a good night's sleep. Just drinking water makes my throat burn. My vision's so cloudy, it makes me worry that if I let my guard down, I'll go totally blind.*

Yeah, it's true. I admit it... I've lost—again. This life in which I've never won even once—I'm sick of it. I thought that if I had Schwi I'd be able to endure this world. If I could talk to Schwi, see her face, hold her hand...I could even forget this misery.

Riku recalled Schwi's words:

...You shall not, die...you shall...live, until I...die...

Yeah, come to think of it…now that Schwi had died, couldn't he? Just fall back into this chair, let go, and drift away…as if to sleep… yeah…

——……

"—Spieler Riku."

Just as his consciousness was fading—seemingly about to carry his soul down with it—a voice called him back. At the nostalgic— somehow mechanical—sound he'd never heard before, he turned slowly. However it had gotten in, however long it had waited…there stood a cloaked figure in shadows.

"……Who are you?"

He didn't ask "What are you?" He didn't have to. The thing visible through the opening in the robe spoke for itself. It was the body of a machine—not Schwi, but an Ex Machina.

"…I have no name, but you can call me as I am called: Einzig."

Riku cautiously attempted to inquire what it wan—

"—The will of Preier Schwi is my mission."

The Ex Machina man who'd cut him off, Einzig, extended his palm while saying this. Taking what was offered……Riku stiffened in a daze. A small, metal ring. Dirty and deformed—but unmistakably Schwi's—

"—Spieler Riku, you have not yet lost."

"…I…what?"

To the still-reeling Riku, Enzig the Ex Machina calmly announced:

"The Rules specified by the Spieler do not imply that *tools may not be broken*."

——Impulsively, Riku swung a fist to bash that face. This guy had some balls calling his wife—Schwi—a *tool*. Ex Machina or whatever, he didn't give a damn, this bastard was—!! As he clenched his fist in mid-swing—the texture of the token inside it froze him. Einzig had said his mission was the will of the Preier. The ring he'd delivered to Riku spoke to that eloquently.

—*Believe it.* If he just believed…

"If I believe that…then Schwi's failure doesn't constitute a loss… Is that what you mean?"

…………*Don't mess with me.* Riku turned his eyes down and fell silent. Einzig responded:

"—Message: 'Check…Riku…please take care, of the rest—' —End of message."

"…Is that all?"

"——————Yes."

Smirking and raising his eyes, Riku glimpsed the boy sitting in the empty chair again, mouthing: *The game isn't over yet.*

"Ha-ha… Goddamn, Schwi… How can you do this to me…?"

The words came out in a cackle, as if Riku had been holding something in, and he turned his gaze to the ceiling.

Ah, you never did really understand the "heart," Schwi. How would you admire a piece of shit like me…?

…*Of all things, you're gonna make me do this*—was what Riku almost whined, but he just barely managed to swallow it. Instead, clutching the ring, he chanted the incantation he'd long since forgotten.

If it was Schwi's will…Schwi's wish from the "heart"… If she'd determined this was the only way to turn around their predicament—as her husband, Riku's only choice was to have faith…even if it was painful enough to break him.

Because Schwi, in burdening him with this wish, must have hated herself even more.

For her sake, he'd do it, take what Schwi had broken and—for the finale, just one last time—lock it up tight.

——, —*Crnk.*

⏻ CHAPTER 5
1 ÷ 0 = SELFLESS

"Nya-ha, Jibs, you worry too muuuch! ♪"

The eldest sister among the Flügel—the first article, Azril—beamed as she bounded through the air.

"You always get mad so easilyyy… Oh, but! That's cute in its own waaay! ♥ And you're so, so cute as li'l Jibs… Hhh… Rites of restoration are such a bore."

Azril was terribly fond of the Irregular Number—currently the youngest of her sisters, Jibril. The unpredictable, uncontrollable, freewheeling Jibril would go out alone and come back having slain a Dragonia. The purpose and reasoning behind the Irregular Number's wild eccentricity were beyond all comprehension, but as both were part of the "imperfection" granted the youngest by their lord, it made her seem all the more adorable.

Meanwhile, Jibril was peeved from the bottom of her heart. All the vast power of the Flügel collected and discharged in a single strike—her Heavenly Smite—had reduced her to the body of a child, and Azril had been rubbing her cheek for a week straight. Finally snapping after being temporarily sidelined, Jibril had applied for a rite of restoration to restore her lost power. Frankly, Azril felt her little sister could just wait for natural restoration—five years—but…

——……

Returning to the throne room, Azril folded her wings, lowered her halo, and slowly kneeled.

"What of Jibril?"

Lounging on the supreme throne was a man exposing muscles as hardy as crags—the most powerful of gods, the god of war, and the creator of the Flügel: the Old Deus Artosh. A frame that seemed twice the size of his creations. Black hair flowing as tenaciously as steel, eighteen wings enrobing him like a mantle from his back. When those sharp, liquid-gold eyes looked down from his deeply carved countenance upon her, it was enough to make Azril feel as if her brain had gone numb. But Azril knew. That majesty, before which one could not help but succumb to awe and ecstasy, was but a sliver of her creator. A drop of the great ocean, a pale reflection of the immense power presenting it.

"Having engaged an Ex Machina while operating independently, she has exhausted herself on a Heavenly Smite and is under a rite of restoration, my lord."

Azril reported as reverently as if she were praying, but honestly, she had no idea what the big deal was. Mere scraps of metal crawling about… Even collectively, they represented little more than an unpleasant heap of rubbish. It was Azril who had forbidden laying hands on them, but not because she considered them a threat. Seeing the mighty power bequeathed to the Flügel by their lord disgraced by clockwork knockoffs simply filled her with bile. Were the Flügel to attack together, they could eradicate that scrap before they had time to adapt.

And yet… Why had Jibril unleashed their greatest weapon—her Heavenly Smite—against one of those hunks of junk?

"—Is that so? Heh-heh, is that so—?"

And why did her lord find it so amusing, as if having gleaned some insight…? Both questions were beyond Azril.

* * *

Her lord was a god of few words, and consequently, Azril could never fathom his ways.

—*No.* She repented of her pride. For her to even suggest a comprehension of her lord's profundity, the heart of her god, was blasphemy. Her lord was all-powerful. He was the zenith. The strongest of gods, Artosh, god of war—the god of all gods. Supreme. Her lord, the very embodiment of the concept of war, had no rivals. He was strongest because he was the strongest. But it had been long since Azril had seen her lord's smile—that proud, fierce grin. For how many thousands—how many tens of thousands—of years had her lord perched languidly on his throne, jaw on his fist? Yet now he was in fine spirits, as anyone could see.

"It cometh—at last, one who will attempt to slay me."

Azril gasped at this prediction—*surely not!*—furrowing her brow as she responded.

"Lord, there can be none on this earth who might rival you."

As for her lord's discontent, Azril knew the cause: Her master was the god of battle.

Battle meaning slaughter. Fighting, clashing, killing and being killed. Wagering their lives and deaths, they polished their souls, their beings. This cycle of struggle was the concept that had birthed her lord, his ether. Therefore, he stood on the field of battle, calling for malice. *Hate ye! Rage ye! Rise ye! Stake your petty lives, spend all your wisdom on the dares of fools. For it is to crush it all—to smash it underfoot with overpowering force—that makes you strong.* Who can cover the land with force, who can define strength—it is he who is lord.

…But a one-sided massacre can be no battle. Therefore, her lord had fallen into perpetual ennui.

"What meaning hath all-powerful strength…without a challenge?"

As her lord wiped away his smile and turned his steely gaze to the world below, that was when—

■■■

<All Kämpfer: Himmelpokryphen—*Lösen*—>

In the sky behind Avant Heim, following in the Phantasma's wake...

<—Aim—Correct for movement—Fix—Don't **kill, okay?**>

<<<Jawohl.>>>

...more than 1,200 Heavenly Smites (an historical salvo that would alter the fate of the planet) suddenly discharged, targeting—the Union.

■■■

Reacting to the sudden flash that razed the sky and earth, Azril emitted a squeal.

"Wh-wh-whaaaat?! Who just fired a Heavenly Smite?!"

"I-it's unclear! There's no sign within Avant Heim—"

The Flügel crowding the throne room went helter-skelter. Some cast detection spells while others shifted to fly out in the open sky. In the midst of the chaos, Azril was struck by Jibril's story. Functioning alone, behaving erratically, one forced the Irregular Number to fire her Heavenly Smite...

"—Ex Machina...the junk piles that can copycat..."

What would this act of aggression accomplish? It would be assumed that the Flügel themselves had launched a preemptive attack—and there would be a full-scale confrontation.

"Nya-haaa, you underestimate us, you scrap metal...!!"

Having assessed the situation, Azril surfaced a dire smile and fired off orders one after another.

"Rafil, take down every last Dwarven battleship that looks like it could launch the E-bomb, by nine-wing group. Sarakil, take Wings Ten through Eighteen, all of them, and rush down those Elves—"

"Heh—heh-heh—heh-ha-ha-ha-ha!"

* * *

Hearing that roar of laughter, all the Flügel hushed.

"Ha-ha-ha! I see, 'tis thou who hast come to slay me, is it? I did not expect thee so soon, ha-ha-ha!!!"

As her lord rocked Avant Heim with his laughter, Azril addressed him meekly.

"I...I hesitate to inform you, Lord, but the notion that mere Ex Machinas could possibly destroy you—"

But, as ever, her lord was a deity of few words. As if his divine insight, or perhaps his capacity as the god of war, told him all— No, it must have.

"Ex Machinas? *Of what speak'st thou?*"

Having said enough to undermine Azril's assumptions, her lord chortled. Perhaps knowing everything, perhaps welcoming what he had waited and longed for, he cast his gaze to the distance.

"Indeed, it is right that the one to face me, the *strongest*, should be the *weakest*—is it not, 'monkey'?"

With this pronouncement, her lord raised his right arm. That gesture—and that alone—rocked Avant Heim, made space and time creak. The Flügel in attendance voiced small shrieks. Their lord spoke.

"All troops——*prepare for battle.*"

That one phrase that overrode all of Azril's orders meant only one thing:

The war god—the strongest god, the king of all kings, their lord—would summon all his power. Drawing upon even the Heavenly Smites of his Flügel host, whose powers were but shards of his, he would unleash a single strike: matchless, peerless, divine and devastating.

His Godly Smite.

"I...I hesitate to suggest it, Lord, but isn't that exyactly what those toys hope to provoke?!"

The Ex Machinas' objective was for him to fire his Godly Smite in the engagement with the Union, which the scrap would then emulate and reproduce. Azril's plea, however, simply elicited the immodesty that was the exclusive province of a god.

"What of it?"

With both of her lord's savage, golden eyes fixed on her, Azril was stunned as if by lightning. Her lord was the supreme god, and they were his servants. Her lord was absolute. Her lord was all-powerful. *Strong* meant her lord, and *weak* meant—*all others.* If the weak devised tricky little schemes, the strong—the king, the god, the lord—would what...?!

Ashamed to have forgotten this even for a moment, Azril shouted:

"All Flügel—ready your Heavenly Smites—and surrender them to Lord Artosh!"

Their lord had no need of words as, like Azril moments earlier, those around him who feared Ex Machina's emulation faltered. His savage smile alone charged Azril with his divine intent.

"Our lord is all-powerful—without peer anywhere between this heaven and earth! So, let the weak devise their wily little tricks!! What have we to fear? Why should we hesitate? What should give us pause?!"

Responding to Azril's speech, the Flügel revved their wings as one.

"He revels in those who hate, feasts on those who rage, stands for those who rise! It is our lord who loves their folly, and we Flügel—created by this lord—shall now devote our wings to the decree of our one true king, the embodiment of strength, our lord, and sing it on high!"

To those ignorant fools who knew not the glory of their lord—

"That exercising one's force freely——*trampling indiscriminately*——*is what makes one strong*!!"

As the Flügel released the power they had summoned, their lord's satisfied smile deepened, and even his whispered warning rattled the heavens and earth.

* * *

"Pitiful creatures and prideful creators who call yourselves gods before me—ye be nothing."

Whoever they might be, they amounted to nothing but a herd of rabble. Before the overwhelming, all-encompassing power of total and universal destruction, unto dust they should return.

Such was the verdict of Artosh, god of war, strongest of all, lord of the entire world. The Flügel host transferred the power of their Heavenly Smites, the entirety of their spirits, to the raised arm of their lord.

But despite this, Azril still could not fathom the blessed heart of her lord. As the laws of the universe wailed, as the order of the planet bent around his arm—

"I have waited for thee, O *true enemy*."

—the meaning she was able to derive from her lord's soft whisper was still...

"If it be the fate of the strong to be overthrown by the weak, then to be strong must at last be mine ether."

His power became manifest, proclaimed the law, defined strength. In his right arm gathered his truth, which no one in this world could contravene. Without bothering to rise from his throne, his cheek still planted on his left fist, he unleashed his savage smile. His immaculate white wings spread, and his holy countenance glowing with a joy that filled his chest, the lord spoke.

"Come what may—today, I shall answer an eternal question."

■■■

Think Nirvalen, after rejoicing for a few minutes, briefly cursed herself for having done so. The scene before her eyes—a storm blowing the world to its end—raised an unthinkable question:

"...Just...what are Old Dei?"

——......

A United fleet had been positioned around Artosh, staring down his forces—when suddenly a Heavenly Smite had been fired. Think immediately recognized that it was *not a Flügel attack*, and she directed the Elven Alliance response appropriately. The evidence could not have been clearer—the spirit response was different. Also, the strike had yielded no fatalities. Most importantly, there was no point in Artosh's camp firing Heavenly Smites. Had that been their intent, they'd have fired a Godly Smite, fully aware that only that could deal a decisive blow to the Union. So she knew—having met the ghost that day, Think knew—that though masked as a first strike by Artosh, this action was, in fact, a gift of time for them to strike first with their maximum firepower: an attack disguised *to catch the god of war unawares*. Think promptly ordered all the Elven forces to *release every rite in the arsenal* of Áka Si Anse. There were eighteen, half of which would be directed at Artosh—so that, immediately thereafter, the remainder could strike the Dwarven Alliance. Just as she received the report that the release of the rites was nearly complete—it happened.

A power emerged from Avant Heim that shattered conventional descriptions like *absurd*.

A power beyond all law…a destructive pulse radiating outward to make gods high and low cower in fear.

The boundless force, beyond the faculties of even an octa-caster like Think to grasp or measure, demanded at a primal level that she take action. Think ordered all fleets—including those of the Dwarven Alliance, their hypothetical enemy—to share intelligence. While all fleets of all stripes scrambled to assess the situation with their respective means of observation, every report came back the same. It was impossible to quantify. Even the two Old Dei allied with the Union—Kainas, god of the forest, and Ocain, god of the forge—were silent. A pulse that shook the planet. At this late hour, at last, everyone understood.

A Godly Smite—its power universally and entirely underestimated. The threat laid bare, the Union unanimously decided on the spot to unleash *all firepower* on Avant Heim. In the face of *that*, the squabbles between the unions were secondary, tertiary— The power was too inexorable for them not to finally see. And then, as if to say, *I've been waiting—*

——......

The *god* of war's peerless, singular *blow*—the *Godly Smite*—pitted itself against the doomsday weapons of every race most proficient in carnage, each onslaught capable of razing the continent. The attacks collided in a firestorm, yet were incapable of canceling out one another... Instead, *it* whirled like a vortex. Sparkling radiant, a power that eclipsed natural order. A catastrophe that would slay heaven and earth and still rage. Áka Si Anse—a rite that detonated the cores of Phantasmas, releasing their unbridled power. An attack designed to fell multiple Phantasmas in one strike. Elf had fired every blast they had—eighteen rites in all. At the same time, Dwarf launched their E-bombs, comparable in their capacity for devastation—twelve of them. Meanwhile, the eight Dragonias fulfilled their contracts by sacrificing their lives to contribute eight Far Cries—

"To be undeterred by this—*what are Old Dei*?!"

The Old Deus Artosh—indeed, his power was fearsome and divine. One might also mention that Áka Si Anse operated under the protection of the Elves' creator—Kainas, god of the forest—as a *186-fold rite*, likewise divine. So why was their relative scale like the difference between heaven and earth? The sight of the planet crumbling before her eyes evoked in Think's mind the sound of Artosh's answer.

Know your place, O schemers of dust. Writhe. Squirm.
Learn at last, O worms of the earth, that, rail as ye may, ye may never reach the heavens.

...Lashing down her reason, which threatened to fly off, Think ground her teeth and thought. It was impossible to stop this devastation, even to understand it. Accept it. This was reality. In which case, this whirling power—what would become of it? A vortex formed by the collision of powers surpassing this world. A force whose merest ripples would vaporize all possessed of spirit corridor junction nerves on contact... Even for such an inconceivable power, the result—as prescribed by the laws of energy dispersal—was predetermined. The whorl would ultimately converge, diffuse, and radiate——*in all directions*.

"Attention all ships! All mages mobilize—deploy Kú Li Anse! Nooow!!"

Bellows pumped at Think's command, but the Elf knew—it was *futile*. Twenty-five years earlier, a rite of protection deployed by three thousand had failed to block the Heavenly Smite of a single Flügel. In light of this, Think had composed a greater rite of protection—no, of *sealing*—Kú Li Anse. Such a rite, deployed under the protection of the Old Deus Kainas, would stand against a Heavenly Smite. Of this, she was utterly confident. However, watching the nebula before her, she snickered.

Why, facing this, I doubt its protection would be more effective than a scrap of papeeer...

The turbulent range of this effect once it converged, diffused, and radiated—was impossible to measure. But taking into consideration the range of an Áka Si Anse rite, one could *imagine* it. In the most optimistic scenario, at least half of this continent was gone. Everything would die. On this land where nearly every race had gathered, most likely all but Artosh would be eradicated.

"—Great War...Suniaster...Old Deus—ether..."

—"Don't second-guess," "Don't think"— Sentiments that had lingered somewhere in her unconsciousness, faced with this mad vision decrying the end of the world, blew away, leaving only doubts to surface. The Old Deus Kainas...creator of the Elves, god of the forest—the concept of nature. Old Deus: a concept that, through the activation conditions of prayers and wishes, accumulated ether—assumed identity.

*A concept made sentient...? Is that really a god? Just what is—
Ether*—her mind would have kept racing, but—
...Huh?

The mad storm of annihilation heralding the end of the world——
swerved. Like a drifting cloth snatched away by the wind, it flowed
southwest. As everyone exhaled as the lawless power mowing
through the continent moved off, Think alone followed it. Casting
her full capacity of eight spells simultaneously, she stretched her
vision far, far beyond the horizon to see—

"...Ex Machina.........? Why—?"

Then, beyond where the world-ending light fluttered like a cur-
tain, rending the continent as it ran, beyond the thousands of Ex
Machinas who were swallowed up and vanished—Think Nirvalen saw it. For an instant, a thought flashed through her mind: *It
couldn't be. It couldn't be, it couldn't be, it couldn't be...* Think worked
a complex web of rites thick enough to burn out her spirit corridor
junction nerves. She searched for something, and finally—she spied
two figures. That meant— In short, "just as planned," to the bitter
end—someone had *played her.* The realization elicited a brutal grin,
and she whispered maliciously:

"—...Why, youuu were the ghooost...were you, *monkey*?"

■■■

Atop a faraway hill, where the collapse of heaven and earth seemed
distant...

"—Zeichner report—Reproduced successfully with seventy-two-
point-eight percent output—Synchronizing."

Her report delivered to Riku, an Ex Machina woman raised
her arm.

"Lösen—Org. 0000—Stalemartyr—This is for you."

Appearing out of thin air, a gun the size of a small tower pierced
the earth. The vortex of violence they'd just witnessed, portending

the end of the world—the combined energy of the Godly Smite, Áka Si Anse, the E-bombs, and the Far Cries, all intermingled—over 70 percent of that energy had been reproduced in this object. Riku alone—no, any number of people—would likely have been unable to lift it. Towering several times Riku's height, it was too gigantic to be rightly called a gun... It was more like a stake. The "gun"—muzzle thrust in the ground, barrel standing on its own—quietly waited for someone to pull its trigger. That is, it waited for the signal...for Riku to draw it. His eyes black and unreflective, Riku gazed at it, mute and expressionless, until the Ex Machina broke the silence.

"Report: Well, then, unit will return to battlefront, so, with that—"

It turned to leave, but a question from Riku stopped it.

"Just now...making this... How many *tools...broke*?"

"—Answer: Twenty-one clusters input. Five units remaining. Four thousand eight hundred two units *lost*."

"...Five units remaining, huh?"

"Affirmation: Do you have any other questions?"

"Not a question so much as a confirmation... I just wait for you guys to strip Artosh's ether, then I pull this guy's trigger and pierce the core of the planet—and the Suniaster will manifest. That's it, right?"

"——Affirmation: Neither Artosh nor anyone else will die. Rules upheld."

Closing his eyes like darkness, Riku clenched the ring Schwi had left him and reminisced.

—Huh, it was so simple...

■ ■ ■

"Reporting frankly—there was error in Preier Schwi's calculation."

At Riku's hideout, the Ex Machina called Einzig went on to explain that convergence—even if thirty-two Umweg stations were aligned—was impossible.

"There is a 10^{-609}-second gap that would prevent the Umwege from drawing all of the combatants' attacks downward. Instead, the power would collide and form a vortex. Assigning it directionality and causing convergence thereafter—is impossible."

An error in Schwi's calculation, so minute as to cast a pall over the quiet of nirvana. This was the conclusion Ex Machina had reached via parallel processing across multiple clusters. Hearing this, Riku lowered his eyes and smirked. Even if everything had gone well, they'd still have failed. Riku had just about resigned himself, *but*—Einzig wasn't finished.

"With the twenty-four 'detours' installed by the Preier—it is possible to *divert* it."

"…And?"

"Under the original conditions, the whirling power nebula would converge, then diffuse in all directions. However, because your plan to install thirty-two Umwege in a circle was aborted at twenty-four—*there is a hole to the southwest*."

—In other words, Riku saw where he was going and jumped in:

"So it's not possible to aim it down—but southwest is feasible, you mean?"

Nodding once, Einzig continued.

"I shall provide supplementary data—"

Just like a tool.

"One: Ex Machina has an armament called Himmelpokryphen that emulates the Heavenly Smite."

Nothing more than data captured by instruments.

"Two: As the Preier, in fact, also recognized, if the Suniaster is manifested using the power released by piercing the planet, the probability is fifty-two percent that it will appear in the hands of Artosh. This is representative of the extent of his ether."

The remark made Riku wonder again—*What the hell is ether?*—but ignoring his reaction, Einzig continued.

"Take these facts into account, Spieler. *To correct strategy—Input command*."

Yes, they were machines. Mere tools. And the one who utilized them—the one who made the decisions—was the user: Riku.

*   *   *

"—That makes things simple. We'll fake a preemptive strike from Artosh's base."

Cutting off emotion, gazing at the strategic map with eyes that reflected no light, Riku elaborated. Flat, calm, cold, calculating—thorough.

"Fire Heavenly Smites from behind Avant Heim at the Union *without killing anyone*. That should be enough to prompt Think Nirvalen to move—then they'll smash all their firepower together for us. After we get that off to the southwest, then—"

Riku's hand, arranging the pieces on the board, almost stopped for a moment...but he kept going.

"*A weapon that emulates, reproduces, and focuses the energy*—I'm sure Ex Machina can make one, right?"

"Affirmative. If twenty-one of thirty-two clusters are input, at least seventy percent reproduction is possible."

Moving his hand to his chest to grab the lock that creaked, Riku continued.

"And will that be enough to pierce the core of the planet and materialize the Suniaster?"

"Affirmative. If four thousand eight hundred and seven units are sacrificed to converge seventy percent of the original power and fire it through the core, the source of the spirit corridors will fail—erupting with sufficient magnitude to manifest the Suniaster."

Which means a death sentence for five thousand of Schwi's—my wife's—breth——

Riku shook off the flash of sentiment and once more chanted as if ripping his chest.

—*Lock it.* And he reiterated as if to remind himself:

"'The Rules' do not prohibit the destruction of tools—just like I threw away my arm."

"Correct."

With that, Riku posed the final question.

"Can the remaining twenty-one clusters neutralize Artosh without killing him?"

"—Affirmative."

......

"The Godly Smite is a strike that aggregates all the Flügel's Heavenly Smites and Artosh's power into a single blast. The Flügel will be neutralized, and Artosh will be weakened. In this window, we shall strip Artosh—of his ether."

"...An Old Deus stripped of his ether is likely to be deactivated for one hundred years. If we achieve this and then bore through the source of the spirit corridors, it is almost certain—that the Suniaster will manifest in your hand, Spieler."

The way he said it made Riku avert his face to hide a smirk. *This guy's really awkward*, he thought. *Just like Schwi. If he's gonna pretend to be a heartless machine, he should figure out that machines don't say "likely" or "almost certain."*

"We are machines without hearts, mere tools, faithful executors of commands—so."

And, most fundamental of all, thought Riku as he lowered his eyes—

"When you see the light of Artosh being stripped of his ether, do not hesitate. Pull the trigger and acquire the Suniaster."

—don't look away when you tell a lie...damn "machine"...

No sooner had Riku completed his reminiscence than the female Ex Machina bowed, saying:

"Report: Well, then, I—unit will join battlefront. Spieler Riku—"

So the race professing themselves mere machines to the very end left him with words they didn't even realize they hadn't got the hang of:

"—Fortune in battle be yours..."

And she leaped.

<—From: Einzig—

<To: Julius, Kafma, Luis, Marta, Nord, Ohto, Ökon, Paula, Quelle, Richard, Samueh, Schule, ß, Theodor, Uhlig, Über, Wil, Wilhelm, Yksati, Ypsilon, Zacharia—All 9,177 units remaining in Größt-Cluster.

<—*Befehl ist nur einer.* Stake the souls we have been granted by Preier Schwi to support Spieler Riku—as follows. *Terminate* the ether of the Old Deus Artosh. Eliminate all obstacles and ignore all damage to achieve this... As a supplement, I conclude this command with a declaration somewhat uncharacteristic of an Ex Machina—

<—Let us go without life, go without life—and go away with life—*Aus*.>
<<<Jawohl—!!>>>

Mocking himself as hardly an Ex Machina, Einzig apologized for his lie.

I am sorry, Spieler. Even after the Godly Smite, to face Flügel, Avant Heim, Artosh... To strip Artosh of his ether without killing anyone is impossible—to conquer him at all strains limits. Please—I hope you will think of it this way: that tools without hearts went haywire on their own.

...Thus, the living things that professed to be lifeless things now shouted aloud:

"All units: Permission granted to use all armaments without restrictions—!"

""—Lösen...Enderpokryphen—!!""

■■■

"—Who do you think you are—you scraaaap!!"

Azril shouted as she took up a position in the corridor leading to

Artosh's throne room. She wrung out what little remained of her power to light up the crimson sky with countless blades of energy, several of which intersected with the enemy. She just barely could make out several Ex Machinas launching blue light just before they blew to bits.

The full-power—Godly Smite—had just been fired. The Flügel had all but lost their power. Some couldn't even move. As if they'd planned it—no, they must have—the machine legion approached as if to cover the sky. Aranleif, a Ruler of Dragonia, had been put down by one-fourth of the forces now descending *in full*. Only a few Flügel, like the later articles, still preserved a modicum of power, and Azril, together with Avant Heim, defended vigorously—but they could only do so much. The anti–air cannon steadily blasted Ex Machinas, but the machine legion stormed forward seemingly heedless of damage.

What struck them must have been what Jibril had described, the weapon imitating Aranleif's Far Cry. A volley struck them broadside, blowing away the handful of Flügel who still had a bit of fight left in them, one after another. The Ex Machinas didn't spare a second glance for the Flügel who were immobile—who they deemed no obstacle. But that wasn't the half of it. What were they doing? The machines were even attacking the Union fleet as it attempted to seize this opportunity to invade. But the attacks weren't lethal. They just robbed the ships of their combat capabilities.

—Do not resist. We wish to kill as few of you as we can.—

This seemed to be the message as the machine swarm attempted to flood past Jibril, who'd been brought to her knees.

"…You—screwing with me…? Huuuh, you specks of duuust—?!"

She knew where they were heading. Straight to the throne room—to Lord Artosh.

"You telling…me…to stand by while our lord is slain—is that it, you heap of scraaap?"

As she screamed, Azril's halo deformed and broke irregularly. The swarm of Ex Machinas closing on her, she thrust her hand out in front of them—

"Yew think all we know how to do...is cast Heavenly Smite over and overrr?"

That instant, the distance between them exploded. She'd applied the Flügel shift—to space. The air itself was gouged out, and the rebound tore forward and shattered everything. Space twisted, warped, and everything in its radius was reduced to steel chunks.

How many dozens were caught in that attack...? But that was her limit.

"—*Hff...! Hfff...hff...!*"

Her back against the door leading to the throne, Azril, like Jibril before her, had exhausted all her power and assumed the form of a child, panting.

Even so, Azril stared daggers, making it plain that none would pass, but a cold voice reached her ear.

"—From Prüfer, to Befehler... Analysis of Flügel shift mechanism—complete."

"___!!"

So this is what it means to feel the blood drain from your face? Azril recognized her error a bit too late. The Ex Machinas analyzed the "attack" they'd just suffered and commenced construction on a device to replicate it. They'd never been able to analyze the shift before, since it was directed at the caster—but as an *attack*... The implication was confirmed by the communication she overheard.

"—From Zeichner, to remaining units—Design of 'Shurapokryphen' complete. Synchronizing."

At the same time, behind Azril, a flash of light shot through the door to Artosh's throne room—

"Target location *observed*. Sharing across all units—immediate enemy neutralization is complete—shifting."

"Crya—!"

"—Lösen—Shurapokryphen!"

Not even giving Azril time to regret her failure, the Ex Machina issuing this update vanished. Flying be damned. Azril could hardly even walk straight at this point, but even so, as if crawling, she passed through the shattered doorway...to the foot of her lord—

■ ■ ■

Shifting to his final destination, the throne room, Einzig found himself greeted by a massive man. It was the first time Einzig had observed him—to be precise, no unit had previously observed him and survived long enough to share the data. Therefore, no data was available. But he didn't need reference data for positive identification. The *thing* seated on the throne, its presence overwhelming, its golden eyes savage even in its state of repose, chin resting on its fist—bold, proud, and unmoved. Its very being announced itself the strongest of all, the god of war, and his target: the Old Deus Artosh. To the Ex Machinas who, one by one, joined Einzig, their ranks swelling into a swarm—

"I permit it. Name thyself."

—Artosh extended a courtesy, his simple utterance rocking space and introducing variation into their collective observation equipment.

"Rejection: Tools do not name themselves."

Artosh laughed at Einzig's response—"Such jest."—and time creaked.

"Wherefore shall I ask the names of tools? I ask the name of mine enemy."

"_____."

Einzig did not answer. It was not his answer to give. Maintaining his silence, he simply assessed the battlefield and waited for the remaining units capable of combat to arrive. Surviving forces: 872 units. Units able to assimilate "Asura Apocrypha": 701. In other words, even if all units arrived, their maximum force would be 701 units—not even enough for two conventional clusters. *To think that we could be so depleted by exhausted Flügel and a single Phantasma—* Einzig smirked. The Spieler had pointed out that the tools' mathematics were critically incomplete. For a machine to acknowledge this was a strange twist of irony. As Einzig silently considered this, Artosh's smile—

"Mm, I approve. That is as it should be."

—simply deepened.

"That the strongest of all, who resoundeth across three thousand worlds, should face the weakest of all, on whom nothing in the world looketh twice... It is meet."

And, sliding his cheek off his fist—

"I have awaited thee, O warrior fit to be mine enemy."

—Artosh rose from his throne. With that mere motion...

<From Einzig to remaining units... Is this unit error?>

...all Ex Machina observation equipment indicated that his mass increased. No, Einzig's assessment was incorrect. This was no optical error. It was simply that the man before them had stood.

Correction. The quantity of associated energy had increased... Recorrection. Not energy. The entity data itself was increasing, as if what hadn't existed was coming to be. But finally, all 701 units gathered in the throne room answered Einzig's astonishment.

<—*Nein.*> They all observed the same phenomenon.

It was impossible. It violated all laws of thermodynamics. Even magic only twisted the laws of physics using spirits within the scope of exchange of energy. This defied all explanation.

Nevertheless, every unit's sensors produced the same conclusion— namely: that his mass was increasing. That concepts which enveloped the heavens, the earth, and the planet were taking shape and form.

<Impossible! What is happening...?!>

After discharging his Godly Smite, Artosh's power should have been less than 12 percent its usual level. This was the unanimous estimate of every Seher and Prüfer—and yet. As if reading their thoughts—or perhaps actually doing so—Artosh professed:

"The strongest is strongest for that he is the strongest. What meaning hath *increase or decrease of power?"*

——.

I see. Einzig accepted it. Though the sentiment was entirely irrational, the machines that now possessed emotions could not help but react with: *True.*

The concept of *strongest. If that is what this is...,* considered the automatons who had gained "hearts," and being somewhat anomalous themselves in a not dissimilar fashion, they derived a hypothesis about something long unknown.

<A concept that has gained an identity. Is this not—a law with will?>

Which meant that ether was—

"There is nothing over which ye must fret. The strongest is I, and the weakest is all others."

Hearing Artosh's fierce yet somehow self-mocking declaration, Einzig smirked.

<All units. Units who share my thoughts: If any of you survive, reassess this hypothesis.>

<Jawohl.>

If ether *conformed to this hypothesis,* then overthrowing Artosh was theoretically *impossible. But—* Einzig put forward a query.

<All remaining Seher and Prüfer—is ether an observable physical entity?>

<<<—Affirmative.>>>

In that case, there was no issue.

"All units prepare the algorithm compiled by the Preier to *combat the unknown*—Lösen—!"

Before his eyes, still increasing in mass—a giant, a concept, a phenomenon, or perhaps a law. Before the true god who seemed likely to swell until heaven and earth were enveloped, Einzig issued his command. At the moment, it was just a hypothesis.

To gauge the enemy's power is impossible. Then what to do? All that remains is to act as the souls we have been granted command. That is to say—if the enemy is unknown, then all you have to do is anticipate everything you can't anticipate. Don't try to understand. Don't try to calculate. Just believe what you feel and move—isn't that right, Schwi?

Avant Heim. In the throne room staring down a god, 701 living things that professed to be machines roared:

`<Target Artosh's` *ether*`—hypothesized capacity to distort space-time and even alter natural law every second—>`

In which case...

`<`*Adapt every half-second* `accordingly. I ask all units—is this beyond us?>`

`<<<Negative!>>>`

No—no matter the foe, no matter the obstacle.

`<If it touches us, we will adapt—that is who we are. All units, I pray you fight valiantly. Aus!>`

`<<<`*Jawohl!*`>>>`

Linking with one another, all units faced their divine enemy—who continued to manifest, to swell—and shouted as one:

"—Lösen—!!"

Gazing upon the oncoming Ex Machina swarm, Artosh delivered a single sentiment in a voice that reverberated across the continent.

"Come, display mine ether—show the quintessence of battle to the world, my dear, true enemy—!!"

—...

——......

■■■

The Stalemartyr entrusted him by Ex Machina in hand, Riku's mind wandered.

What the hell am I doing here? Ruining a game that's a certain loss with mad—

"—Shut up. It's not time yet. Don't think."

Cutting himself short, he checked the lock that seemed to be loosening on his heart.

It was fine. Still locked. He wasn't done yet, not yet… Far, far, so far in the barely-visible distance, Avant Heim. There, the tools were operating to strip Artosh of his ether without killing anyone. All he had to do was wait for the signal—and pull the trigger. Then, a voice out of nowhere—no, a convulsion shaking the entire planet. *O heavens, O earth, O all in every place—listen*, the voice demanded. With the absolute roar of a true god, of the strongest of the Old Dei, it said:

"So this is defeat—I see. It was an enjoyable battle, such that it made mine heart boil."

It went on as if convinced, *I am certain thou canst hear me*.

"Nameless weak one—thou mayest hold thine head high, having truly proved thyself worthy to be mine enemy."

——Then, in Riku's single eye like night. Far, far away—a white light flared to paint out the red sky. Emptily, he noted that it looked just as Einzig had described. It was their signal, indicating Ex Machina had succeeded in stripping the Old Deus Artosh of his ether.

At least…that's what they'd agreed to.

"……"

In truth, he knew—but he had to admit, he didn't know it for a fact. He shook his head at that and, alone—placed his finger on the trigger of Stalemartyr. None of the Ex Machinas would come back… Unaware what that meant—no.

Keep pretending you don't know. Just like Artosh must have known but presumably never said the words, *I am slain—*

"…You've held for me somehow, huh…?"

Checking the lock on his heart, which seemed on the verge of breaking, Riku remembered the Rules that he himself had set:

—One: No one may kill.

—Two: No one may die.

—Three: No one must know.

—Four: All means are fair.

...Yes, there was a loophole in these rules. If he didn't recognize Ex Machinas—Schwi—as living beings, but tools. And no one knew what foul means the tools had employed. If he just pretended he didn't know—*it wouldn't break the Rules at all.* Chuckling, Riku thought: *Now this is the height of sophistry and fraud.* Schwi—an Ex Machina—had fallen back on *a false premise.* Knowing what this meant made it impossible for him to refuse. It was Schwi's wish from the "heart." Letting go of each other's hands—the mistake that placed them in this overwhelmingly inferior position that guaranteed defeat...

Checkmate might be beyond their reach.

But this gave them one last move that could potentially earn a stalemate, gouging the planet and destroying the board in the process—hence Ex Machina's name for it:

Stalemartyr.

"So now it's gonna be a draw... Sorry, gods—"

Muttering, Riku gripped the trigger of the giant gun thrust into the ground like a stake—and pulled, with immediate results.

Far taller than himself, Riku felt that stake start sucking up all the gods of heaven and earth—everything. A magnificent influx of power—at which point, the buried muzzle erupted in light. Seventy percent of the force that incinerated the continent and scorched the very planet. That power converged into a single-stripe beam and pierced the planet like a needle, penetrating its core and destroying the spirit corridors.

From Riku's perspective, it all transpired in an instant, but in that same instant, he felt the lock on his heart explode—

"...What part of this shit is a stalemate...? How do you call this—a draw—?"

As if he'd literally come undone, light returned to his eyes, and

Riku let all the emotions he'd locked away erupt. The lock broken, his heart could no longer be contained.

How many had died? Schwi's comrades. *Living beings.* Flügel—how the hell many had died?! Deluding himself—pinning it on Schwi's last wishes! The final sacrifice to end the war that demanded infinite sacrifice… Now that he was here, he wanted to murder the Riku that had come up with all those excuses.

How is this a stalemate? You're just a shitty little bastard. A loser. You can squawk all you want about how it's what Schwi wanted or whatever! But you! Have lost! Pathetically—Riku!!

……

"Hey, Schwi. What was I missing, I wonder…?"

…Yeah. He didn't have to ask. He knew…

"Hey, Schwi. If you and me were two in one…"

…*Yeah. Next time, I wanna win, Schwi. With you… Next time, no one will die. No one will have to die. Not in our game…*

The planet's crust obliterated, its core gutted, the source of the spirit corridors detonated. The unfathomable power that had been unleashed moments before seemed like the prick of a pin by comparison. The power that forged the world—sufficient to blow it away without a trace—was unleashed. As he was being consumed, Riku——saw it.

"……Is……that it…?"

The Suniaster.

Glowing, a star-shaped dodecahedron, its sides embossed with five-pointed stars. It materialized where all the expelled power released converged… *Huh. It really did appear to the winner…* But when he stretched out his hand—Riku couldn't reach. Dropping his gaze, he chuckled.

"…I see. Guess I wouldn't be able to reach it…"

Having lost his right arm now, too, he had nothing to reach with. Besides…he hadn't won. In the glitter of the spirit corridors as they

spilled out power beyond measure, his body was swallowed, broken down...and his essence slipped away.

When had it started? He finally realized now, after everything, as he shamelessly, pathetically gushed tears... The armless man covered in bandages breaking down and sobbing like a little kid—

"...Ha-ha...I'm such...a dork..."

He'd figured he might as well live awesomely and die the same. But here was his life, not a single victory to his name.

A ludicrous death befitting a loser. It was too late for shame or pride.

"Hey, Schwi. I've got a million things I regret... Sorry for being such a dopey husband."

Countless, countless regrets were the only things that flashed through his mind. The faces of the people he'd let die passed by one by one. The sight of the 177 ghosts who'd indulged his arrogance elicited a guilt that threatened to crush him, but then it dawned on him that there was something even direr—his greatest regret.

Mystifying even himself, he laughed aloud at his immeasurable disgrace.

"Ahh, damn it... I should've got down on my hands and knees and begged Couron if that's what it took to make love to you, Schwi."

Riku. Virgin. Twenty. Married, but dying without knowing the touch of a woman. Hmm, when you think about it, isn't that kinda cool in its own way?

"Nah, guess not... Can't dress that up... Ha-ha..."

In any case, it seemed he'd exist without dignity right to the bitter end. And at that point, why not go all the way—at the end? Throwing away his last shred of pride, he pleaded to a god.

"...Hey, if gods are born from feelings—*god of games*."

If the hands you already took—

"Though this life of mine is rubbish, I offer you all I have. I'm praying for the first time in my life—please."

—belonged to a loser and were too dirty to seize the Astral Grail. If they were too blood-soaked to hold the throne of the One True God...

Please. I beg you. At least tell me our hearts meant something. It doesn't have to be me. It can be anyone. Just...anyone. As long as they'll end this war. Anyone... Let them have it...the Suniaster...a... ny......one............

......And with that, his consciousness faded away.

"*Hh—*"

Riku saw someone approach the Suniaster, and he smiled. The figure striding forward against the light was no one he'd seen before. He wore a large cap, and his pupils were a diamond and a spade. The boy didn't look familiar—but Riku knew who he was. Because the boy had always—always, always, always, even after Riku was sick about it—beaten him, and always wearing that bold grin in the darkness.

"...Ha... Ha-ha-ha-ha— Ah-ha-ha-ha-ha-ha-ha!"

—The hell? I knew it. You do exist... Little bastard...

"—Hey, let's play again... 'Cos this time, I'm gonna show you, all right..."

—Together with Schwi... I swear......I'll...

......

Leaving these words in his wake, Riku was swallowed by light and disappeared. Born of the faith of just two—Riku and Schwi, the weakest—the last Old Deus returned a forced smile, as if straining to hold something back. Softly, he reached for the Suniaster, and then......

The entire world witnessed this moment. Therefore, it is one of the few facts in this story recorded as history...

First, light enveloped the world. A light spreading from the horizon whitened the red heavens and the blue earth, stealing the border between them. When it stopped, spreading without a sound—the world had lost all color. Everyone was befuddled as they searched the heavens and earth, and then, after a beat, they realized. The ashes drifting through the sky had frozen there, and the flames of war had forgotten to flicker. Everything had stopped.

Even time. Everything that did not live. Gaping in wonder, every living thing was lost as to what was happening, and then—

—A shock tickled the planet. It clearly wasn't destructive. The gentle force just sort of brushed up against the world like a lick. At the same time, those who turned to the skies...marveled. A sight that defied expectation that every race—every living thing—just gaped at, dumbstruck.

Except. One hundred seventy-seven ghosts and one human saw and understood...

■■■

——......

A ghost that once had a name, its body corroded by dead spirits, leaned on a crag.

"...You really did it...General..."

With what little vision it had left, it looked up to see the dust that tinted the sky red—just flap away in the breeze, disappearing like cards snatched off a table, before disappearing into nothingness as if it had all been a joke.

——......

Another ghost that, likewise, had once had a name had been afflicted by the bite of a Dhampir.

"...Ha-ha... Damn, he pulled it off—that son of a bitch...!"

Bathing in light for the first time, he felt his body sear, but at the same time, he felt the mountains—ravaged and devastated—regenerating themselves as if by a magic trick to assume their proper form.

——......

One hundred seventy-seven ghosts, in their respective locations, with their respective bodies, understood what was happening and watched with chests brimming with individual emotions. An irresistible, absolute command was being echoed by all things as the world was remade. Humans had no way to detect magic, but they knew just the same. They didn't know why—but. They knew that the War—the long, long Great War—had ended. With this conviction teeming inside them, they laughed aloud—from their "hearts."

——......

Lastly, there was just one other besides the ghosts who watched and understood what was happening. On the continent of Lucia, she peered out of Riku and Schwi's bedroom window.

"...You really...got the Suniaster...everyone..."

Before she knew it, the ash had stopped falling. Turning her eyes to the heavens, Couron discovered that the tale about the sky being blue was true. And for the first time...

...she saw the sun.

"...That's my—darling little, brother...and...sister..."

Despite closing her eyelids, the dazzling sunlight still stabbed through them, stinging her eyes. That had to be it... Riku, Schwi, everyone—her darling, darling brother and sister—those two...had really—really—ended the eternal War. As their sister, as their loving sister...more than anyone—she could take pr——

"...Uh—wuh...waaaaaauuughhhhh!!"

I knew it... It's impossible— I just...you know...!
"Hey, Rikuuu, Schwi, your sister still can't take thiiiis!"
'Cos—you both made her a promise...and broke it!

"I said—I didn't want to lose any more family... Why? How could you—?!"

Weeping at the absurdity, Couron called her siblings' names. Cradling the blue stone engraved with all their names, she shed pathetic tears and wondered:

Why'd it have to be them? Couldn't it have been me? Why can't I do anything?

Fair enough, the long Great War had ended. The days of cowering before death and grieving in despair were presumably over. In exchange, Couron had lost the one most important to her, her brother, and her sister, whom her brother had loved. After that—what in the world was she left with—?

"This is, too much...for me... Why does everyone leave me behind...?"

"—Hey, Couronne Dola."

Suddenly, her last conversation with Riku came rushing back to her.

■■■

After hearing out Riku, who'd turned up with an Ex Machina—Einzig—in tow, Couron insisted:

"——Don't."

As she stared into those eyes as black as obsidian she'd thought she'd never see again, eyes that reflected no light, her brother went on undeterred.

"Then, if everything works out—"

"—I said don't...didn't you hear me?!"

Couron's hysterical scream cut him off.

"You've never called me by my full name before—not once!! And now what—"

Watching his sister—Couronne Dola—wailing with tear-filled eyes, Riku continued.

"If everything works out, I think you'll see. And then—"

His gaze still black, Riku nevertheless summoned a pleading smile.

"The chessboard on the table. Can you move the white rook...to e6 for me?"

"...Why don't you...do it—yourself?!"

Couronne Dola clenched her fists as if it had taken everything to wring out those words.

Really, she knew. Their relationship was not so shallow that she didn't understand what he was saying. Self-proclaimed or not—they were family. Their relationship was anything but shallow. But for that very reason—she couldn't say it. That one thing: *Don't go.* Because Riku...Riku and Schwi—

Riku peeled his attention away from Couron, turning it to the empty seat at the table in the room. Narrowing his vision, staring somewhere beyond where they stood, he muttered as if in prayer:

"...Hey, God. If you're not just my hallucination and you really exist..."

——.

"...will you remember that there was a hopeless twit who tried to eliminate war using games?"

He turned back to Couron.

"...Couronne Dola...no—"

He bent to pick up his pack.

"—*Sister*... Thanks for everything. And also..."

With that, he took his leave, his last words trailing behind him.

"Humans, 'next time,' 'after'... I leave it all to you. You're my sister, and I believe in you."

■ ■ ■

Ruining her face with tears, Couron staggered to the table. Then, as per Riku's "will," she placed the piece and muttered:

"...Check...mate...isn't it...Riku...?"

Wiping her tears with her sleeve, Couron stood.

Much had been left her...many things to do. She had no more time for crying. To insure that what Riku and others had created would not be for nothing, she first had to dispose of all the evidence that Riku and Schwi...the ghosts...had ever existed. Burn the records, the notes, the scrolls—everything. Wipe all evidence that Riku, Schwi—the human race—had played a game in the shadows. She'd leave nothing. In the world to come, it would be the same—so no one could notice them. So they'd all believe humanity too weak to bother with. For next time. And the time after that. Looking down at the blue stone engraved with their three names, Couron mumbled.

"Hey, Riku, Schwi... You two really are amazing...you know that?"

Sure, in the game that Riku had outlined their deaths meant that, even in the most generous assessment, it had been a draw. They'd achieved their objective but lost the game.

"But still your sister thinks the same... You two are too amazing to believe."

They'd challenged the gods, taken on the world. Never spotted and without a trace, they'd ended the eternal Great War—in just two years. With no memories and no records, they would never become legend. They wove a myth that could never be sung...for the people who came after. Was this defeat? It was impossible for Couron to see it that way. If it wasn't a feat, an epic victory, then what was it?

"But, still, it's weird... Why......?"

After all this, she wondered, *Is this it? What Riku had been feeling his entire life?*

"...Why, am I so...frustrated...?"

She'd decided not to cry anymore—so. Couron just covered her face, leaning on the wall as she left the room.

——......

"—Because the game's not over."

The empty room Couron had vacated.

Who knows how long he'd been there, the boy wearing a large cap with a front brim. The boy with a mischievous smile and a star-shaped regular dodecahedron—the Suniaster—floating beside him. He walked up to the chessboard, softly moved the black queen, and under his breath—he corrected Couron's *mistake.*

"It's not checkmate—it's *check.* But with this…"

Contemplating the board, the boy painted out in his mind all the moves he could conceivably make. Seeing that, no matter how he moved, the final result would be endless repetition—he grinned.

"You got me in perpetual check… That's the first time you've forced me to a *draw.*"

To the end, to the bitter end—he'd never given up. Even from a position of overwhelming disadvantage, he'd said, *At the very least, I'm gonna bite you hard, even here—*

—Hey, let's play again… 'Cos this time, I'm gonna show you, all right…

—Together with Schwi…I swear……I'll…

Recalling this, the boy—the Old Deus born of the faith of just two, just as he was in those days when Riku was young, when he was still just the most powerful of gamers dwelling in the dark recesses of Riku's imagination—grinned, boldly and impudently, and held out the Suniaster.

——……

All intelligent life-forms in this world were created by the Old Dei. *Except for one: humans.*

"O ye created of none, wished for by none, asked for by none. The only race that, by its own will, hath stood from beasthood on its own two feet to seize wisdom—and that therefore hath no name—O *humans.*"

Only they had succeeded in ending the futile, fruitless, fatuous War. Even if the result had been a mess—it was still only them. Could one speak of them in the same breath as beasts…? Surely not.

"For these reasons, I, the One True God, grant you a name: Immanity...after *immunity*."

A fitting name for those who kept learning, built up endurance, never stopped resisting, never surrendered though they might be reduced to one. Who, in the end, put a halt to this foolish scourge, serving as the immune system of the planet itself. The race that concealed within itself the concept of progress—infinite possibility.

Gently, Tet smiled and continued.

"Come, then—let the games *continue*."

It wasn't his thing to leave after he'd been stalemated, so he'd give *those guys* what they wanted—

"I've got a game that's fun for everyone, where no one will die, and I'll be waiting."

In this world, there was no reincarnation. Even so, till the end, they believed in "next time"—*so why don't I try believing in it, too?*

"All right. With that—"

With these words, the weakest and last Old Deus held out the Suniaster and proclaimed in a voice that reached throughout the heavens and across the earth:

O Ixseeds that claim yourselves wise—!

And so the myth that would never be sung continued into the myth that still is told. That is:

By the vow of *achéte* and the bonds of *aschent*,
the One True God, on his *ascente*, setteth forth the Ten Covenants.
Which ye shall heed. For this day, today, the world hath changed.

—*Aschente*—!!

⏻ ENDING TALK

——.

Before you knew it, the sun had slid low and was casting scarlet light through the alley in Elkia. As Tet finished his tale, his vision somehow distant, Izuna's immediate reaction was:

"...How much of that story is true, and how much of it is bullshit, please?"

Her eyes half-closed, she smelled some bullshit. Tet laughed at Izuna's tearful glare which warned, *depending on which part's a lie, I might not forgive you.*

"Whaaat? What makes you think it's not all true?"

"Riku and Shibi...sound kind of like those assholes Sora and Shiro, please. Don't screw with me, please."

Izuna snorted up some snot, served as an assertion that she didn't need her Werebeast super-senses to figure out that much. And her eyes imparted that she knew she was being played with, too.

"Ah-ha-ha! ☆ You sure are sharp, yep, yep! ♪ Of *course* I dramatized it a little. I mean—"

Tet, who'd related his story while he played with her until the sun set—*never once letting her win*—looked up with childlike innocence.

* * *

"If I actually told you everything, then it wouldn't be an untold myth anymore, now would it? ☆"

The entity farthest from *maturity* smirked like a *kid*.
"Damn it. You are a little bitch, please."
Izuna glared hard at Tet, but...
"...But you're good at petting, so I'll forgive you, please."
Being all *fluffy-fluffed, there's a good girl*, she purred and dropped it. Stroking her, Tet, his eyes now assuming the manner of a kind and loving god, thought, *This child, Izuna Hatsuse, is young—and foolish.*

And that was also why...she was bright, clever, and perceptive. Tet took her words—"kind of like those assholes"—very much to heart. Sure, he'd embellished what facts he knew. But those two who'd *inspired him to create* this world were indeed like " "—but somewhat. For they, compared to Sora and Shiro—the ones whose names spelled Blank—

—were *far stronger.*

After all, " " had turned their backs on that challenge, whereas those two had played the game with no rules—reality—and pulled off a stalemate.

Even if it ended in a mess, a brawl through the mud in throes of anguish... Well, after all—that's what a stalemate was. Stalemate or perpetual check. Either meant coming from a position of certain defeat—but refusing to surrender, landing back a blow along the way. But even so...

"To me, it was just so dazzling. Enough to make me want to believe in them, you know? ♪"
"...? The hell are you talking about, please?"
Izuna purred and looked up, but Tet returned only a smile. Sora and Shiro—" "—were just what *they'd* aspired to be...*two in one.* Would they ultimately reach the place their precursors never could? Would they make good on their declaration and defeat him? *Or*

perhaps...to the contrary...? Ha-ha! ☆ While Tet was lost in thought, Izuna suddenly insisted—

"...I ain't gonna let you quit while you're ahead, please."

When the god came back to himself, Izuna had stopped purring and was sizing him up with the eyes of a gamer.

"Sora and Shiro are gonna get together with everyone else—and kick your ass, please."

Goodness me. He laughed giddily.

"Tee-hee! ☆ You figured it out?"

The jig being up, Tet—the One True God—brandished the Suniaster and smiled merrily. Izuna watched him coolly and replied:

"I'm a kid—but I'm not a dumbass, please."

"—Yeah, you're absolutely right. I know. ♪"

Youth was folly, yet unrestrained by the *illusions* of half-assed understanding—wise. Because even when the world looked complicated and outlandish, more often than one might expect, its essence—was precisely as it seemed to the sensibilities of a child. Exactly how *those two* saw it...

——......

"Heyyyyy, Izunaaa, where are youuu?"

"...Iz-zyy...where'd you go...?"

Tet was quicker to react to the approaching voices than Izuna, hopping to his feet.

"Whoopsie. Guess it's time for me to go. It was fun talking to you! ♪"

"Wait. The hell did you even come for, please?"

Izuna'd finally gotten to the most important question—what was the One True God doing there?—but Tet simply responded with a rather bemused expression.

"Mmm, actually, I was gonna go give ' ' a cheer—but it's okay. ☆"

With that, he allowed light to pour out of the Suniaster.

"'Cos I ended up picking up something *even better*. Izuna Hatsuse, I'll be waiting for you! ☆"

Noting Izuna's blank reaction to hearing her name (which she didn't remember giving) and beaming with wily content at surprising her in the end—*foop*—Tet vanished into thin air. But...

"......Damn frickin' bastard! He whipped me and ran, please...!"

Realizing she'd been punked, Izuna puffed up her tail, her solitary growl echoing through the alleyway...

■■■

"Oh, there you are! Man, where'd you go, Izuna? We were so worrieeed!"

"...Izzy...did you...get lost?"

Their reactions were immediate when the black-haired young man and contrastingly stark-white girl—Sora and Shiro—spotted Izuna.

"Izunaaa, you can't go off wandering by yourself like that! There are some creepy people in this world!"

"...Yeah. Like, Brother...or, like, me..."

And making noises anyone (including those two themselves) would consider creepy, they proceeded to hug and stroke her. Apparently, they'd been genuinely worried, though the notion of something "happening" to a Werebeast was absurd.

"...I, uh... Sorry, please..."

Izuna remembered Tet's story and apologized with conflicted feelings, her face downcast.

"—Oh! You found Miss Izuna?! *Hff*...that's a relief!"

The red-haired girl covered in sweat who showed up a bit late—Steph—similarly ran up to her.

"Miss Izuna, you mustn't go off by yourself! Look at these creepy people!"

Raising her eyes to apologize to Steph (who was pointing at Sora and Shiro), Izuna's gaze paused on the girl's chest—which was pinned with a brooch set with a blue stone.

"Hey, hey, Stuch."

"——Ehh, yes, I'm used to it by now... What is it?"

"Where the hell'd you snatch that stone on your chest, please?"

"Can you not phrase it as if I stole it?!"

Having vented her initial offense, Steph presented the brooch carefully.

"I received this from my grandfather. It is a treasure that has been passed down through the Dola family for generations."

"Let me see that shit, please."

"Uh, all right... I don't mind, but please don't break—"

Izuna nodded solemnly at the admonition as Steph reluctantly surrendered the broach.

—Snap.

"Eeeghyaa—aaaahhhh, my family's treasure! My family's treasuuuure!"

Propping up Steph as she shrieked, frothed, and collapsed, Sora muttered with a squint:

"Look closer. She just took it out of the setting...but what's your deal, huh, Izuna?"

Izuna turned over the stone, which had been covered by the decoration, and smiled faintly. Noticing this, Sora and Shiro peered into her hands, but—

"...? What's this, writing?"

"...It's not, Immanity...Jibril... Can you, read it?"

Shiro called the name of someone who wasn't there as if it was quite natural.

"Ohhh, yes, yes, yes. ♥ It is I, Jibril, who fly at your beck and call. My masters, what need might you have of me, who can interpret over seven hundred languages in forms both modern and ancient with ease? ♪"

"...As if, you don't know......? Izzy, what's up...?"

Jibril's sudden appearance had set off Izuna, who was glaring and growling fiercely.

* * *

"......When I think about it, it's *all this bitch's fault*, isn't it, please...?!"

Izuna's hackles rose as she stared daggers, but no one understood what she meant.

"I—I don't know what all that's about...but, Jibril, can you read this?"

"—Goodness, but these are some ancient glyphs. From before the Immanity tongue was standardized... Hmmm..."

Even Jibril prefaced her translation with *If I'm not mistaken...* before she read:

—*Couronne Dola*

—*Riku Dola*

—*Schwi Dola*

"...? Who are they? Your relatives or something, Steph?"

Steph bristled with pride and honor.

"Couronne Dola...the founding queen of Elkia. No one saw her cry in her life. She brimmed with smiles and wisdom—the great lady who led Immanity after the Great War concluded...the pride of the Dola family."

"—Shyeet! You're the direct descendant of the founder of the country?! The Great War was over six thousand years ago, wasn't it?!"

"...Steph...you *were* a princess...?"

"Can you not use the past tense?!"

But—Steph said, cocking her head as she looked at the brooch.

"It's strange... I do not recognize the names of the other two at all..."

"...Hmm, I do, but then, she wasn't an Immanity... A coincidence, then! ♪"

Though Izuna growled at Jibril's comment, Sora thought, *No, the real question is*—

"Izuna, how'd you figure out something was hidden behind the decoration when even Steph didn't know?"

Gleaning Sora's point, Shiro, Steph, and Jibril all fixed their eyes intently on Izuna—but she just gave a little smile and kindly replaced the stone in its setting. There must have been a reason he'd only told her. So her Werebeast—no, her own sense—advised her to keep quiet.

——......

Well, then. Sora formally surveyed everyone's faces.

"So, you've all got your luggage, right? Shiro?"

"...I'm good..."

"Jibril—well, I don't see anything on you..."

"Not to worry, Master. I have compressed space and placed it in my bosom. ♥"

"What, you have a fourth-dimensional pocket...? Uh, Izuna?"

"Mm, I got my shit, please."

"And over here we've got way too much... Steph?"

"Yes, yes, I've got it. The heavy luggage..."

"—It's our secret weapon, so handle it carefully, okay? Wait... Hey, where the hell's Plum?"

"H-heeere...albeit not exactly of my wiiill... I'll leave as soon as the sun goes doooown."

"Great. Looks like everyone's ready."

"What? Sora—aren't you going to wait for those two?"

"We'll meet up with 'em there. In the worst case, y'know, they can always join in late. So, with that—"

With bold grins, Sora and Shiro looked around, asking:

"Right—*shall we go*?"

■■■

——......

Under the red moon, Sora chatted as he led the party.

"Since we came to this world and heard about the Ten Covenants and the Ixseeds, I've always wondered—"

Sixteen seeds—each assigned a Race Piece. Gathering them all gave one the right to challenge Tet, the One True God. That was this world. This game. But it raised a question.

"...How do you, collect...the Race Pieces...of races, that don't form groups...like Old Deus?"

Walking alongside Sora, Shiro completed his thoughts, little by little.

—The Seventh of the Ten Covenants: "For conflicts *between groups*, an agent plenipotentiary shall be established..." Plodding along behind them, Steph hadn't realized something so obvious until it was pointed out.

"Right, Old Deus hasn't designated an agent plenipotentiary. The Old Deus Piece—can't be taken."

Pattering along behind Sora as he summarized this implication, Izuna still wasn't sure she fully understood.

"At least, that's whatcha think if you're an Old Deus, right?" The corners of Sora's mouth twisted sarcastically as he said it.

"This world Tet's created—it's all a 'game where we collect the pieces of the other races.'"

Yes, the difference between a player and a prayer. The Old Dei assumed that they were the players and the rest were just prayers, so they'd just prop their feet up in heaven, Sora imagined. After all, these were guys who'd warred for an eternity. So—one could easily imagine some races would *assume the same*, give up, and surrender to them.

"—Buuut..."

Sora pursued this line of reasoning as if mocking the gods he imagined.

"They're waaay off the mark, you know."

Walking beside him in fine form in the moonlight, the Dhampir girl—pardon, boy—sneered.

"Yeeess... Because to begin wiith...?"

Yes, to begin with—walking with her hand in Sora's, Shiro smirked.

"...If you don't...*have to take, the Race Piece...that, changes things...*"

Jibril beamed at that as if awed by Sora and Shiro's—her masters'—insight.

"Too true! After all, if it is the agent plenipotentiary of Old Deus you seek—"

They all stopped in their tracks with a *zump*.

"—*why let the Old Dei decide who that is*, right?"

Sora's eyes narrowed as if to verify the identity of the person before them and said:

"—Shrine Maiden of *something*?"

Kannagari, capital of the Eastern Union—the Garden in the Central Division of the Shrine. On the red bridge over the pond illuminated by the divine light of the moon, sitting on the railing, gently ringing her little bells...

—The Shrine Maiden, agent plenipotentiary of the Eastern Union, of Werebeast, swayed her two golden tails and smiled bewitchingly.

■■■

Beyond the horizon. Having returned to the peak of the black king, Tet looked down upon the land and spoke—not for anyone to hear. He simply played with the cards in his hands, tossing words into the void.

"The world really is very simple...just like he thought."

The way everyone must have seen it when they were children. What complicated and made things difficult wasn't the world, but the terribly boring people who lived in it... Such were Tet's thoughts on the matter.

"I went to the trouble of creating such a simple game, and those guys are totally screwing it up—but I'm sure you guys can show them, right?"

The guys screwing it up. Yes—those boring guys. Those condescending ones who thought they knew everything, like some kind of gods.

Thus, with a sigh, Tet—the creator of the game—glared at the ones misinterpreting his rules and totally wrecking the game's balance. With a malicious grin and eyes tinged with childish venom, he mused.

"Guess you're the one who'll be dragged down first... That's karma, huh?"

To slay a god for the third time in history—to kill a god without killing them... Tet's eyes suddenly sparkled, and he rocked his feet excitedly.

"I know you guys. You can do it. I'm waiting for you. I believe in you, so hurry up—"

"Drag down those wet blankets and come here!!"

■■■

"—Ether manifest, deity revealed—divinity configured...base."

Wind and clouds swirled around the Shrine Maiden. In the center of the vortex (which took even Jibril's breath away), the Shrine Maiden finally...deferred.

"Mr. Sora, Miss Shiro, and all of you... I shall leave you my last move—"

And with that—

"The continuation of my dream...that I once dreamed of seeing to its end..."

But Sora interrupted her line, picking it up.

"Is never-ending—yeah, we'll prove it. Don't worry. Just leave it to us."

As if satisfied with his answer, the Shrine Maiden closed her eyes, at which point, the air, the clouds, the ground creaked. The manifestation of a concept blotted out the world—and formed words:

* * *

"—How reckon ye the one ye call, O mortals?"

Someone who was not the Shrine Maiden opened her eyes and posed this question. As the being's authority and presence, its overwhelming pressure, overcame them—

"We reckon you're a bigheaded old parasite mooching off people and the planet."

"…You're a worthless organism, worse than a shut-in, loser, friendless virgin…like me or Brother."

—Sora and Shiro just taunted the tempest, *otherwise known as*:

""Ixseed Rank One—Old Deus, you ooold god.""

"Come on. Let's start the game already. Frankly speaking—you're in our goddamn way, bitches."

⏻ AFTERWORD

Let me tell you a story... Oh, just a little story from a few months ago. It was, yes—just around the time I was writing the ending of Volume 5. Suddenly, my mobile phone rang and vibrated, whereupon I picked it up to discover it was my editor, Ms. Fishboard.

"I know you're not done with Volume 5 yet, but, if you please, make sure you finish the next one by the time the anime airs! ♥"

...I see, so she calls me before I've delivered Volume 5—well aware of the hideous state I'm in—to solicit the next. That's my editor for you. I must commend her gumption. If she didn't have such a *fine personality*, I suppose she wouldn't make much of an editor, and it makes me shed a tear for the deep karma in which her trade is mired—but that's one thing, and this is another.

At this point, Volume 6 was supposed to be about the game against Old Deus. I didn't have confidence that, before the anime aired (when I'd likely be swamped with illustration work), I'd be able to pull it off in time. When I told her this frankly and forthrightly, she suggested:

"What about that idea for 'Volume 0' you described? Could you make that into Volume 6?"

I see, the age in which the Old Dei and their relations ran amok—the Great War. *The plot relating to its end and how Disboard was created*—I did have something like that. It's also true that I was somewhat hesitant to head into the game against Old Deus before working up how absolute Old Deus is. I hadn't entirely nailed down the plan for the game against Old Deus, either, so—

"All right. Let's go with that."

Even a jellyfish would have been aghast to witness the fool who'd given this response. To describe the Great War and its conclusion in a single volume, fully developing all the characters and races involved and making that work with the main story—even someone with a working brain the size of a mitochondrion should have been capable of grasping what an epically unreasonable task that would be. At the time, though, the magnitude had not occurred to me in the slightest, you see......

——......

With that in mind... Nice to see you again! It's that fool Kamiya. I have survived up to now by means of a canon of friends and acquaintances singing my folly. Still, I would like you to imagine for a moment the great and wise figures who made massive, revolutionary contributions to modern man—to our civilization. For now, I would like you to imagine Columbus.

—Christopher Columbus. I am sure I need not tell you that he discovered the Americas. Well, we'll put aside the argument for now of whether that was a good thing... He embarked across the vast Atlantic Ocean when no one knew for sure what lay beyond, pressing only this courage, wisdom, knowledge to his bosom: *Go west*. His crew burdened with fears, they just went west, west, west. And, at last, at the very west, they arrived in the Americas—and came back! Their safe return could only have been supported by their wit and knowledge, their wisdom! For that, he is called a great man, and he is called a great man because he was a wise man!!

But still. I'd like you to step back for a moment and think about it objectively now. Certainly, those who ventured on a great journey and returned were wise. Considering that if they weren't, they'd probably never have made it back. Then, yes, I'm sure the perceptive among you, my dear readers, have already realized—if they hadn't made it back, they'd just have been called fools. Of course, they would have. It's fundamental. What kind of idiot sets sail for some continent that may or may not be there? *If they really had brains, they'd stay the hell on land*, you'd say. What kind of wise man would take that kind of risk? What's the point of risking your life on a gamble like that?

Yes! As I have just illustrated, that in which humans should truly take pride is not wisdom. Folly is the driving force of humanity, and it is by avoiding being killed by that folly that we hone our wit! Therefore! At this juncture! I shall stand proud, cowed by no one! To say it loud! **Yes—I—am a fooooool!!!**

QED—self-justification complete! What do you think of this bulletproof theory? You can fall in love with me, you know!

"...Are you quite done spouting self-satisfied sophistry in an attempt to excuse your wanton trampling of our deadlines?"

But of course, Ms. Fishboard. Thanks for getting on your hands and knees in front of everyone on my behalf. (*chomp chomp*)

"Excuse me, this time, we were really, *reaaally* pushing it. I polished the floor with my forehead three times, you know?!"

Well, of course I'm very grateful for all that.

—But, um, can I say what I'm thinking?

".......Uh, uh, well, um—"

You had me write a new side story for the official anime site, write more for all the various bonuses, check the scripts, check the licensed stuff, draw a boatload of new illustrations— I don't know how much I'm allowed to disclose, so I'll stop there. But you wrote, "Hurry and get the damn manuscript in," and on the very next line, you wrote, "Also, I need you to do these things, too, okay?" What followed was a huge list, and all this forces me to question your human integrity. (*dimpled smile*)

* * *

"Ah-ha-ha, why blame me for that? You could blame the producer."
(*casually*) Oh, can I?
"(*casually*) Sure, why not? ♥"
Then let us declare that the war criminal who plotted to work me to death is "P."
"I concur! So now's the time—(*glance*)"
Oh, yes. For promotion, you mean. You're telling me to blatantly advertise it, are you? Ahem...

Now—!! *No Game No Life*, the TV anime—!! By the time this book is on store shelves, it should already be airing. I participated in just about every script conference, and by the producer's suggestion, the first episode is intentionally based not on the original novel, but the manga version my wife and I are drawing together. It has the structure I redesigned for the manga, and I even wrote one of the scripts myself. The visual specifications were set by me and the director while laughing our asses off, and all in all, I have no complaints about how it turned out as the author. I suppose that you, the readers, should be able to enjoy it as well. I fervently hope that you find both it and this volume to your liking.

So with that, it's about time for me to—oh, just one last thing, a request I have.
...Please don't hate Jibril. Now she's a different—well, I guess she isn't, but...anyway, you know. Yeah...
"What? After writing it yourself—?!"
All right, here I go. I hope you pick up the next volume as well.

WHAT THEY WOULD TAKE
ON THE WORLD TO GET—

WHAT THEY WOULD
FLEE FROM THE WORLD
AND STILL SEEK—

TO KILL IXSEED RANK ONE, OLD DEUS, WITHOUT KILLING—

NO GAME NO LIFE, VOLUME 7

Please wait for... ~~WAIT~~ THE FOOL AUTHOR WHO'S PUSHED
HIMSELF TO WHERE HE'S SHAKING!

Story by Yuu Kamiya, the creator of *No Game No Life*

Read the manga & watch the anime streaming on Crunchyroll!

In a steampunk future where the entire planet is mechanized, high school dropout and prodigy mechanic Naoto's spends his days tinkering with machinery - and the intricate, clockwork world is his playground. His quiet life is changed when an automaton girl crashes into his home. Her arrival means disrupting Naoto's life, societal order, and maybe saving the world!

KC
KODANSHA
COMICS

CLOCKWORK PLANET

"Clockwork Planet is filled with clever characters in a compelling science fiction world that's hard to put down... I'm desperate to see what happens next."
- AiPT!

"The world of Clockwork Planet is both physically fascinating and potentially narratively unique. The series has a lot of promise, and I'll be keeping an eye on it."
- Taykōbon

A NEW GAME IN A BIZARRE
WORLD WITH ALIEN SPECIES!
PLAY, IF YOU DARE!

No Game No Life

THE MANGA

NO GAME NO LIFE VOL. 1 © MASHIRO HIIRAGI & YUU KAMIYA 2013. © YUU KAMIYA 2013

Seven Seas

IN THIS FANTASY WORLD, EVERYTHING'S A GAME—AND THESE SIBLINGS PLAY TO WIN!

A genius but socially inept brother and sister duo is offered the chance to compete in a fantasy world where games decide everything. Sora and Shiro will take on the world and, while they're at it, create a harem of nonhuman companions!

No Game No Life © YUU KAMIYA
KADOKAWA CORPORATION

LIGHT NOVELS 1–6 AVAILABLE NOW

No Game No Life, Please! © Kazuya Yuizaki 2016 © Yuu Kamiya 2016
KADOKAWA CORPORATION

LIKE THE NOVELS?

Check out the spin-off manga for even more out-of-control adventures with the Werebeast girl, Izuna!